# *The* Faculty Lounge

## Also by Jennifer Mathieu

*The Truth About Alice*
*Devoted*
*Afterward*
*Moxie*
*The Liars of Mariposa Island*
*Bad Girls Never Say Die*
*Down Came the Rain*

# *The* Faculty Lounge

*A Novel*

⸻

## Jennifer Mathieu

**DUTTON**

**DUTTON**

An imprint of Penguin Random House LLC
penguinrandomhouse.com

LIBRARY OF CONGRESS CATALOGING-IN-PUBLICATION DATA

Names: Mathieu, Jennifer, author.
Title: The faculty lounge : a novel / Jennifer Mathieu.
Description: New York : Dutton, 2024.Identifiers: LCCN 2023047223 |
ISBN 9780593475393 (hardcover) | ISBN 9780593475409 (ebook)
Subjects: LCGFT: School fiction. | Novels.
Classification: LCC PS3613.A82844 F33 2024 |
DDC 813/.6—dc23/eng/20231213
LC record available at https://lccn.loc.gov/2023047223

Printed in the United States of America
1st Printing

BOOK DESIGN BY TIFFANY ESTREICHER

*For anyone who has ever worked in a school.*

*And in memory of Linda Balkin,*
*who many years ago took a chance on a naïve*
*young woman with no experience who wanted*
*to be a teacher. I am forever grateful.*

*The best teachers don't follow methods but are richly informed and widely interested and interesting themselves—the difference between a doctor and a mere druggist who spoons out the advised doses.*

—Dawn Powell

*And gladly would he learn, and gladly teach.*

—Chaucer

# The
# Faculty
# Lounge

# BALDWIN HIGH SCHOOL

*2022–23 School Year*

———

Principal Kendricks

Assistant Principal Baker

Assistant Principal Garcia

Ms. Jackson—Guidance Counselor

Ms. Fletcher—English

Mr. Fitzsimmons—Mathematics

Mr. Williams—English

Ms. Sanderson—Social Studies

Mr. Rayfield—Biology

Ms. Brennan—English

Ms. Jimenez—Social Studies

Mr. Lehrer—Substitute

Nurse Honeycutt—Clinic

Ms. Guevara—Custodian

## *One*

You really had to hand it to Mr. Lehrer. While dying at work is never ideal, he had the decency to do it during his off period. And not only that, but at the start of it, too, giving the clerks in the main office plenty of time to find someone else to cover Ms. De La Rosa's Spanish II classes, even as they scrambled to figure out who should be telephoned when an eighty-two-year-old substitute teacher lies down on a ratty couch in a high school faculty lounge and dies.

He was found in a poignant, circle-of-life sort of way by the youngest teacher on campus, a fresh-faced twenty-two-year-old named Ms. Sanderson, who taught geography to remedial freshmen, although Ms. Sanderson insisted on referring to them as "first years" in an effort to avoid sexism. Short and cherubic, with hormonal acne scattered over her chin, she was regularly stopped in the halls by colleagues who hadn't yet met her and asked to present a hall pass, something she found beyond infuriating.

While grading in the lounge during her off period, she had noticed Mr. Lehrer splayed out on the couch, his skinny frame draped almost comically over the dated patterned fabric. At first she thought he was just napping, but something seemed off. Although she called his name loudly more than once, he didn't stir. His long, slender face seemed paler than normal, his thin-lipped mouth was open and twisted, and when she collected the bravery necessary to approach him and hold her hand inches away from his nose, trying not to look too closely at the graying hairs poking out of its nostrils, she counted to one hundred before she had to admit that the worst was probably true.

Racing down two flights of stairs to the clinic, she was out of breath by the time she pulled open the door.

"Mr. Lehrer, the substitute," Ms. Sanderson began, holding out her teacher's badge on a lanyard as she spoke, prepared to have her identity questioned. "I believe he's . . . expired?"

*These young people and their soft language*, thought Nurse Honeycutt, frowning at Ms. Sanderson. "Do you mean he's dead?" she asked, already standing up and moving for her medical kit.

"Yes," Ms. Sanderson said, as scared of the nurse as she was of most of the adults in the building. In truth, she was scared of the students, too.

"Let's go," announced the nurse. As they left the clinic, Nurse Honeycutt realized this was the first dead body she'd had to deal with on campus, and she was struck by the fact that even after all these years, she still held the capacity for surprise.

An hour or so later, an all-faculty notification had been sent out from Principal Kendricks, received via text and email.

Baldwin family, I have some sad news to report. Bob Lehrer, former Baldwin High English teacher who retired in 1997 and who returned last year to substitute for us, has died of what appears to be natural causes. Sadly, Mr. Lehrer passed away in the third-floor faculty lounge, and we have been informed that it may be some time before the medical examiner's office is able to remove his body. Nurse Honeycutt has covered him with a sheet, and we ask that those who must use the third-floor lounge be aware of this extremely sensitive situation. Students are never allowed in the lounge, but on this day it is absolutely imperative that they not be allowed entry nor should they be informed of this development. I want to take a moment to express my appreciation to Mr. Lehrer for his years of service to the Baldwin High community. Ms. Jackson and the counseling department are available should this event bring up any feelings for you that you would like to discuss.

Of course, this news immediately caused a stir.

"Did you see this?" said Ms. Brennan incredulously as she stepped into the classroom of her neighbor Mr. Williams during a brief and hectic passing period between classes, her phone outstretched in her hand. The two of them taught advanced English to juniors.

"How can he offer his appreciation to Mr. Lehrer if Mr. Lehrer is dead?" responded Mr. Williams, peeved. "It should have been worded, '. . . to express my appreciation for Mr. Lehrer's years of service.'" Ms. Brennan nodded in agreement. The English teachers loved to pick apart the principal's frequent, wordy missives; after all, Principal Kendricks had taught geometry before heading into administration. Following their exchange about the message, naturally Ms. Brennan and Mr. Williams crossed the hall and entered the third-floor faculty lounge, the one closest to the English department, to see the evidence for themselves.

There was the body, tucked under a snowy white sheet from the clinic. Teachers were gathering in clumps, assessing the situation and murmuring quietly to one another. One veteran, a curmudgeon of a man named Mr. Fitzsimmons who taught math to sophomores and had worked with Mr. Lehrer for much of the 1980s and 1990s, shook his head in disbelief.

"So it's really Bob Lehrer under there," he muttered. "What a way to go."

Suddenly, a loud voice punctuated the relative quiet.

"Is it true there's a dead fucking body in here?" asked Ms. Jimenez upon arrival. Ms. Jimenez was a teacher of U.S. history, the longtime campus smart-ass, and a total terrorist known for jamming the copy machine on a regular basis before walking away, blissfully unbothered.

"See for yourself," said Ms. Brennan, motioning toward the figure on the couch.

Ms. Jimenez peered at the body of Mr. Lehrer, and for a moment half the room thought she just might march over there and lift the sheet to be sure.

"This is a hell of a way to start the school year," said Ms. Jimenez, pressing a forefinger into the deep vertical wrinkle that ran between her eyes. "And the crazy thing is that this isn't even the most fucked up thing that's happened at this place." Many of her colleagues in the lounge nodded in agreement.

Depending on the length of time they'd served at Baldwin, they had either experienced firsthand or learned through oral tradition about the following events: the time a young math teacher was caught receiving a blow job from a female student in the faculty parking lot after hours; the time an eleventh grader delivered a full-term baby in the girls' second-floor bathroom; the time it was discovered that one of the assistant principals,

Mr. Ellis, had lost his home to foreclosure and was essentially living at the school, showering in the boys' locker room and sleeping in his office; not to mention the time there was a four-hour lockdown due to an alleged gun on campus and poor, beloved Mrs. Cardoza had been forced to urinate into a trash can while partially hidden in her classroom's storage cabinet. (She had taken early retirement that spring.)

So Ms. Jimenez had a point. A dead body in the lounge was not, in fact, the most fucked up thing to ever happen at Baldwin High School.

"I'm eating lunch in my classroom today," continued Ms. Jimenez. "It doesn't seem sanitary to eat near a dead body, right?"

At this some of the teachers looked meaningfully in the direction of the biology teacher Mr. Rayfield, who merely shrugged his shoulders, as unsure of the answer as the rest of them. Mr. Rayfield had taken this teaching gig only after spending his years at a prestigious university on a consistent diet of mushrooms, marijuana, and benzodiazepines, causing him to flame out on his MCAT exam and destroy his father's biggest dreams.

"I always found it strange he came back to substitute after so many years away," said Mr. Williams. "I mean, the man was eighty-two years old."

Of course, it was natural for retired teachers to return to substitute in an effort to supplement their meager pension checks, although Mr. Lehrer was exceptionally old for such a taxing venture. While these retired-teacher subs could be revered for their ability to do the job better than most, they had a tendency to annoy younger teachers with their constant litany of what was different now, ranging from the surprising to the offensive.

(*"Back in my day, you could smoke in this lounge." "Back in my day, we had to calculate grades by hand." "Back in my day, there weren't so many Mexicans here."*)

"He told me he was bored," said Ms. Sanderson, the young teacher who'd discovered the body. There was a ripple of confusion over her presence until some of her colleagues spotted her teacher lanyard. She continued on, her voice still uncertain and high-pitched, that of a child more than a woman's: "I talked to him a few times when he substituted for Ms. De La Rosa, next door to me." Her cheeks were pinking up now that she realized she had the attention of the room, but she went on, glancing at Mr. Lehrer's body as if looking for permission to share all of this. "He said coming here was better than sitting at home alone and reading crime novels and watching PBS, and that substituting reminded him of some of the best times of his life, just being with students and other teachers and stuff."

"The best times of his life?" said Mr. Rayfield, disbelieving. He was desperately trying to imagine an exit strategy after four short years at Baldwin.

"Yes," Ms. Sanderson said, nodding. "The best times of his life."

"Did he have any family?" asked Ms. Brennan. She was an experienced teacher, but since she'd only recently moved to the area, this was her first year at Baldwin, and she was still getting to know names and faces.

"I don't believe he ever married," came a voice from the back of the gathering crowd. Everyone turned to look. It was Ms. Fletcher, a respected veteran English teacher with a full load of advanced seniors. "At least, he was unmarried when I first met him. He had a son who lived with his mother in . . ." She wrinkled her brow, trying to recall. "Arizona, I think. I mean, this was ages ago, of course."

"I didn't realize you'd worked together," said Ms. Brennan. "Did you know him well?"

"Not really," said Ms. Fletcher, shaking her head. "We only overlapped for one year, his last full-time and my first." As she said this, she looked at the body in front of her and her mind was transported.

———

In the fall of 1996 and right out of college, Amanda Fletcher had taken a job teaching English to sophomores at Baldwin High, a comprehensive public high school in Houston, Texas, with four thousand students and a good reputation, housed in a three-story red brick building constructed in the middle of the century on a campus with large, mature oak trees that gave the entire place a solid feeling. It was located not far from the university where Amanda had secured her degree and roughly two hours from her hometown, which to Amanda seemed like a good enough distance away to start her adult life.

Her parents were not pleased with her choice of career. Amanda was smart, they said. She should aim for something in law or finance. Something that made real money. But Amanda loved literature, she loved school, and she loved learning, and her time as a student teacher at a smaller high school in the same district had cemented for her the belief that the classroom was where she belonged. She couldn't quite explain it, not even to herself, but in her gut she knew that this was what she was supposed to be doing with her life.

She rented a one-bedroom apartment just five minutes from the school, in a neighborhood known for its eclectic, artsy shops and ethnic restaurants that stayed open late for the young people who were curious enough to try them. Not that Amanda planned on going out much. Her longtime high school boyfriend turned college boyfriend, Dave Saunders, was in graduate school in Colorado, earning his master's degree in engineering. Dave's parents and Amanda's parents and Dave and Amanda themselves were all certain of Dave's eventual return as well as the couple's eventual marriage, children, and grandchildren. Dave's secure financial future helped buffer the anxiety Amanda's parents had over what they considered to be her otherwise poor life choices.

During the week before classes began, Amanda worked tirelessly in her classroom, trying to stretch the small decorating budget she'd allowed herself to make the space look homey and welcoming. Peeking shyly into the rooms of others, who'd had decades to make their classrooms look inviting, only sparked frustration. Veteran teachers kept coming by to introduce themselves, but their names exited her mind just as soon as they'd entered it. She also quickly discovered that they seemed to see her as a dumping ground for all their old materials, donated under the guise of helping out their new young colleague.

One afternoon, as she sat flipping through dusty textbooks from the mid-1970s, there was a knock at her open door. She looked up to see a tall, slender man with salt-and-pepper hair, a large nose, and a kind smile. Since graduating from college, she'd realized how bad she was at guessing the ages of other adults—they all seemed to be anywhere from twenty-five to fifty-five—but she would later learn that this man, Mr. Lehrer, was fifty-six and planning to retire in May. He taught the seniors taking AP Literature, he told her, and he enjoyed encouraging young teachers.

"What made you get into this profession, Ms. Fletcher?" he asked, leaning against her doorframe, relaxed, his smile open and warm. He was the first teacher to stop by that she didn't wish would leave right away. He didn't try to foist any materials on her, and he seemed genuinely friendly.

"I think teaching was just always what I wanted to do," she said, wishing she had a smarter answer. Then, because she felt compelled to keep talking, she added, "My parents wanted me to go into law or finance."

"Ah, law or finance," said Mr. Lehrer, nodding sagely as if he partly agreed with Amanda's parents. "Impressive professions to be sure. But they're not teaching."

"No, they're not," said Amanda as if she had the experience to know.

"It sounds like you were called to this career," he said. "For some of us, it is a vocation, not just a job. It's what I have always referred to as good work."

She nodded in agreement, and privately, she liked how he seemed to be putting her in the same category as him, a respected veteran teacher with the top students in the school.

The first day of the academic year arrived, and Amanda quickly sensed that she was drowning. She came to realize almost immediately that one reason her lessons had gone off so easily when she was a student teacher was that her cooperating teacher had already established her as the authority figure. Now Amanda had to establish that for herself, which was difficult when she looked almost as young as the students.

She spent hours at home crafting lessons down to the minute, practiced delivering them in the mirror, and annotated every story and novel she had to teach within an inch of its life. She lived in fear of a student asking her a question she wouldn't have the answer for, and despite all her hours of extra work on the weekends and in the evenings, she fretted that when it came to their writing and reading-comprehension skills, her students were going backward. When administrators wandered through to observe her, she could feel her face and chest bursting into itchy red hives, and she almost expected them to fire her there on the spot.

She was exhausted most nights, and when she wasn't working, she watched stupid television or tried and failed to read for pleasure. She wrote a letter to Dave every Sunday, and late on Friday nights, the two indulged in an expensive long-distance phone call that could last hours.

"You work too hard," said Dave as she recounted the week. "How much do you get paid again?"

When she told him, he quickly calculated the hourly rate based on the extra time she put in outside of the school day. The amount stunned Amanda.

"You'd make more money working at the mall," he told her.

"I wish you hadn't told me that," she said.

One October afternoon after a particularly lousy fifth period class, she found a folded note on the floor that a student had left behind, on purpose or by accident she'd never know. She opened it to read the message, written in a worn-out pencil.

*This class is so fucking boooooooring.*

Grateful that she had sixth period off, she shut the classroom door, sat at her desk, folded her arms, and buried her face in them. Then she sobbed.

A few moments later, there was a knock at the door. Wiping her eyes, she sat up and tried to make herself look professional.

"Yes?"

It was Mr. Lehrer. He'd come to ask her if she had any staples, but upon seeing her face, he knew something was wrong. When he asked what it was, Amanda burst into tears again. She held out the note before embarrassment could stop her.

Mr. Lehrer took it from her and read it.

"Little shits," he said. The response surprised her, but it also made her laugh a little, too. "God bless them and everything," Mr. Lehrer continued, "because their brains are still developing. But sometimes they can really ruin our days."

"They're right, though," said Amanda, sniffling. "The lesson *was* boring. I was bored. One of my professors always said if you're bored, the kids are bored."

Mr. Lehrer nodded sympathetically. "It's not a bad point," he said. "But we're also not here to entertain, remember that. We're here to teach. Don't put so much pressure on yourself. It takes time to be good at this job. Even for someone who was called to it like you were."

"I'm not sure I was called to anything," Amanda said. She sighed.

"Listen," Mr. Lehrer said. "How would you like to come and observe me? I could give you a couple of pointers. Aren't you off third?"

Amanda nodded, and they agreed she would visit his class the next day.

When she arrived a few minutes before the bell, Mr. Lehrer motioned toward an empty desk by the windows. It was just the two of them for now. The classroom had a cozy, lived-in feeling, the walls covered with all sorts of blown-up book covers, including *The Great Gatsby* and *Brave New World*; there was hardly any blank space left. The bulletin board behind Mr. Lehrer's teacher desk was jam-packed with thank-you cards, handwritten notes, pieces of student artwork, and wallet-sized photographs of graduating seniors dressed in caps and gowns.

*This class changed my life!* read one note, written in bubbly cursive. *Thank you Mr. Lehrer!*

Mr. Lehrer noticed Amanda's eyes coming to rest on the photograph of a boy, maybe thirteen or fourteen, tucked into the corner of the bulletin board. He looked remarkably like Mr. Lehrer.

"That's my son, Matthew," he said. "Sort of a late-in-life surprise. I've never been married, but . . ." He paused, suddenly uncomfortable. He'd never spoken of his personal life. "Anyway, he lives with his mom in Arizona most of the time, but I see him during the summers. Good kid, but he prefers video games to books, so . . ." His voice trailed off.

"Maybe you can spend more time with him once you're retired," she offered, unsure if this was the right thing to say.

"Yes, possibly," said Mr. Lehrer. "I also have a novel that's sort of in progress. Something I'm trying to finish and hopefully get published. But I don't know."

"What's it about?" asked Amanda, but Mr. Lehrer just smiled and shook his head.

"I'm too bashful to share," he said. "It's probably not very good." Mr. Lehrer's reaction surprised Amanda. Normally, he seemed so assured. At this, the bell rang and students began to stream into the room, and suddenly his confidence was again on full display. Almost instantly, Amanda was reminded of what she loved about school. What she loved about sitting in a classroom with a beloved teacher who could make the material explode with color and feeling.

But she watched him like a teacher now, not just as a student.

She noticed how, when two boys started goofing around in the back row, Mr. Lehrer didn't call them out. He simply went to stand near them; his hovering presence made them stop. When he read a passage of the story they were studying out loud, he wasn't afraid to do the characters' voices, even if this was a class full of seniors. And in a moment that shocked Amanda, when he made a spelling error while writing on the overhead projector, he took a moment to call attention to it.

"See?" he told the class. "Even I make mistakes. There's a lesson in that. Everyone screws up sometimes."

When the bell rang to end class, Amanda felt inspired. She rushed up to Mr. Lehrer and told him so.

"Well, I'm glad," he told her. "You're welcome anytime. And be patient with yourself, okay? You'll get there."

"Thank you," she said. "Thanks a lot." As she started to head out—her fourth period class was entering her room as she stood there—she turned back and asked, "Why are you retiring now? You're still so great at this."

Mr. Lehrer smiled, obviously flattered. "That's nice of you to say," he answered. "But I've been teaching since longer than you've been alive, you know. I actually could have started collecting my pension a few years ago. There's a part of me that wants to make sure I quit while I'm ahead. I never wanted to be one of those teachers who was phoning it in."

Amanda nodded like she understood, but the idea of retirement was something so far away and foreign to her that she couldn't grasp at all what Mr. Lehrer meant.

As the months passed, things improved for Amanda in the classroom. She was learning to anticipate things, trust herself more. She was finding ways to meld her teacher personality with her actual personality, and the results weren't half bad;

once, when she made a wry joke about the ending of Shirley Jackson's "The Lottery" and some of the smartest kids in the class cracked up, she felt a shiver of happiness. She wasn't great. Not even close. But she was getting better. She was becoming Ms. Fletcher. She took to observing Mr. Lehrer whenever she needed a boost, and she also liked dropping by his room to share little victories, like her first thank-you note from a student or a lesson that had gone especially well. He cheered her on every time.

"See?" he said, smiling. "You're getting there!"

On a Friday in April, just six weeks or so before the end of the year and not long before the bell to begin seventh period, Mr. Lehrer popped his head into Amanda's room, where Amanda sat during her off period grading papers, or trying to.

"A few of us are heading over to La Casita Bonita for a little happy hour," he said. "You should come." It was not the first time he'd asked.

"Well," she said, trying to drum up an excuse that sounded plausible. She'd grown friendly with Mr. Lehrer, yes, but the idea of interacting socially with him and lots of people decades older than her seemed strange, and interacting socially with people she worked with even stranger. She was aware that some of the other veterans probably saw her as standoffish or even rude, but she wasn't. She was just twenty-two and somewhat shy.

"Come on now," he said, slapping the doorframe for emphasis. "Almost the entire department will be there. It's sort of an early retirement party for me." He smiled, and the skin near his eyes crinkled. He looked like such a dad. "You won't last in this profession if you don't unwind from time to time."

Amanda glanced at the papers in front of her and thought of

her apartment at home, the Lean Cuisines for one stacked like little monuments to loneliness in her freezer. She could arrive late and leave early, and be back in time for her regular Friday evening phone call with Dave.

"All right," she said. "What time?"

"Just right after school," he said. "You'll find us there."

When she got to the restaurant, she found her colleagues at a cluttered table in the back, half of them smoking and all of them drinking.

"Ms. Fletcher!" Mr. Lehrer shouted out, waving her down. She forced a smile and found an empty seat toward the end of the table, in between Mrs. McCarthy and Ms. Gray, the latter a notoriously easy grader students referred to as "Get an A with Gray." Sweating goblets filled with melting margaritas and half-empty red plastic baskets of tortilla chips dotted the table. Amanda ordered a margarita and made a silent prayer of gratitude when the waiter didn't ask for her ID, then sipped her drink slowly, making sure to alternate between the alcohol and a glass of ice water.

She pasted a smile on her face as her fellow teachers—the one closest to her in age was almost thirty, she guessed, and had already had a baby—gossiped with the ease of those who'd known each other and worked together for years. The room was raucous and loud and the conversation was so full of inside jokes as to make Amanda feel even lonelier here surrounded by people than she would have been at her apartment. Not to mention that it was hard to keep track of who everybody was when they referred to each other casually and affectionately as Gary and Carol and Sharon and Donna. In her mind, these people existed only by their last names. It struck Amanda, not for the first time, that all of them could have easily been her own teachers when she was in high school.

Amanda sipped on her margarita, trying to laugh at the right moments and trying not to chew on her plastic straw, a nervous habit she knew made her look twelve years old. At last Mrs. McCarthy seemed to remember she was sitting there and turned toward her.

"Well, Ms. Fletcher, you've almost made it through your first year!" she said, holding up her drink in a little salute. "It really is the hardest one, you know."

"*Not* true!" bellowed a teacher named Mrs. Dixon, raising a finger to accentuate her point. "The first *five* years are the hardest. You gotta get through at least *five* years before you know what the hell you're doing in this business." She shook her finger at Amanda and cackled, and Amanda could see smears of pink lipstick on Mrs. Dixon's yellowing teeth.

"For God's sake, Dorothy, don't frighten her," Mr. Lehrer said, rolling his eyes. "I swear to God, this profession eats its young." He gave Amanda a sympathetic look, and Amanda smiled back. She longed to get out of there.

After a little over an hour had passed and Amanda had uttered about three sentences, she felt she could leave without appearing rude. As she motioned to the waiter for her check, Mr. Lehrer waved his hand.

"It's on me," he said, pretending not to hear her protests. "I'm about to be making that retired-teacher money, you know." He laughed a little too loudly. After thanking him, Amanda stood up and pushed her chair back, then noticed that Mr. Lehrer was mirroring her actions.

"I'll walk you out," he said. "Just to be safe." La Casita Bonita was in a decent part of town, and Amanda could see through the big pane windows covered in string lights and painted-on notices advertising dinner specials that it wasn't even dark yet.

"Okay," she said.

Her ancient Honda Civic was parked around the side of the restaurant, near the dumpsters. It had been the only spot she'd been able to find when she'd arrived.

"Pee-yew!" said Mr. Lehrer, wrinkling his nose as Amanda pulled her keys out of her canvas tote. "Sure does stink back here."

"Yeah, it does," she said, sliding the key into the lock. She sensed him hovering behind her, and she wondered why he wasn't leaving. "Well, thank you."

"Amanda," said Mr. Lehrer, and as she turned to face him, she realized just how close he was. So close she could see how red his cheeks were under his five o'clock shadow, so close she could see his pores under the field of gray and black hairs blooming from his ruddy face. He blinked slowly. His blue eyes were glassy.

"I just want you to know that I've really enjoyed working with you this year," he said. Was he slurring his words? "Your enthusiasm," he continued, "your youthful energy and idealism . . ." He struggled to pronounce that last word. "Anyway, it's helped me remember why I got into this profession in the first place . . . and I'm . . . really going to miss you."

"Oh," said Amanda, her mind blank but her well-trained polite response functioning on autopilot. "That's . . . so nice of you to say." He was inches away. No, centimeters.

In the instant it took for Amanda to consider what could happen, it happened. Mr. Lehrer was kissing her, his lips were on hers. His body was pressed up against hers, too, and his stubble scraped the bottom of her mouth, just under her lip. It lasted maybe three seconds and an eternity, and it was the least sexy thing in the whole wide world.

"Mr. Lehrer!" she said, able to react at last, pulling back, her heart racing. Her mouth was wet from his spit in a way that could only be described as disgusting, and she longed to wipe it off with her hand but didn't. "Mr. Lehrer, I have a boyfriend," she said. Her cheeks were aflame.

But Mr. Lehrer was already stepping away, looking down at the ground.

"Oh my God, what am I doing," he murmured, more to himself than to Amanda, and then he backed up even farther, turned, and headed toward the restaurant. Somehow, Amanda managed to open her car door, get inside, and drive out of the parking lot and onto a side street before pulling over and exhaling. Her body was shaking ever so slightly, and she was already imagining what she would tell Dave over the phone. She finally did wipe her mouth, then grimaced with repulsion.

Glancing at her reflection in the mirror, she asked loudly, "What the hell was that?"

At home she got a beer out of the refrigerator and called Dave and told him everything.

"Did he, like, slip his tongue in your mouth?" Dave asked.

Amanda frowned. It had all happened so quickly she couldn't be sure, but anyway, why did Dave care about this fact?

"I'm really not sure," she said.

"How could you not be sure if he put his tongue in your mouth?"

Amanda took a sip of her beer. "Dave," she said, annoyed, "my fifty-something-year-old coworker kissed me in the parking lot of a Mexican restaurant. Why are the specific details so important to you?"

Dave didn't respond right away. When Amanda didn't say anything else, he finally said, "Well, he'd better not try it again."

This statement struck Amanda as funny. She was an inch taller than Dave and probably weighed more, too. "Or what?" she asked. "You're going to beat him up after school?"

Dave didn't like this reaction. "I guess I just don't find this whole thing funny," he said.

"Like I do?" responded Amanda. Part of her was regretting saying anything to Dave in the first place, but since they were basically engaged, how could she not?

Given the era they were living in, neither one of them brought up the possibility of reporting Mr. Lehrer. It had been a kiss between two adults, off campus and after hours. And honestly, as Amanda made clear to Dave before she hung up the phone, mostly she wanted to forget it. What had Mr. Lehrer been thinking? He had always struck her as so smart, so capable. She'd been in awe of his command of the classroom. His brilliance. His charisma. Upon reflection, Amanda had to admit that what upset her most of all was not the kiss, but the realization that adulthood did not prevent otherwise reasonable, intelligent people like Mr. Lehrer from doing stupid things. The thought made her nervous about her own future.

On Monday morning in her faculty mailbox, Amanda found a small envelope, cream-colored and thick between her fingers. It reminded Amanda of the paper on which her high school and college graduation announcements had been printed. Her teacher name was written on the front in well-practiced cursive. Ms. Fletcher.

Curious but able to delay gratification enough to wait till she was alone, she quickly climbed the stairs to her classroom, shut the door behind herself, kept the lights off so no one would know she was there, walked to her desk, and opened the envelope.

*Ms. Fletcher,*

*I must apologize for my unprofessional, thoughtless, and downright rotten behavior on Friday evening. I am old enough to know that alcohol is not an excuse in such situations, but I fear that contributed to my idiocy. It was an impulsive and stupid act, and I ask for your forgiveness. Certainly, you are not under any obligation to extend it to me.*

*In a few weeks I'll be gone from this place, and you'll never have to see me again. I can only hope this incident does not prevent you from continuing on as a teacher here at Baldwin. You are too gifted to leave us, and Baldwin surely needs you.*

*Again, my deepest apologies.*

Amanda's first reaction was to wonder why on earth Mr. Lehrer would think she was a gifted teacher, given that he'd never seen her teach and, more importantly, that she certainly was not. She read the card through a few more times, then slid it into her tote bag so she could take it home. She resolved not to share it with Dave. That day as she moved through her lessons, at least 10 percent of her brain was at all times focused on the card in her bag.

In the weeks that followed, Mr. Lehrer made every attempt to avoid her, including one horribly awkward moment when they both happened to walk toward each other in an otherwise empty hallway during a shared off period. Amanda slowed down, uncertain—she would have been willing to say hello and nod and keep going—but Mr. Lehrer spun on his heel and raced in the opposite direction, the *tap tap* of his feet on the tiled floor growing more distant by the moment.

Amanda thought about writing him back, but what would she even say? *It's weird that you're older than my dad and you kissed me in the parking lot of a Tex-Mex restaurant, but thanks for the note of apology.* No, best to let it go. It was awkward for only a few weeks and then, as Mr. Lehrer had promised in his note, he was gone for good.

Almost.

Years later, when Mr. Lehrer started substituting at Baldwin, he looked so radically different to Amanda she could hardly believe it. So much older, his skin mottled with liver spots, the wisps of his thinning gray hair forever askew. *Wizened* was the word that came to mind. Naturally, Amanda was older, too. She had stayed at Baldwin, married Dave, had two boys back-to-back who were now by a good twist of fate regulated and mature college students, amicably divorced Dave when they both realized that they had very little left in common and even less to talk about, gained thirty pounds and lost ten, lost her father to pancreatic cancer, lost two students to suicide, and graded approximately twenty-three thousand student essays. In recent years she had fallen into a comfortable, low-stakes relationship with a widowed father of one adult daughter who lived two blocks over and who had a rescue dog named Elvis, after Costello, not Presley. The sex was good and the conversation was even better, and on Sunday mornings she would leave his place with a tender kiss and head off to grade student essays over morning coffee and then sink into a good book. All told, it had been a pretty good life thus far.

Although Amanda was uncomfortable admitting it because it felt like such a brag, on her best days she thought Mr. Lehrer had been right about her being a gifted teacher. Over the years she had experienced moments of divine transcendence in the classroom, tiny treasures full of sacred meaning, exchanges she would think back on fondly and sometimes recall and retell to her closest teacher friends and the young ones she mentored, both formally and informally. Books and poems and stories and essays had been cradled gently, like fragile, breathing things, and on good days she pressed them carefully into her students' open hands with so much love. Students liked to keep in touch with her, come back to visit, send photographs of their weddings and their babies. Her desk and bulletin board were filled with sweet little thank-you notes dotted with grammatical errors and spelling mistakes that rhapsodized about what a wonderful English teacher she was. (As for Mr. Lehrer's note, she'd felt compelled to save it, too, but it was stashed in a shoebox in the hall closet at home.)

She had also experienced difficult moments, lately more often than before. She questioned her relevance, her ability to connect with the kids, the way every text she introduced in class was classified as *problematic* by her students, who struck her as far more sensitive and humorless than she had ever been at that age.

She bemoaned the way public education had become corrupted, seemingly never able to escape an ever-growing obsession with metrics, data points, objectives, strands, formative assessments, standards-based learning, and the weeping lesion that was high-stakes, state-mandated testing. Old enough to recall the world before the Internet, she grimaced with embarrassment when she was forced to ask her younger colleagues for help with all the online platforms she was now expected to master and was admittedly turned off by that generation's dependence on Kahoot!, Nearpod, Padlet, Pear Deck, AppleTree, DooDad, ClickClack, and so on. Still, she kept at it, being in as deep as she was. She could collect her pension in just six more years.

When the #MeToo wave crashed ashore, Amanda, like countless men and women, performed an inventory of her life. The old man's grope in the supermarket when she was only seven. The father of the family she babysat for in high school casting glances at her breasts, rather than her face, as he drove her home in the dark. The frat boy trapping her in a cramped, sweaty corner until she managed to dart under his arm in escape, catching a whiff of his Old Spice that would stay with her for so long that she refused to buy that brand for her own sons. But Mr. Lehrer? Surely some would think what he did counted. Probably most would. Amanda could even imagine the language she could use in her Facebook post, and the vitriolic comments she could command with a few choice words. ("I was a shy, 22-year-old first-year teacher when an older male colleague pushed himself against me and kissed me without my consent by the dumpsters at a Mexican restaurant.")

But the truth was, this was not how she considered the situation with Mr. Lehrer. When she had cause to think back on that evening in her life, which was actually not often at all, mostly she just felt sorry for him in his middle-aged loneliness, his graying-at-the-temples awkwardness. She could easily picture his walk back to La Casita Bonita as she drove away in her

Honda Civic, his tequila-filled head already swimmy and aching with regret. It was not difficult at all to visualize him sitting in a poorly decorated bachelor's apartment, writing out his apology note, ripping up draft after draft before taking out a fresh piece of good stationery. Or perhaps he went and *bought* the stationery for that very purpose? That detail seemed plausible, and this made Amanda even sadder.

The situation had not been pleasant, certainly. But it had not been horrific. It had not ruined her. She hoped it had not ruined Mr. Lehrer.

His return to substituting at Baldwin the year prior struck Amanda as a bizarre sort of swan song. She was one of a handful of teachers left on campus who had worked with him back in the 1990s and the only one left in the English department. Naturally, they ran into each other here and there, and there were pleasant nods of the head, *hello*s, and *hasn't it changed*s. She almost asked him if he'd ever published that novel before realizing that she already knew the answer. The awkward kiss in the parking lot of La Casita Bonita seemed so long ago to Amanda it was as if it had happened to someone else. She hoped that Mr. Lehrer, being in his eighties, had almost certainly forgotten about it by now, but Amanda suspected that because he was the sort of good man who had the decency to die during his off period, probably he had never forgotten it.

Now, instead of being just a few years older than her students, Amanda was much closer to the age Mr. Lehrer had been when he'd kissed her. Time was a funny thing. Very slowly and then all at once, she was closer to the end of her career than the start, a black-and-white fact printed on her annual state pension statement that was impossible to ignore.

Would she suggest to a young, bright-eyed college student

that she should go into public education? On her worst and hardest days, probably not. Things had changed, and not for the better. This job now felt less like an art form and more like a factory line.

That said, and all things considered, Amanda could say with total honesty that when she sat down and thought, really thought, about how she had spent the past twenty-six years of her life, she was glad that she had not gone into law or finance.

————————

Mr. Lehrer's body lay on the couch in the third-floor faculty lounge under the clinic's white sheet for all of second, third, fourth, lunch, fifth, and sixth periods. Teachers darted in and out all day on an as-needed basis, occasionally texting photos of Mr. Lehrer's covered body to colleagues on other floors.

    **Still here. #bodywatch**

    **Can you believe we work here? #lehrerbodywatch**

    **How long before he starts to smell? #iamgoingtohell**

Toward the end of sixth, one of her off periods, Ms. Fletcher went into the lounge to use the bathroom. She avoided glancing in the direction of the body. Upon exiting the bathroom, she found young Ms. Sanderson standing off to the side, gazing at Mr. Lehrer. She also noted that Ms. Jimenez was busy and unbothered at the copy machine, most likely jamming it up again.

"I can't believe I found a dead man at work," said Ms. Sanderson, not really to anyone but perhaps just to herself. Her voice was flat.

"It's got to have been disturbing," said Ms. Fletcher. She

allowed herself to glance toward the couch. Mr. Lehrer's feet looked like two snow-covered mountains.

"He was always so nice to me, so encouraging," said Ms. Sanderson. "Poor old man."

"I know," said Ms. Fletcher, her throat a sudden ache. "He was nice."

The two stood there for a moment, the *zip-chunk* of the copy machine the only noise in the room.

"It's almost like a soldier dying on the battlefield, isn't it?" said Ms. Sanderson in a soft voice. The language was a little much, to be sure, but after all Ms. Sanderson taught social studies, not English. Ms. Fletcher noticed that Ms. Sanderson's voice had cracked when she'd spoken and that little tears were pooling in her dark eyes, so she went over and wrapped an arm around her young colleague and gave her a little squeeze.

"Yes," said Ms. Fletcher. "In some ways it is just like that."

"Well, I sure as shit am not dying here," said Ms. Jimenez from her reign at the copy machine, a hand on her hip. "I have my time-share in Tampa. That's where I'd like to be when I go."

At this, the lounge door opened and three men entered, rolling a gurney. They wore black jackets that announced they were from the medical examiner's office.

"Excuse us, we need the room," said one of them.

"But I'm not finished with my copies!" said Ms. Jimenez, annoyed. Just then, the bell to signal the passing period to seventh, the last class of the day, rang long and loud. Ms. Jimenez cursed.

Ignoring the others and turning her attention to Ms. Sanderson, Ms. Fletcher asked, "Are you okay? I mean, can you go back to class?"

Ms. Sanderson sniffed and nodded, but she didn't seem sure.

The men from the medical examiner's office crowded around Mr. Lehrer, murmuring to one another in technical language. Ms. Fletcher figured that at any moment they might remove the sheet Nurse Honeycutt had so carefully placed. Gently pivoting Ms. Sanderson toward the door of the lounge, she began to move her colleague in that direction.

"You've had quite a day, haven't you?" said Ms. Fletcher, reaching for the door handle.

"Yes," said Ms. Sanderson. "Oh my God, yes." She was crying in earnest now.

They exited completely into the hallway, and Ms. Fletcher made sure the door to the lounge was shut behind them. As they huddled off to one side, silent tears running down Ms. Sanderson's cheeks, Ms. Fletcher placed a hand on the younger teacher's shoulder and waited. A few minutes passed like that, with neither one of them speaking. The hallway was filled with the shouts of teenagers liberated for a few moments between classes. Profanity mixed with the screech of shoes on tiled floors. The odor of cheap perfume mingled with sweat. The children did not seem to notice them.

"There are some days when all you can do is just make it until the last bell," said Ms. Fletcher. As she said this, she was somewhat embarrassed she'd offered such oft-repeated advice, but the advice really was true, which was one reason why veteran teachers kept giving it.

"Yeah, you're right," said Ms. Sanderson, pressing her fingers to her eyes to wipe away her remaining tears and taking a shaky breath. "Thank you."

"Of course," said Ms. Fletcher, lifting her hand from Ms.

Sanderson's shoulder. "Now, you're sure you're okay? They can find someone to cover for you, you know. You can go home early."

Ms. Sanderson shook her head no. She had managed to compose herself.

"Thank you so much, Ms. Fletcher," she said.

"Of course. Anytime. And you can call me Amanda, you know." But Ms. Fletcher knew Ms. Sanderson never would.

Just then the staccato warning bell went off, alerting them to the fact that there was just one minute left until seventh period officially began. In front of them was a churning sea of adolescence, full of trauma, curiosity, anxiety, and joy. The two teachers were drawn into it, swept up by it. Unable to resist, they allowed it to carry them all the way to their classrooms, where their students were waiting for them.

# Two

Mr. Lehrer had requested that his ashes be spread in the front courtyard on the campus of Baldwin High School. It had been stated explicitly in his will, according to the attorney who contacted Principal Kendricks not long after the former veteran teacher and substitute lay down and died in the faculty lounge.

"He . . . what?" said the principal, an affable man and a good leader who, having just turned fifty, had been stricken with recurring thoughts about his own mortality. He was closer to Mr. Lehrer's age at death than to his own birth—there was no longer any denying it. His thirties, for instance. Had that decade actually even *happened* to him? But it must have, because now he was fifty and the principal of the largest high school in the city, and he was taking a phone call about a dead man's ashes.

"Didn't he have family?" Principal Kendricks asked.

"One son," said the attorney, "but they weren't especially close, and he's asking that his father's wishes be honored. He lives out of state and said he won't be attending the ceremony."

*The ceremony?* Principal Kendricks considered the idea, trying to imagine how much of an event this would have to be while mentally running through his chain of command at Central Office. Which one of his superiors would have to sign off on such a thing? The deputy superintendent of secondary schools? The assistant deputy superintendent over human resources? The chief assistant deputy superintendent of you'll-never-believe-this-shit? The latter would be a useful office in the world of public education, he admitted to himself, shortly before telling Mr. Lehrer's attorney to have the ashes shipped to the school, attention his name.

They arrived in the main office on a Thursday morning in late September, and Principal Kendricks, who had been something of a rebel in his youth, decided—not for the first time in his career—to do what he believed was the right thing, even if the powers that be might have disagreed. A quick search had revealed that while it wasn't explicitly *against* school policy to spread ashes all over a school campus, it probably wasn't something that was encouraged, either. Perhaps this was a time when it was better to ask for forgiveness than permission, Principal Kendricks decided. Besides, it had clearly meant something to Mr. Lehrer.

He fired off an all-staff email, being careful not to put the matter of the ashes into print.

Dear Faculty and Staff,
I hope you'll join me in the front courtyard today after the final bell. We'll be having a brief ceremony to honor the legacy of former substitute and longtime Baldwin teacher, Mr. Bob Lehrer. As you may recall, Mr. Lehrer died of natural causes on campus a few weeks ago while he was here

substituting. Mr. Lehrer did not have much family, and he specifically requested a memorial of sorts here at Baldwin High because this place was so special to him. A home away from home, if you will. So let's please gather in the front courtyard together and share a few moments together to celebrate the life of Bob Lehrer. No one is required to speak, however if you're one of the folks on campus who worked with Mr. Lehrer all those years ago, I hope you will consider sharing a few words. It will be good to be together to honor Mr. Lehrer.

Thanks,
Mark Kendricks

"Do you think this ceremony will at least be briefer than this wordy email?" said Ms. Brennan to Mr. Williams in their usual hallway gossip spot.

"Seriously," answered Mr. Williams with a roll of his eyes. "Also, would I be an asshole if I explained to our principal that he should have used a semicolon before the word *however*?"

"Probably," said Ms. Brennan. "I also loved the part where he suggested we might not remember the fact that a man died in the lounge."

"'As you may recall,'" Mr. Williams mimicked, with air quotes for emphasis. "Like I'm going to forget that?"

"I know I won't," said Ms. Brennan. "Anyway, are you going to go to this thing?"

"Sure," said Mr. Williams, shrugging. "I feel sorry for the old man."

Ms. Brennan agreed to join him. All over campus, teachers and staff members were debating whether to attend. In the end, only a handful did. Some, like Ms. Fletcher and Nurse Honey-cutt and Mr. Fitzsimmons, had actually worked with Mr. Leh-rer and felt it was owed. A few junior administrators hoped it would score some brownie points with Principal Kendricks if they made an appearance. And still others, like the young and idealistic Ms. Sanderson, believed it was the right thing to pay honor to a man who had spent his life doing good work in ser-vice to something larger than himself.

Mr. Lehrer probably deserved more than a rushed, hurried ceremony on a Thursday after the final bell while kids ditched after-school detention to go vape by the bus lane, but this is what Principal Kendricks and the Baldwin High community were able to offer him during these first few weeks of fall, when the wheels of the school year were still gaining traction and the busy days were only growing busier. Those who had chosen to attend the ceremony began to gather in the courtyard, on a scraggly patch of grass that—like the old building it stood in front of—had seen better days. The place was often littered with empty chip bags and the sad, lonely plastic caps of ball-point pens. Several scraggly bushes as well as a few functional metal benches lacking any character (they had been donated by several graduating classes during the 1980s and 1990s) dotted the perimeter. On this gusty late September day, the American and Texan flags on the flagpole in the center of the courtyard fluttered and occasionally snapped in the wind.

"Thank you all for coming," began Principal Kendricks, the small wooden box in his hands already sparking curious looks among those in attendance. "We're here because we want to fulfill the wishes of one of our own, Mr. Bob Lehrer, an En-glish teacher who worked here for many years and recently came back to substitute. Bob started here at Baldwin in . . ." It occurred to Principal Kendricks that he was not sure of the year. Why hadn't he taken the time to look up this information? Or anything at all about the man? He'd intended to, of course, but between meetings and angry parent emails and a fire drill and some suit from Central Office paying him an unexpected visit, he hadn't even had time to eat lunch.

"I started here fresh out of college in eighty-four," barked Mr. Fitzsimmons, the veteran math teacher. "And he'd been teaching here at least twenty years by then."

"*Damn*," muttered a voice, and the crowd turned to look at Mr. Rayfield, whom most were surprised to see in attendance as he normally fled his biology classroom for the faculty parking lot the moment the final bell rang. "Sorry," he continued. "That's just . . . like, he started here in the *sixties*? Just wild."

A few of the older teachers chuckled, then Ms. Fletcher began to speak.

"I only worked with Mr. Lehrer for one year, the 1996–97 school year," she began. "I had the pleasure of observing his classes several times. I was a struggling young teacher and he offered to let me visit in an effort to improve my practice." At this Ms. Fletcher paused, a small smile forming on her lips. "Mr. Lehrer was an artist in the classroom. A master, really. I suspect he was a natural right from the start, although he was too modest to ever admit such a thing. I'm sure the number of lives he touched are in the thousands, and I'm glad I had the chance to learn from him."

There was a murmur of approval, and Principal Kendricks shot Ms. Fletcher a grateful look.

"What I know about Bob Lehrer was that he didn't tolerate any BS from Central Office!" It was Mr. Fitzsimmons again. In addition to being one of the most senior teachers on campus, he was also one of the grumbliest, never passing up an opportunity to illustrate the many ways the Baldwin faculty was mistreated and maligned by the public education hierarchy. Apparently, memorial services were not an exception to this rule.

"Bob was always the first to make it about the kids," Mr. Fitzsimmons continued. As he spoke, the wisps of his unkempt white hair blew about in the strong breeze, and his jowls shook ever so slightly. "Now, thank God he got out of the game before all this junk about high-stakes testing really took off, but still, there has always been meaningless crap in this business. Crap from the higher-ups who think we are cogs in a machine, not teachers to children! Anyway, Bob Lehrer was very vocal in faculty meetings, and he spoke out against crap. That's what I remember most about him, and that's one thing I really liked about him."

Principal Kendricks nodded, unfazed. "Thank you, Mr. Fitzsimmons," he said. "I know Mr. Lehrer would certainly be thankful to you for carrying on his legacy." Mr. Fitzsimmons grunted in response, while there were some titters from the others.

"Could I say something?" came a tentative voice from the back of the loose circle of people. It was Ms. Sanderson.

"Of course," said Principal Kendricks.

"Well," she started, tucking a loose strand of dark hair behind one ear, "I just wanted to say that . . ." At this Ms. Sanderson's young, thin voice cracked, and the pink of her cheeks turned to scarlet. Ms. Fletcher moved toward her and put a comforting arm around the young woman's shoulders. One of the assistant principals present, Ms. Garcia, gave the first-year teacher a sympathetic look.

"I know he was special," said Ms. Garcia, trying to help Ms. Sanderson out.

"Yes," answered Ms. Sanderson. "But I think the reason I'm crying is that it just seemed so undignified the way he died. On an old, nasty couch in the lounge." At this Ms. Sanderson shot a panicked look at the principal, worried that by insulting the furniture in the teachers' lounge she was somehow insulting him.

"It's all right," said Principal Kendricks, understanding her worry. "The furniture in there is pretty awful, but we haven't had the budget to do anything about it for years."

There was a collective sigh then, followed by an awkward silence. The other assistant principal there, Ms. Baker, asked Principal Kendricks if there was anything special that Mr. Lehrer wanted as part of this memorial, gently helping him refocus on the event at hand. The most senior of all the assistant principals, Ms. Baker was often tasked with attempting to keep Principal Kendricks on track.

"Well, funny you should ask," he answered, his voice tightening a little in anticipation of the news he was about to deliver. He lifted the wooden box and looked around the circle of expectant faces. "It turns out that Mr. Lehrer asked us to spread his ashes here, in the courtyard of Baldwin High."

There was a beat or two of shocked silence, broken eventually by stately Nurse Honeycutt's old-school Texas twang. "I'm sorry, I don't think I heard you correctly," she said. "He asked us to do *what?*"

The principal repeated himself, now well aware of the eyes not on him, but on the box in his hands.

"He's . . . in there?" asked Ms. Baker, her eyes widening.

"He sure is," responded Principal Kendricks, his voice matter-of-fact.

Bemused glances were exchanged, and several teachers looked around themselves, wondering if this was part of some strange, elaborate prank or some sort of bizarre, forced professional-development team-building activity concocted by Central Office. Ms. Jimenez, the snarky queen of copy machine jams, loudly declared that *this* was the most fucked up thing that had ever happened in this place.

"Are we sure this is allowed?" asked Ms. Baker, frowning slightly while running a long list of persnickety Central Office bureaucrats through her mind.

"Well," said Principal Kendrick, "there isn't anything saying we *can't.*"

"I say we do it," bellowed Mr. Fitzsimmons. "If it's what Bob wanted."

Mr. Rayfield could not hold back. Spreading his arms wide in an *are you seeing this place* gesture, he stared at his colleagues, his expression one of total bafflement.

"Here?" he asked. "*Here?* I caught two kids skipping class the other day taking a leak in those bushes!" He pointed to the bushes in question, two featureless shrubs that were surprisingly hardy despite their recent abuse. The tone of his voice suggested dismay bordering on near panic. "This can't be someone's final resting place."

"I think," said Ms. Fletcher, piping up, "that Mr. Lehrer most likely asked us to do this because this was a very special place to him." She cast a gentle gaze in Mr. Rayfield's direction. "I know perhaps not all of us can grasp this. But for Mr. Lehrer, Baldwin High was a source of joy. He spent some of his happier days here. It gave him purpose."

Somewhat cowed, Mr. Rayfield shrugged and slipped his hands into his pockets. Part of him wanted to leave, but he knew it would only draw more attention to him. He caught the eye of Ms. Sanderson, who offered him a sympathetic look. She seemed to understand what he was feeling. After all, she'd been troubled by the fact that Mr. Lehrer had died on a ratty couch. Certainly she would be bothered by his ashes being spread where kids cut class to make TikTok videos.

"I don't think we have to understand it to want to honor his wishes," said Principal Kendricks, democratic as usual in his approach. "It may make you feel better to know that his son expressly gave his permission." At this, the principal removed a clear plastic bag filled with the gray cremains of Mr. Lehrer from the wooden box before handing the box to Ms. Baker, who was standing next to him. Principal Kendricks, whose deceased loved ones had all been buried, had expected what was in the bag to be more, well, ashlike. He'd also expected that they would be easier to access. His faculty and staff waited patiently as he tugged on the thick plastic, willing it to tear even a little. At last Ms. Garcia, whose office was off the courtyard, volunteered to run over to get a pair of scissors, leaving the crowd to murmur uncertainly as Principal Kendricks held the plastic sack in his hands.

"Perhaps we should say a prayer?" asked Nurse Honeycutt.

Principal Kendricks looked around to gauge interest. While he was personally an atheist who believed fervently in the separation of church and state—a tall order sometimes, given his home state—he understood the need for ritual.

"I don't know if he was religious, but I suppose it would be fine," he said.

"Heavenly Father," began Nurse Honeycutt, and immediately

most of those in the crowd bowed their heads, "we thank you
for your humble servant Bob Lehrer, who dedicated so much of
himself to this school community for so many decades. Now he
goes to his reward, and we know his spirit is at rest. In your
mercy, may you give peace and comfort to Mr. Lehrer's family
and to all of those who knew him. Amen."

The prayer finished just as Ms. Garcia returned with the
scissors, and soon Principal Kendricks was faced with the task
at hand. Not sure if it would be disrespectful to touch the cremains themselves, he tugged the cut he'd made in the thick
plastic wide open and began shaking the bag repeatedly up and
down, causing the ashes to leap up and fall to the ground as if
he were operating some sort of defective lawn sprinkler. He felt
like a fool.

And there was so much more than he'd anticipated! He had
seen Bob Lehrer once or twice, and the man had grown fairly
gaunt in his old age, but by what was left in this bag, you would
have thought he'd been a world-class bodybuilder.

A wave of discomfort moved through the group, although
no one present blamed Principal Kendricks for it. It was simply
a discomforting situation; those in the crowd with partners and
families waiting for them at home were already imagining how
they would explain this event to their loved ones. There was so
much about their jobs that could not be explained well, especially to those who had never worked in a school. It often felt
like trying to describe some strange supernatural phenomenon,
some bizarre thing outside the laws of nature.

Upon seeing how much was left in the bag, Ms. Fletcher
suggested that Principal Kendricks simply pour the rest out
along the bushes, although she was clear to point toward the
bushes that hadn't been urinated on.

"That's a good idea," replied the principal, his cheeks almost as red as young Ms. Sanderson's. He moved toward the edge of the courtyard closest to the street, the bag in his hands.

As Principal Kendricks crouched and began to pour out what remained of Mr. Lehrer, three women came around the corner and entered the courtyard. All three were middle-aged ash blondes who had given up high-powered careers to be the sort of women who had the time to be very *involved* at a school. They did a lot of advocating for Baldwin, and they mostly meant well. But it was hard not to be a little bit scared of them.

"Principal Kendricks, we were looking for you!" said Jessica Patterson, the tallest of the ash blondes. She was the formidable PTO president, the mother of a sophomore and a senior at Baldwin, and she projected her clear, crisp voice with confidence. "For the fall safety walk, remember? We've already found areas of concern that need to be addressed as soon as possible. For example, we found a door by the gym that isn't locking, which makes that a very vulnerable soft target. Do you have plans to address this?"

As she finished speaking, she was also processing what was happening around her. The group of teachers and staff. The plastic bag in Principal Kendricks's hands. The pained looks on so many of their faces. "What's going on here?" she asked, her voice tightening. Unlike Principal Kendricks, Jessica Patterson had experience scattering ashes, having done so with one mother-in-law and two grandparents; what was in the bag in the principal's hands looked unsettlingly familiar to her.

One of her companions pulled out her cell phone and started recording.

"It's a long story, Ms. Patterson," said Principal Kendricks. He sighed audibly. The teachers and staff members surrounding him looked around at one another, their eyes transmitting the same message: *Oh shit. This isn't good.*

At this moment—a moment that would be discussed ad nauseam and shared on social media, even making it onto some local news broadcasts, a moment described later by advanced English teachers Mr. Williams and Ms. Brennan as both "spectacularly cinematic" and "grippingly surreal"—a large gust of wind blew across the courtyard. On any other warm September afternoon in Texas, it would have been welcomed, but this gust of wind did more than provide a bit of cool relief to those standing in attendance. This gust of wind had other plans.

By the time it had moved on to wherever, PTO President Jessica Patterson was left sputtering and shouting, totally coated in what was left of the remains of Mr. Bob Lehrer, former Baldwin High teacher and beloved substitute.

# *Three*

Mr. Rayfield did not like teaching biology to tenth graders, but his fifth (and hopefully last) year at Baldwin High had offered a respite of sorts.

He had discovered a hiding spot.

On the third floor of the school, at the end of a rarely used hallway, sat the English department book room. It was a dusty, musty space, about fifteen feet by fifteen feet, a breeding ground for wolf spiders and disturbing patches of dark mold, and it served as a repository for haphazard stacks of *Romeo and Juliet* and *The Stranger* and *A Farewell to Arms* that threatened to collapse at any moment.

Most of the English teachers kept sets of the novels they needed in their classrooms; the younger ones allowed and encouraged e-books. So the book room was often empty, a quiet space for Mr. Rayfield to come during his off period. There, he could feel sorry for himself while sitting on the floor, which was covered in a tattered gray carpet that had not been vacuumed since the first Clinton administration.

The cell reception was terrible inside the cinder-block walls, so he didn't come to fool around on his phone. He didn't come to grade. He didn't even come to cry. Mostly he came to enjoy the quiet.

Oh, how much he craved quiet, and oh, how *not quiet* was Baldwin High School!

But in the book room? In the book room there were no teenagers asking him for extra credit or hall passes or extensions on already-extended homework assignments.

There were no administrators asking him to reply to parent emails and attend meetings and keep discipline logs.

And there were no colleagues asking him to watch their classrooms for five minutes while they went to the bathroom or darted out early to a dental appointment. But on this Thursday morning when he unlocked the door to the book room, he was surprised to find not a place to hide away but, instead, his colleague Ms. Sanderson, the teacher who had discovered the body of Mr. Lehrer a few weeks ago, standing in a corner wiping her face with a Kleenex. She was crying. Not sobbing, but definitely and audibly shedding tears.

"Uh, hello?" said Mr. Rayfield, caught off guard and unsure of what to do. Ms. Sanderson startled, taking in Mr. Rayfield's presence just outside the doorway.

"I can come back," he said, trying to brush off the irritation he felt because someone else had discovered his spot.

Just then, three electronic blips crackled over the school's PA system, indicating an incoming announcement.

"Attention, faculty, students, and staff, at this time we are asking that everyone follow procedures for a lockdown," came the voice of Principal Kendricks. "Again, please immediately follow the procedures for a lockdown drill as stated in your

emergency manual. We will be back shortly with an update."
While the principal's voice was steady, Mr. Rayfield could hear
a sliver of anxiety coursing through it.

Mr. Rayfield froze, but Ms. Sanderson immediately moved
past him with purpose, peeking her head out the door, scanning the empty hallway.

"We're supposed to gather any roaming students inside with
us," she said. She was no longer crying; instead, she seemed
calm and in control. "But I don't see anyone."

Stepping back into the book room, she said to Mr. Rayfield,
"Well, I think you need to come in." Following her order, Mr.
Rayfield stepped inside. Ms. Sanderson locked the door behind
them and shut off the lights. Now the only light in the window-
less space came through the glass transom above the door. It
cast a small spotlight in the center of the room.

"Is this for real?" said Mr. Rayfield. "I mean, did they say we
were having a drill today?"

Ms. Sanderson was peering at her phone, biting her bottom
lip. "I barely have reception in here," she answered. "And no, I
don't remember them saying anything."

Mr. Rayfield moved as close as possible toward the door and
held his phone toward the glass above it, as if the magical ether
that made the Internet work could move more easily that way.
He briefly got a single bar of reception, but there were no emails
or texts offering more information.

"Jesus Christ," he said, sliding his phone back into his pocket.
"I *hope* it's not for real."

"Same," said Ms. Sanderson, setting her phone down next to
a stack of tattered *Frankenstein*s on a shelf near her. She placed
her Kleenex from earlier there, too.

"I don't *hear* anything," said Mr. Rayfield, trying his best to listen for any commotion coming from outside and sensing nothing.

"I guess we could sit down," said Ms. Sanderson. "I mean, the carpet is gross, but . . . we're probably going to be stuck in here for a while."

At this suggestion, Mr. Rayfield lowered himself to the floor, then leaned back against a bookshelf full of well-worn copies of *The Catcher in the Rye*. He pulled his knees up to his chest. Ms. Sanderson, a fair-skinned, petite brunette who was wearing a black pencil skirt and a pink Oxford blouse, carefully arranged herself across from him. As she did so, Mr. Rayfield could not help but notice that she possessed a pretty great figure, with ample curves in just the right places. He took in a careful glance, making sure he didn't let his eyes linger. Mr. Rayfield wasn't a particularly good teacher, but he also wasn't a creep.

"Maybe it's just one of those things where they want us to practice without a heads-up," said Ms. Sanderson. "I mean, a drill you know is coming is sort of pointless, I guess."

Mr. Rayfield let his head rest against the shelf behind him. "There's a lot of stuff about this job that seems pointless some-times," he said. "Honestly, I guess I'm something of a fatalist. If some asshole is going to come in here shooting, it's going to happen whether we do these drills or not."

At this, Ms. Sanderson nodded, acknowledging his point. Born just months after the Columbine shooting, she, like Mr. Rayfield, had been performing lockdowns since elementary school. Even now in the book room during this unexpected drill, the two young teachers possessed a preternatural calm that came only from growing up aware that at any moment they might be shot dead at school. First as students, now as teachers.

While their older colleagues were known to hold back tears during these practices or post long social media diatribes about how they should not have to work under such conditions, Mr. Rayfield and Ms. Sanderson were part of a generation that had absorbed an absurd atrocity as normal.

For a while, the two sat in something of an awkward silence, until Mr. Rayfield said, "So, current situation notwithstanding, how have you been holding up since the ashes incident?"

Ms. Sanderson sighed in response and gave Mr. Rayfield a knowing look. Among Baldwin faculty and staff, the situation involving Mr. Lehrer's ashes was referred to as "the ashes incident," "the Lehrer debacle," or "the craziest shit since Cardoza," among other even more colorful phrases. In the two weeks since its occurrence, it had sent the school into crisis mode.

"I just feel so bad for everyone," said Ms. Sanderson. "I feel horrible for Mr. Lehrer, for Principal Kendricks, and even for that mom. I mean, she was just on campus to try and help prevent stuff like *this* from happening." At the word *this* she waved her hand in the air, indicating their current lockdown status.

"Yeah," agreed Mr. Rayfield. "And now the aftermath. It sucks."

To say that Jessica Patterson had been upset would be speaking in the mildest of terms. She had been livid. While the indignity of being stood up by Principal Kendricks for the all-important fall safety walk and her disgust at being covered with a dead man's cremains were probably at the root of her reaction, her angry claims on social media, in PTO meetings, and with local television reporters were focused elsewhere. Her well-crafted, clearly delivered comments homed in on Principal Kendricks's decision to dispose of Mr. Lehrer's remains on the school campus ("unsanitary, disrespectful, and traumatizing to our community") and on her discovery of how Mr. Lehrer's death had been handled in the first place. ("Regardless of the medical examiner's response time, school administrators should have contacted parents to inform them of a body on campus, yet they never did. Imagine if a young person had accidentally walked into the lounge and encountered a dead body! The potential for trauma could be enormous!")

Jessica Patterson had her supporters—many of them—and soon the district initiated a formal investigation into the matter. There was talk of repercussions in the form of heavier oversight from Central Office, and even a concern that Principal Kendricks's position was at risk. Not to mention the damage done to the Baldwin High reputation. As was true with all school communities, the adults who worked at Baldwin and the students who attended it wanted to be proud of their school, not see it serve as the butt of jokes. (At the last away football game, against Baldwin's biggest rival, Lanthrop High, several Lanthrop students had chanted, "Ashes to ashes, dust to dust, Baldwin High is gonna get crushed!" Baldwin had lost 21–0.)

"I heard that the district is going to mandate some sort of trauma counseling session for those of us who attended the ceremony in the courtyard," said Ms. Sanderson. "I'm not sure if they actually will, though."

"You know it would just be for the optics if they did," said Mr. Rayfield, waving his cell phone in the air again, fruitlessly searching for a signal or any sort of communication from outside the book room. Ms. Sanderson nodded in agreement.

"God, that was a weird afternoon," Mr. Rayfield added.

"My roommate is an accountant at a consulting firm," said

Ms. Sanderson, "so I definitely had the better work story that day." She raised a single eyebrow.

Mr. Rayfield smiled, pleased by her witty remark. While he'd had the bad fortune to grow up during a time when school shootings were commonplace, he'd been lucky enough to be born into a generation of men who were not as threatened by funny women as their fathers and grandfathers had been.

"And the day you found him in the lounge," Mr. Rayfield continued. "That must have been . . ." He searched for the right words.

"Oh, it definitely messed with my head," she answered. "I should have gone home early, but I hate to miss a day."

At this Mr. Rayfield gave her a suspicious look. This was not something he could relate to. He used all ten of his personal days every year, and he told Ms. Sanderson as much.

"You're not that into this job, are you?" Ms. Sanderson said, tilting her head and assessing him. "I was surprised to even see you at the memorial." She flushed slightly. She didn't want him to think she'd noticed him, even if she had.

"I can't quite explain it," said Mr. Rayfield. "I mean, why I chose to attend. I guess I just felt like it was the right thing to do, you know? I used to see that guy walking down the halls, all hunched over and old and, like, gripping his substitute teacher folder for dear life. And the way he would just nod and smile at all the kids even if they didn't smile back." Mr. Rayfield sighed deeply and his voice dropped into a softer register: "The whole thing sort of broke my heart."

Privately moved by Mr. Rayfield's display of sensitivity, Ms. Sanderson pressed her hands together, forming her response. "I found his death heartbreaking," she said. "But I don't think *he* was heartbreaking. It's like Ms. Fletcher said. He loved it here. He loved being good at this job."

Mr. Rayfield nodded in acknowledgment and then—because he felt at ease with Ms. Sanderson—bluntly stated, "I suck at this job."

"I'm sure you don't," said Ms. Sanderson, even though she wasn't actually sure. It was only mid-October, but she had been at Baldwin long enough to know that her colleague wasn't a joiner or a leader or a rising star on campus; in fact, he often sat at the back of the auditorium during faculty meetings, looking like he'd rather be anywhere else. She had noticed his forlorn face and his brooding brown eyes, and she had also noticed that he was not bad-looking. In fact, there had been an appeal to him, even in his disaffection.

"No," insisted Mr. Rayfield. "I do suck at it. I think that's why this guy's death just hit me. Like . . . what if I don't get my act together and end up here at the age of eighty-two, dead in the lounge after having sucked at this job for decades?" He grimaced. "This isn't the sort of job you should stick with if you aren't good at it."

"I think *I* might suck at it, too," said Ms. Sanderson, trying to cheer him up. "But I also think I like it? Which makes for a difficult situation. I don't know. It's just . . . the kids make me laugh, I guess. I love it when I explain something and they *get* it. Or if I see a kid having a hard day and something I say cheers them up? I like feeling useful. *Needed* in that way. My roommate just sits at a desk all day and answers emails. She says work is boring. This place is never boring. I never leave here thinking I wasted my time, you know?"

"Well, it's for sure never *boring*," acknowledged Mr. Rayfield. "I mean . . ." He motioned around himself for emphasis before pulling out his phone and holding it up toward the glass yet again. Still one bar. Still no information. Still only silence outside the door.

"At first I thought I sucked at it because I was new at it," he continued, dropping his phone into his lap. "Or because of the pandemic. I kept waiting for some magical switch to flip or whatever. Like some moment when I'm like, *Yeah, it's working*. But that hasn't happened." He did not tell Ms. Sanderson that he often felt like a fraud in front of students, leading them through biology lessons that brought him little joy. He was overwhelmed by the grading, by the paperwork, by the constant demands that started from the moment he entered the building and continued even after he left. He could not even take a piss when he wanted to. Put simply, it was not the vocation that it seemed to be for other people. It was just a job. If he was going to have just a job, perhaps he should find one that paid more and did less residual damage to teenagers.

"Why don't you quit then?" asked Ms. Sanderson. "Find something else?" Ms. Sanderson was a proactive person who thrived off to-do lists and monthly goals. She was the sort of young woman who color-coded her planner and loved organizing her desk. On weekends, one of her favorite things to do was to put on a podcast about popular culture or politics and listen while she rearranged her closets.

"I should," said Mr. Rayfield, his voice flat and with zero promise that this acknowledgment would translate into action. "You're right."

There was a pause, and the two glanced simultaneously at the glass transom, then checked their phones. Still nothing.

There were no sounds outside the door, either. No footsteps, no shrieks, no gunshots.

"I guess it's good we're at least a little hidden back here," said Ms. Sanderson. "This is a very underused area of the school."

"Is that why you come here to cry?" Mr. Rayfield asked. The question came out directly, but not unkindly.

Ms. Sanderson smiled softly, grateful for the opportunity to acknowledge why she'd been in the book room in the first place.

"This was actually my first time coming here," she said. "I just remembered it existed this morning." She frowned a bit, picked at her thumbnail. "What set me off was a nasty email from this mom about her kid's paper, about how I didn't give her kid an extension even though she was allegedly sick." At the word *sick* Ms. Sanderson made air quotes and rolled her eyes. "But *actually*," she continued, sitting up straighter now, clearly frustrated, "she was on *vacation* in Costa *Rica*. Some of the other kids told me they saw it on her Instagram, and I looked, and her profile is public, so I could see it was true. So the mother was just straight up *lying* to me to protect her daughter's precious GPA!" She harrumphed after this little speech, clearly still prickly over the entire situation.

"See, me?" said Mr. Rayfield. "I would have just let it slide. Give the extension. It's not even worth it." He shrugged.

"But it's the *principle* of the thing," said Ms. Sanderson, holding up an index finger for emphasis; even in the poorly lit room, Mr. Rayfield could see Ms. Sanderson's cheeks redden in anger as her original indignation came flooding back. In addition to being born full of executive function, Ms. Sanderson had also been born with a finely tuned moral compass, and she was not yet old enough to realize that its guidance sometimes made her come across as self-righteous. But Ms. Sanderson really was a person of principle. Mr. Rayfield could not know that the week before, she had unloaded all her groceries into her car at Kroger before realizing she had not paid for the twelve-pack of Diet Coke on the bottom rack of her cart. Well aware that her carton of chocolate ice cream was melting in the backseat of her used Honda, Ms. Sanderson had dutifully headed back inside to pay for the soda.

"I get it, I get it," said Mr. Rayfield, holding his hands up in surrender. They had not been in this book room for very long, but he liked Ms. Sanderson. He also thought she was cute. He did not want to offend her.

"So why were *you* coming in here?" she asked, eager to change the focus.

"I come in here all the time," Mr. Rayfield admitted. "Mostly just to get some peace, I guess. To think. To escape. Like I said, I'm really not happy here." It felt good to admit this truth out loud inside the school building. In fact, it was the first time he'd done so. Even though his displeasure at the job was fairly obvious to his colleagues, Mr. Rayfield had been cautious about speaking too explicitly about how miserable he was at Baldwin. The truth was, most of his older coworkers were nice people who had tried to help him, and he didn't want to hurt their feelings. Mr. Rayfield could be a procrastinator, a depressive, and something of a misanthrope, but at his core he was also a good person, which was one reason why he felt guilty about his inability to unstick himself from his current job.

"Like you said, this job is too difficult to stay in if you don't like it," reasoned Ms. Sanderson. "If you want, you could send me your résumé. I'm a good proofreader." She smiled at him. This offer of some sort of communication beyond their current strange circumstances sent a charge of excitement and pleasure through Mr. Rayfield.

"Thanks," said Mr. Rayfield. "That's really nice of you."

Ms. Sanderson nodded, then stood up and went toward the entrance of the book room. She leaned her ear against the door as if she could somehow hear something, her face screwed up in concentration. From her vantage point, she could see the way Mr. Rayfield's dark hair fell over the collar of his navy blue polo shirt. She could observe how his dark jeans were faded at the knees and that his legs were long and lanky. She was supposed to be listening for a school shooter, yet she was examining—no, she was *admiring*—this young man in front of her. It seemed ridiculous, but the month before she had found a dead body in the faculty lounge, so really, what was ridiculous?

"Do you know what this all reminds me of?" she said, taking her seat again on the floor across from Mr. Rayfield. They hadn't been in the room very long, but Ms. Sanderson had to admit she felt comfortable here with Mr. Rayfield, who was young like her and would get all her references and would not try to regale her with teaching stories of long ago or express shock that she was too young to remember 9/11.

"What does it remind you of?" asked Mr. Rayfield, leaning back and knocking a copy of *Catcher* off the shelf with his head. He put it back carefully.

"It reminds me of this time in tenth grade when we had an unannounced lockdown, only I was in the bathroom when it happened," she said.

"Oh shit," said Mr. Rayfield.

"Yeah, oh shit," said Ms. Sanderson. "And they hadn't really told us what to do, you know? We'd always had these planned drills, which is one reason why I think these are stupid in the first place, because you can't truly *plan* for a random school shooter, but anyways, this one time we had this one that was unannounced. It was still just a drill, but I didn't know that at the time, of course."

"Of course," said Mr. Rayfield, nodding.

"So I'm in the bathroom, and I'm all alone," Ms. Sanderson continued. "There weren't any other kids in there, which was odd in and of itself and also made it scarier."

"Sure," said Mr. Rayfield, his voice serious, his face lined with concern as he imagined a younger Ms. Sanderson in this frightening situation. "Could you lock the bathroom door?"

"No, I couldn't," said Ms. Sanderson, appreciating the fact that Mr. Rayfield was a very good listener. He had been born that way, just as Ms. Sanderson had been born full of principle and executive function.

"Why not?" Mr. Rayfield asked.

"There actually weren't doors," she said. "It was one of those open-air designs, you know, so they could catch kids smoking weed? Not that I smoked weed."

Mr. Rayfield nodded.

"So this lockdown starts, and I'm totally scared and clueless, right?" She frowned. Mr. Rayfield could sense that the same principled indignation that had bubbled to the surface earlier when she'd relayed her story about the vacationing liar of a student was making itself known again. This time, Mr. Rayfield understood it totally.

"So I venture out into the hallway, and my heart is just racing, and there is no one, I mean *no one* in sight," Ms. Sanderson continued. "No kids, no adults, nothing. It was like a ghost town. And I thought, *Shit, this is the real thing. There's some ass-hole with an AR-15 somewhere in this building, and I'm out here all alone.*"

"Jesus Christ," said Mr. Rayfield, placing his own teenage self in the same situation and imagining the surge of panic Ms. Sanderson must have no doubt endured. "What did you do?"

"I didn't know *what* to do, so I ran back to my classroom," said Ms. Sanderson. "I was in world history class, and the teacher was this woman, Ms. Jefferson, who was really cool. It was my favorite class, and she was basically my favorite teacher."

Mr. Rayfield nodded, sensing from the tone of Ms. Sanderson's voice that this story was headed nowhere good.

"So I tried to open the door, which was stupid because of course it was locked," she continued. "And then I wiggled the knob a few times, and then, well . . . I just knocked. I was like—in this sort of loud whisper—I was like, 'Ms. Jefferson, it's me. It's Hannah.'"

Mr. Rayfield was pleased to know her first name at last, and happy that it was a name as soft and lovely as Hannah, but he didn't say this, of course. Instead, he asked if Ms. Jefferson opened the door, even though he was fairly certain he knew the answer already.

"No," said Hannah Sanderson, first-year social studies teacher at Baldwin High and only seven years removed from this awful event. "She *didn't*. I knocked and knocked, and I basically *begged* to be let back in, and I was really starting to panic, you know? I was literally all alone. I didn't know if any second some madman was going to run around the corner and shoot me dead, right there in front of my world history classroom."

There was a pause in this story. Mr. Rayfield could see the

spots of indignation starting to bloom on her face again, and even the base of her throat. She frowned and then continued.

"I started to cry. Like out of total panic. I was totally abandoned." At this Hannah let out a shaky breath.

"I would have lost it, too," said Mr. Rayfield. "I would have freaked the fuck out."

Hannah nodded, acknowledging that it had been a very freak-the-fuck-out situation. "I ended up running down this stairwell and out a door that led to the faculty parking lot, and every second I was flinching, like, convinced at any moment that a bullet was going to take me out. And then it turned out it was a drill anyway, unannounced so we could get a good practice in and learn from our mistakes. And one of the things the school learned because of me is that they hadn't planned for what to do for kids outside the classrooms during a lockdown."

"What *are* you supposed to do?" Mr. Rayfield asked, realizing he didn't know the answer.

"Well, teachers and clerks are supposed to immediately go outside and scoop up any kids in the halls and take them into their rooms and offices." He remembered how she'd checked for any such students when this drill had started.

"But what about kids who can't get swept into a safe place fast enough?" said Mr. Rayfield, frowning.

Hannah shrugged and sighed. "They should hide on top of a toilet in the bathroom stalls," she said. "Or make a break for it like I did. That's what I've told my students to do."

"Great," said Mr. Rayfield, his voice thick with sarcasm. He leaned back and again knocked the copy of *The Catcher in the Rye* off the shelf. He picked up the book and peered at the iconic brick-red cover. "Holden Caulfield may have suffered from, like, postwar angst and Waspy ennui, but at least there weren't school shooters at Pencey Prep."

At this Hannah laughed loudly. The specifics buried inside Mr. Rayfield's witty comment pleased her greatly.

"So many kids hated that book in high school," she said, "but I loved it."

"Same," said Mr. Rayfield, and with this exchange each young teacher suddenly knew much about the other.

He left the book at his side and asked Hannah what happened to the teacher who hadn't let her in during that awful lockdown drill.

"Nothing," said Hannah. "I mean, she was following protocol. She wasn't supposed to open the door, you know? If there had been a shooter holding me hostage, he could have been using me to try to get inside, right?"

"Yeah," Mr. Rayfield said, pretty sure he would have broken that protocol.

"I was so upset that day, they let me go home early," said Hannah. "But when I came back the next day, Ms. Jefferson hugged me and cried and cried. I felt sorry for her, I really did. And I understood the position she was in, but . . . she was relatively safe in her classroom, you know?"

The entire horrible event had been a lesson for Hannah that she had not yet fully absorbed and, in fact, would spend most of her adult life trying to willfully ignore: A person could color-code and list and organize, but in the end, life sometimes just happened to you.

"I'm really sorry you went through that," said Mr. Rayfield, his voice soft and full of genuine compassion. "Really sorry."

"Thanks," said Hannah, simultaneously grateful and uncomfortable with her young colleague's sympathy. "I mean, it's no *I found a dead body at work*," she continued, anxious to lighten the mood, "but it's still one of my wildest stories."

Now it was Mr. Rayfield's turn to laugh loudly. He really liked this girl.

Before Mr. Rayfield could fully appreciate what was happening, Hannah was crouching right in front of him—just inches away, really—and carefully lifting up the teacher identification badge hanging around his neck on a red lanyard. As she twisted the ID around to examine it, her knuckles grazed his polo shirt, leaving behind a pleasant, tingling sensation Mr. Rayfield found hard to ignore.

"Jake Rayfield," said Hannah out loud, nodding appreciatively. "It's like the name of a detective from a black-and-white movie." Then she sat down, but this time, instead of sitting back down across from Jake, she placed herself next to him, directly to his left. Jake could smell her strawberry-scented shampoo. She could tease out the cool, clean scent of Irish Spring mixed with some guy deodorant.

Each liked the smell of the other quite a bit.

Just then, the crackling static and the three blips of the PA system startled them both.

"Everyone, I'd like to thank all of you for your composure and compliance during this lockdown," came the calm, collected voice of Principal Kendricks. This time, the sliver of anxiety Jake had picked up on earlier was absent. "We went into lockdown purely out of an abundance of caution, and while we have determined that thankfully there is no threat to our school at this time, we need to remain in our classrooms for just a bit longer. We hope to release right before lunch."

Hannah exhaled. "Thank God," she said.

"I wonder what the hell happened," added Jake.

As soon as Jake finished speaking, Hannah's phone buzzed with an incoming text.

"Wow, something made it through," she said. "Oh, it's Ms. Fletcher. She really looks out for me since everything that happened with Mr. Lehrer." Hannah's eyebrows popped up. "Look," she continued, showing her phone to Jake, leaning into him in a way that felt warm and pleasant.

> Rumor is a homeless guy with a big backpack somehow got inside the building. They finally found him and I'm sure he is harmless, but I think they need to check all the lockers and stuff to make sure he didn't put something dangerous somewhere. Kendricks has to be super cautious with absolutely everything since the ashes incident. We should be on lockdown for at least another hour. Hope you don't need to pee!!! Did you ever hear about the poor Spanish teacher Mrs. Cardoza who went to the bathroom in a trash can during a lockdown? I'll have to tell you about it sometime.

"Jeez, that's going to take a while," said Jake. He said it in the world-weary tone he thought was warranted, but secretly, he was not at all disappointed.

"*Do* you need to pee?" asked Hannah, putting her phone aside.

"No, do you?"

"No, thank goodness."

Jake drew his knees up to his chin and shifted a bit, trying to get comfortable. Hannah thought it made him look younger, more like a teenager himself. She wondered what he had been like in high school, and if they would have been friends. She'd heard through the grapevine that he had attended a prestigious university in the Northeast, one she probably never would have gotten into, even though she had been a very good student herself. She tried to square the young Jake who had clearly been intelligent and ambitious with the handsome, aimless man who'd wandered into a profession he didn't seem to care for very much.

"Can I ask how you ended up here?" she asked. "Teaching, I mean?"

Jake turned to look at her. Hannah adjusted her posture, too, turning her body toward him. They were relaxed now around each other. It was hard to imagine that not that long ago they had been essentially strangers.

"I worked my *ass* off in high school," began Jake. "You wouldn't have recognized me. I was the biggest nerd. Obsessed with my grades, obsessed with my college applications." His forehead crinkled a little at this, as if he was trying to picture someone he had met quite some time ago, and only once. "I used to joke that it was because I had an Asian mom, but the truth is, most of the pressure came from my dad, who's your standard-issue white guy."

Hannah had wondered about Jake's background, but she knew it would have been weird to bring it up right away. Still, since he'd mentioned it, she asked for details.

"My mom is Korean," said Jake. "But her family has been here forever. Honestly, my mom is the chill one. Like I said, it was my dad that was always pushing me at the start, demanding A's, really cheering me on when I made them, talking about how I'd end up a surgeon like him one day, and then, I don't know, somewhere around eighth or ninth grade, I started pushing myself. He didn't have to do it anymore. It was like I became obsessed with being perfect." What being perfect had meant for Jake had involved him staying up all night on a sometimes weekly basis, tapping on his laptop and annotating his readings and working his problem sets over and over until he knew his work would earn nothing less than a 100. It had meant enduring anxiety attacks on a regular basis, usually in the mornings while brushing his teeth or trying to eat a bowl of Cheerios, still groggy from a lack of sleep. It had meant a wave of relief over his college acceptance letters, accompanied by a surprising, lingering worry: *Congrats, you made it. Now what?*

"Okay, so you were this rock-star teenager. But college?" asked Hannah, knowing that the next chapter in Jake's story would provide the crucial turning point.

"To say I didn't adjust well would be an understatement," Jake told her. "I was sort of a disaster, actually. My freshman year I ended up pledging a frat. It was stupid, but I was desperate to find my place, I guess." Jake did not tell her about his horrible homesickness or the beginnings of something that would evolve into a long depression that he would self-medicate with every substance he could find. He did not tell her how he'd spent the first few weeks of college doubting all of his abilities and missing his parents and his bedroom and his dog, a rescue mutt named Banjo. He did not tell her how he'd spent those early days not meeting others, but instead in constant communication with his equally driven high school girlfriend Olivia—his first love and the first girl he'd had sex with, then at a college on the other side of the country—or how it had taken her exactly one month to jettison him in a thirty-minute phone call that had left him a crumbling shell of an eighteen-year-old who quickly became vulnerable to his worst instincts.

He did not tell her any of these things, there in the book room. But there was something about Hannah that made Jake think that one day he just might.

Hannah's small liberal arts college hadn't had a Greek system, something she was grateful for. Her knowledge of fraternities came from movies, and she quickly conjured up an image of sweaty, shirtless white-dude bros chugging cheap beer and crushing empty cans on their foreheads before doing backflips off poorly constructed wooden decks. This didn't square with Jake Rayfield, who was tall and thin, with a brooding face and a big brain and a cynical sense about him.

She had loved college. Loved her professors and her friends and the nights she'd spent with them drinking cheap wine by the small lake on campus, belting out lyrics by earnest female singer songwriters in her terrible voice. She felt sorry that Jake hadn't had an equally wonderful experience.

"So you join this frat . . . ," she said, leaving space for him to continue.

"Yeah," said Jake. "And . . . it sucked. Honestly. It was so disgusting and stupid and absurd. And one night we got super wasted and . . ." Jake stopped. He looked at Hannah. At her open blue eyes and her kind face. At the face that was probably meant for something like this. Meant to listen and nurture and comfort and advise. She was younger than him by a handful of years, but suddenly to Jake, she seemed older. Wiser. In some ways she probably she was.

"What happened?" she asked. Her voice was a whisper, her pretty face full of concern.

"It's embarrassing," said Jake, looking down, looking away. But somehow, he knew that he would tell her right now. That he *could* tell her. That he could tell her about the night the president of the frat—a muscular, wealthy white boy from Greenwich nicknamed Trip—had forced all the freshmen pledges to consume large amounts of grain alcohol and strip naked, then watch a gay porno in the frat house's common room. And how Jake, to his horror, had realized he'd gotten an erection in front of everyone. And how all the other pledges had laughed at him and Trip had laughed at him and how he had run out of the frat house naked and puked in the bushes out back, then stumbled back inside to try to find his clothing so he could escape.

It had been the most humiliating moment of his life.

"I dropped out of the frat, of course," Jake said. "I ended up hanging around with this other sort of lost dude in my dorm who smoked weed every morning before class. And that led to me doing, like, every other drug I could find for about four years. I barely graduated. My dad's dream of med school was over. When I did finish, I moved back in with my parents, and they insisted I had to get a job. My mom actually had to help me finish the application for the district's alternative teacher certification program." He stopped here, taking in his narrative, realizing that it was, in fact, his. "Anyway, five years later, I'm still here."

Hannah's eyes were wide. She was horrified.

"Oh my God, Jake," she said. "That was abuse. What happened to you at the frat, I mean. That was, like, actual abuse."

Jake shrugged. He didn't know if that was the word he would have used, but he also didn't think Hannah's choice of it was too far-fetched, either.

"I've never told anyone about that," said Jake. "I mean, what happened that night." Then, aware of how that might sound, he added, "I know that's something guys say sometimes to endear themselves to women, but I'm telling you the truth. I've never talked about that with anyone else."

Hannah nodded seriously, taking this in. "I'm glad you felt you could tell me," she said.

"Also," added Jake, "I know that whole stunt the frat president pulled was homophobic as hell, and so immature and absurd, but . . . I mean, what I'm saying is . . . my reaction to that video? I'm, uh . . . I'm actually into girls."

Hannah shrugged, brushing aside this comment. "Human sexuality is very complex," she said. "I took a whole course about it in college. Our bodies can respond in ways that surprise us sometimes." She spoke with an air of authority despite the fact that at this point in her life she'd had sex with exactly one person, her college boyfriend of seven months, a directionless theater major who had been a tender and interesting lover and with whom she'd enjoyed an amicable breakup.

"Well, maybe so, but I wish my body hadn't chosen to respond in that way on that night," said Jake. "Although, I don't know . . . maybe it was meant to be. Otherwise, I might have been stuck in that fucking frat for four years."

Hannah grimaced at the thought. "Gross," she added.

"Yeah, gross," said Jake.

"His nickname was actually Trip?" asked Hannah, incredulous.

"Yeah," said Jake. "His real name was, like, Archibald Pierce the Third, or some shit."

Hannah laughed out loud at this. "Archibald Pierce? Seriously?"

Jake rolled his eyes. "Seriously."

"Are you sure his name wasn't Chandler Brooks?" asked Hannah, affecting a posh English accent. "Or maybe Bergstrom

Cooper? Or, like, Clayton Graham?" She stuck her nose in the air and peered around the book room with the bored manner- isms of a member of the effete aristocracy.

"You may be right," said Jake, enjoying himself. "He's mar- ried to a Bitsy now. Or a Muffy. Or maybe a Topsy, if he's really lucky."

"Well, he's certainly not married to a *Hannah*," said Han- nah, her fake English accent gone all at once, replaced by her flat, middle-class American one.

"No," said Jake, "he's not *that* lucky."

At this Hannah looked at Jake, looked him right in the eyes, and Jake leaned in to kiss her.

Oh, how good it felt to kiss Jake! How warm and soft and inviting was his tender, gentle mouth. In Hannah's relatively limited experience, she'd found that some boys were terrible kissers. Too forceful or too wet. But kissing Jake felt like sink- ing leisurely without a fear of falling. Kissing Jake felt like cozy-on-the-couch.

Jake sensed that she liked it, that he hadn't made a mistake. He pulled away for a moment, and she opened her eyes and smiled at him. Their faces were centimeters apart. They laughed, their laughs coming out in soft hushes. They laughed with de- light both at what they had just done and at the awareness that they could do it again, right then.

So they did.

They weren't going to have sex in the book room, obviously, although that was a fantasy both would revisit later, in private. But for now, fantasies were filed safely away, and they turned their attentions entirely to each other in the here and now, to their pink mouths and the napes of their necks and the swell of Hannah's breasts pressing into Jake's warm chest. They kissed and they kissed and they sank all the way down until they were lying next to each other on the floor. There, they stopped briefly to breathe before they kissed and kissed some more. Hannah was eager, like Jake. Hands went under shirts and skated over soft skin. Palms pressed into heated places and were met with little sighs of bliss. The whole thing reminded Jake of high school, back before he had lost his virginity and he and his girl-friend had negotiated all sorts of pleasurable positions on the sofa that always left him aching and full of desire.

It all felt wonderfully youthful, and it occurred to Jake as he kissed Hannah that he was, in fact, still young. That yes, the world was on fire and for their entire lives damaged men had brought guns into schools and their generation had been dealt a terrible hand and nothing good had seemed to happen for years and years, but! His knees and his back were still strong. He did not have to be a teacher forever if he did not want to be because there was still time to be something else. And this beautiful, smart, funny girl wanted to kiss him. She wanted to touch him and let him touch her. There, in the book room, anything and everything seemed possible. Jake's heart surged with joy at the realization.

They made out for a good twenty minutes, until the piercing PA shattered the silence again.

Grinning, they pulled apart and looked at each other, full of happiness. They could barely take in Principal Kendricks's voice as he explained that the school was secure and, soon, they would all be dismissed for lunch.

"I have to say," said Jake, his smile growing, "this isn't at all what I thought was going to happen to me today."

Hannah beamed back. "Same. But . . . I'm glad it did."

"Same," said Jake. "Like . . . incredibly glad."

They sat there, unsure of what to do next, not really wanting to move, even though they knew they must. Suddenly, they were interrupted by the sound of a key in the door.

"Oh my God," said Hannah. The two quickly scrambled to their feet.

The bright fluorescent light of the hallway blasted into them, as did the presence of Mr. Williams, one of the veteran English teachers, who stood in the doorway of the book room with a rolling cart.

"My God, did you spend the entire lockdown in here?" asked Mr. Williams, incredulous. He was a balding middle-aged man who enjoyed weekly sex with his middle-aged wife, but he had not made out with anyone in many years. He stared at his two young colleagues.

"Yes," said Ms. Sanderson, actually giggling. There were three buttons undone on her pink Oxford blouse, but Mr. Williams knew he could not be the one to point that out.

"We're fine, though," said Mr. Rayfield, not even trying to cover up a satisfied smile. He was almost glowing with happiness, and Mr. Williams thought this was the first time he had seen him seem pleased to be at Baldwin.

"Well, it's lunch now," he informed the two, filling the space between them, realizing they were far too intoxicated by whatever had just happened to feel in any way awkward about this moment. "I just came in to get these." He motioned at several stacks of *The Autobiography of Malcolm X*.

"We'll help you," said Ms. Sanderson, peering carefully at Mr. Rayfield, almost as if gripped by a sudden shyness. Mr. Rayfield gazed back at her, captivated.

"Yeah, we'll help," he answered, not taking his eyes off Ms. Sanderson.

After the three of them had loaded up the cart, Mr. Williams thanked them and told them they should go on and get lunch. Standing in the doorway of the book room, he watched as his two young colleagues made their way down the hall, their shoulders nearly touching. He thought, not for the first time, that the two could have been his students at one point, or even his own children. He read the subtext of their body language with the careful eye of someone who had made a living out of analyzing and interpreting stories. Not lifting his gaze until they rounded the corner, Mr. Williams found himself smiling. He wished the two young teachers a satisfying conclusion, or at least a very good next chapter.

# *Four*

There were a million other things Ms. Lovie Jackson, head guidance counselor at Baldwin High School, would rather be doing at present.

Correction. There were exactly three things. A former math teacher, Ms. Jackson enjoyed being precise. The three things she would rather be doing were as follows: (1) telling anyone who would listen about her genius of a grandson who had just started his first year at Morehouse and was already making a mark for himself on campus; (2) going to yoga; and (3) rereading one of her favorite science fiction novels, either *Kindred* by Octavia Butler or just about anything by Isaac Asimov.

Yet here she was, on a late October afternoon, watching a woman almost four decades her junior take over the Baldwin High library for a district-mandated counseling session. And all because her former colleague Bob Lehrer's ashes had flown into the face of the PTO president.

"I'll just finish putting these out," said Ms. Harper, the slight, peppy redhead from Central Office, as she charged along, putting large pads of chart paper and small plastic caddies full of markers on different tables in one corner of the library. She didn't wait for Ms. Jackson's encouragement or acknowledgment; she was clearly taking ownership of the meeting from the start. Ms. Jackson took a deep breath to calm herself and tried to fix her face into something at least resembling a neutral expression.

There was no one to thank for the use of the space. Due to budget cuts, Baldwin High shared one librarian with two nearby middle schools, and today was an off day for Baldwin. The large, high-ceilinged room, which in its glory days had probably been quite impressive, with its tall windows and gleaming tables and bookcases made of real oak, not particleboard, now appeared tired and worn. The poor, solitary librarian had not had the time, energy, or funds to spruce up the place, and the years had done a number here, as they had on every corner of the school.

Tacked up on the dingy white walls in the area in which they were meeting were several once-hopeful READ posters, most featuring celebrities from the late 1990s that few current students could identify. Still, students and teachers liked meeting here instead of the auditorium, which was rumored to have ceiling tiles on the verge of coming loose at any moment, threatening the unlucky person who happened to be seated below.

As Ms. Harper proceeded to stick a large piece of paper on one of the walls, then used a dying green Expo marker to label it PARKING LOT, Ms. Jackson, aware of what was coming, cringed.

"All set!" Ms. Harper announced, turning to look at Ms. Jackson and practically clapping her hands. "Folks come in right after the last bell, right?" she asked.

*Folks*, Ms. Jackson thought. *Lord have mercy.*

"Yes, they should be in shortly after the bell, but we will have to give them time to use the restroom and deal with any last-minute requests from students and emails from parents," Ms. Jackson answered. "I'm not sure how long it's been since you were a teacher, Ms. Harper, so you might not remember that it's difficult to get out immediately at the end of the day."

Given her age and her astonishing rise within the counseling department at Central Office, Ms. Jackson knew that Ms. Harper had probably taught for only two or three years before getting out of the classroom entirely. Yet she probably earned more than most of the teachers who would soon enter the room. She might even earn more than Ms. Jackson.

"Oh, it hasn't been too long since I worked on a campus!" Ms. Harper responded, a tiny slice of defensiveness cutting through her chipper tone. "Of course, I don't have quite the storied career I'm sure you have!"

Ms. Jackson offered a tight smile and maintained her composure. A demure, petite woman in her late sixties, she was known for wearing tailored suits in a collection of neutral tones, and her outfits were never complete without two single pearl earrings and a small silver watch she'd been given by her husband, George, on their twentieth wedding anniversary. (It was inscribed *To My Girl*.) She kept her hair short and natural; in recent years it had started to turn silver. One of the first Black educators to be hired at Baldwin, she had been employed in some capacity at the school since the late 1970s and was now, she realized, something of an institution.

Principal Kendricks had been the one to break the news to her that the district was sending someone to run a mandatory counseling session for all who had been in the courtyard on the day of the ashes incident, and that in her role as head counselor, she would be required to be there.

"They wouldn't acquiesce to me running the meeting?" Ms. Jackson had asked, frowning, when Mr. Kendricks had appeared in her office doorway to deliver the decree from on high. "It might go down easier if they did. And I could make sure our time together actually had value."

"I'd like nothing more than to put you in charge," the principal had answered. "But Central Office is obsessed with appearances, as you well know, and their desire to monitor, weigh, measure, and document has once again gotten the better of them." Mr. Kendricks had rolled his eyes almost imperceptibly, and the two had exchanged a knowing look.

And so Ms. Jackson found herself on this afternoon simultaneously greeting Baldwin faculty and staff members and explaining the presence of Ms. Harper, who stood next to the tables where the meeting was to take place, a wide smile carefully affixed to her face.

"Oh God, not markers and chart paper," grumbled Mr. Fitzsimmons as he sat down at one of the tables. "Please God, anything but that."

Ms. Harper's face fell for a moment before she recovered.

Ms. Jackson suppressed a laugh as she took her seat next to Nurse Honeycutt; he was Ms. Harper's problem today, not hers. And the truth was, he wasn't wrong. Teacher trainings and district-led meetings were often run this way, with an approach that treated the adults in the room as if they were children, not professionals. Ms. Jackson had sometimes wondered if hedge fund managers and attorneys sat around in meetings being asked to draw a colorful picture that represented the group's consensus or to post clarifying follow-up questions on a piece of chart paper labeled PARKING LOT so that these things could be considered later. It was demeaning, and Ms. Jackson prided herself on never treating her colleagues in such a manner.

As the room filled, Ms. Jackson gazed about, taking in the faces of those required to be there. Baldwin High was, as white people liked to say, "diverse" in its population. The biggest school in the city, it drew its students from a vast area, but among the staff, the so-called diversity was not as robust as it could have been. Principal Kendricks was a white man, and out of eight assistant principals there were only two who were not white: Ms. Garcia and a young, animated Black man and Teach for America alum by the name of Mr. Turner, who was clearly on the ambitious track; he had a popular Twitter account that had more than ten thousand followers and regularly featured pictures of him smiling and fist-bumping students as he enthusiastically participated in classroom activities. Ms. Jackson often wondered when—or if—he slept.

To be clear, the faculty and staff were much more representative of the city than they had been back in 1977, when Ms. Jackson had started at Baldwin as a young calculus teacher. Back then, Mr. Bob Lehrer, the source of this godforsaken meeting, had been a relatively young man in his late thirties. At this thought—as was often the case these days—Ms. Jackson was briefly taken aback by the long stretch of her career, and by how much she had experienced and seen.

Aware that her thoughts were drifting, she tried to focus on Ms. Harper, who had started the meeting by asking everyone in the room to "share out" their names, positions, and a fun fact about themselves. Ms. Jackson thought she saw the English teachers grimace at the grammatically incorrect phrase.

"Um, I'm Ms. Sanderson," began the youngest teacher in the

room, "and this is my first year in the classroom teaching geography, and my fun fact is—" She stammered and started to blush, apparently unable to think of a "fun fact."

"Your fun fact is you're a very nervous driver," offered her colleague Mr. Rayfield, smiling in her direction.

"Right, exactly," Ms. Sanderson finished, grinning back at him.

Ms. Jackson immediately understood that there was something going on between the two of them, and hoped that they would either get married or break up in the summer, not during the school year. At least they were in separate departments.

After a few more voices offered brief, strained introductions (Ms. Jimenez: "My fun fact is I absolutely despise fun facts"), Mr. Fitzsimmons inserted himself into the conversation without bothering to introduce himself by name to Ms. Harper.

"My fun fact is I have roughly forty students per class because the damn state of Texas refuses to fund public education properly, how about that?" he said, smiling broadly. Several of the teachers in the room fought not to laugh audibly.

Ms. Harper's eyes grew wide, and she glanced around uncertainly.

"Okay, Mr. Fitzsimmons," said Principal Kendricks from the back of the room, sighing deeply, "thank you for that."

"Yes, thank you for that, Mr. Fitzsimmons," murmured Ms. Harper, regaining her composure. "I think that just about takes care of introductions. Well, except for me." She pushed her smile into full force again before saying, "I know you're all thinking this woman from Central Office is showing up to tell us how to do things and she's so out of touch, but I'll have you know I worked as a second-grade teacher for three years, so I get what it's like to be in the trenches!"

Upon hearing this—perhaps trying to mentally transport herself elsewhere—veteran English teacher Ms. Fletcher closed her eyes and tipped her face toward the library ceiling.

"After working with the kiddos," continued Ms. Harper, "I decided to get my master's in counseling and increase my impact by taking a job at Central Office, where I'm deputy director of the district's counseling department. And my fun fact is that I love avocados!"

Nobody said anything, and after a few uncomfortable beats Ms. Harper proceeded with the debriefing session, slowly defining words like *grief* and *trauma* and *process* in her affected tone of voice. It all felt highly scripted because it almost certainly was. Ms. Jackson found nothing particularly insightful or helpful in what this young woman was parroting; instead, her mind drifted to the unanswered emails in her inbox and to the lasagna her (happily retired) husband, George, had promised to prepare for dinner.

The session moved on, with Ms. Harper instructing the group to make K-W-L charts on the provided chart paper, complete with three columns, each marked with a *K*, a *W*, or an *L*. "In these columns we will place what we *know* about our grief over Mr. Lehrer's passing and the event in the courtyard, what we *want* to know about that grief, and what we will *learn* about that grief," Ms. Harper explained cheerily.

As Ms. Jackson worked with Nurse Honeycutt on their chart, she could overhear the English teachers at the next table.

"I *know* I want to die right now," said Ms. Brennan to Mr. Williams. "Write that down."

"And I *want* to know how to die," Mr. Williams responded quietly, "right here in this library, so we don't have to sit through any more of this shit."

"After you do it, I will *learn* how to do it, too," finished Ms. Fletcher dryly, completing the joke.

Being longtime veterans, the three were easily able to fill their chart with appropriate, vacuous nonsense that would appease Ms. Harper, even as they joked about darker, unwritten content. It was how they managed to survive such moments.

The session droned on as Ms. Harper blathered. While Ms. Jackson worked, she noticed Principal Kendricks and Ms. Garcia, the newest assistant principal, putting their heads together. The other assistant principal present, Ms. Baker, worked quietly with the two younger teachers. Even the grumbly Mr. Fitzsimmons and the snarky Ms. Jimenez played along. She felt a swell of affection for everyone in the room as they dutifully complied with Ms. Harper's idiotic directions. In the end, they knew, it would only help them shed this undue burden the district was forcing them to carry.

With about fifteen minutes left in the session, Ms. Harper moved toward a blank piece of chart paper hanging next to the still-empty PARKING LOT poster. In careful print, she wrote, "How Does Managing Trauma Create a Value-Added Education for Students?" She punctuated the sentence with a large smiley face, then turned to face the group.

"We know that healthy teachers are better teachers, right?" said Ms. Harper. "So to sum up our learning today, let's guide our thinking through an outcomes-based lens and brainstorm and share out all the ways that our work here answers one of the district's essential questions for this school year: How can we measure our impact on student growth in relation to the socio-emotional learning we've done here today?"

Ms. Jackson sighed. Was Ms. Harper honestly trying to tie the events surrounding Bob Lehrer's death to the school's

T-SOAR scores? But of course she was, even if she didn't come out and explicitly state it. Standardized test scores were everything, and that fact wasn't even Ms. Harper's fault.

The Texas Standards of Academic Readiness tests (T-SOAR, sometimes casually referred to by teachers as *bedsore*) were the bane of their existence—high-stakes, poorly written tests that caused unreal amounts of stress for students and faculty alike and transformed normally enthusiastic, creative classrooms into drill-and-kill multiple-choice factories where students ceased to be human beings and instead became data points. Championed in equal measure by the state's conservatives (who longed for concrete reasons to defund public schools and sell them to charters) and bourgeois neoliberals (who saw college degrees and white-collar jobs as the only measures of "success"), these tests had so damaged public education that Ms. Jackson worried their deleterious effects would be felt for generations to come. It took an exceptional amount of strength and commitment not to become worn down by the constant focus on the T-SOAR and instead remember that the children they served were real, actual people with unique gifts and needs.

As the room began to understand the next step on Ms. Harper's agenda, there was uncomfortable shifting in seats and open eye-rolling. Ms. Jackson wondered again just how much Ms. Harper earned, and if it was enough to make up for the hostility she almost certainly had to face on a regular basis. Maybe she was oblivious to the hostility? Or maybe she—like some in the profession—had actually swallowed the lie that the T-SOAR mattered and was a good judge of ability, both of children and of teachers. Who could know?

The question of how their meeting about Mr. Lehrer might connect to standardized testing hung in the air unanswered.

Ms. Harper did not relent but instead projected her fixed smile at the room without stopping.

Ms. Sanderson, clearly an overachiever who couldn't help herself, raised her hand.

"Great!" Ms. Harper almost shouted. "Let's hear from you!"

"Um . . . ," the young teacher began as Ms. Harper poised herself by the chart paper, marker in hand, ready to take notes. "I guess we could, like, do an assessment after this meeting and compare it with one from before and then, like, see if there has been an impact on the data?"

Ms. Jackson thought Ms. Sanderson's tiny voice sounded defeated. Sad. She noticed the first-year teacher glancing shyly about the room, seeking approval, and Ms. Jackson wondered if her young colleague had ever imagined that such a dry and soulless meeting would be a part of her work as a teacher. She also wondered how much better this meeting might have been had Ms. Harper bothered to actually address the loss of Mr. Lehrer with the group in an authentic way. Ms. Jackson had heard through the grapevine that Ms. Sanderson had been the one to discover the body and that, naturally, it had shaken her up. She made a mental note to check in with the young teacher later, one-on-one.

"An assessment is a great idea!" Ms. Harper exclaimed, enthusiastically affirming Ms. Sanderson's tepid response. She wrote PRE-TEST/POST-TEST on the paper, then turned to look back at the group. "What else?"

From the back came the voice of Mr. Kendricks, and the entire room shifted in unison, the faces of the teachers and staff members in the room now focused on him. Their principal stood up and smiled congenially.

"You know, Ms. Harper, I want to thank you for your time

today," he said, and Ms. Jackson could tell he was choosing his words carefully. "I'm going to be sure to tell Anna Dowell over at Central Office what a help you've been for us, but I think given the sensitive nature of what happened in the courtyard, this last activity might be better completed just by those who are a part of the school community."

He was so affable in his delivery, so unthreatening in his approach, but as he spoke he walked toward Ms. Harper in much the same way an experienced bouncer gently approaches a drunk to guide him out of the bar. As if he can get the drunk to believe it was his idea to leave all along.

"Oh!" said Ms. Harper. "Well, I think . . ." She was somewhat uncertain. In the hierarchy of the district, she outranked him, even though he was more than twenty years her senior. That said, Baldwin was his school. His turf. On some level Ms. Jackson knew that Ms. Harper would have to respect that, even as the head guidance counselor worried what such a bold move might mean for their principal. She noticed Ms. Baker, Principal Kendricks's second-in-command, nervously appraising what was going on.

"We can help you gather your stuff," Principal Kendricks said, still smiling. Understanding what was being asked, some of the teachers began gathering Ms. Harper's chart paper and markers and packing them up.

"Again, I can't thank you enough for this guidance," said Mr. Kendricks. "You deserve and will receive a glowing report."

These words seemed to relax Ms. Harper. Ms. Jackson knew she was the sort of district employee who found value not in her work but in glowing reports about her work.

After Ms. Harper was packed up, Principal Kendricks volunteered to walk her out.

"Let's talk tomorrow," he murmured quietly to Ms. Jackson as he passed her. "Just go home and unwind."

Ms. Jackson shot him a look of gratitude—hers certainly not the only one he'd received over the last couple of minutes—and waited for the library to empty before she started to gather her things.

A young custodian arrived, pushing her janitorial cart through the library doors, ready to get to work. Trying to quell her worries over what had just happened, Ms. Jackson excused herself and got out of the woman's way. She was the last one to leave the meeting.

# *Five*

November 10, 2022

---

FROM: vanessa.hollins123@hollinsfamily.com
TO: Andrew.Williams@district181.org
SUBJECT: Serious Concern About Book Choice in
Classroom!

Mr. Williams,
Good morning. I write to you with a serious concern. As you
know, my son Cayden is in your 3rd period AP English
Language class. Today he came home with some upsetting
news, namely that you would be teaching a book called *The
Autobiography of Malcolm X* in your class. After doing some
research about this book, I was really shocked that it would
be taught in a high school setting. I can tell you that when I
went to Baldwin High in the 90s, this book was not on any
reading list!

I have always been a supportive parent who strives to help her children learn and grow at school, but I regret to inform you that this novel choice is not acceptable for my family as it is an example of Critical Race Theory (CRT) and is racist against white people. My children have been raised not to see color and to love all people equally no matter if they are white, brown, black, or purple! This book does not support that worldview.

It is my request that Cayden be given an alternative assignment during this unit. To be honest, I do not think *any* Baldwin child should be forced to read this book, but my main concern right now is protecting my own son.

I look forward to reading your response.


Sincerely,
Vanessa Hollins

---

FROM: Andrew.Williams@district181.org
TO: vanessa.hollins123@hollinsfamily.com
SUBJECT: RE: Serious Concern About Book Choice in Classroom!


Mrs. Hollins,
Thank you for taking the time to reach out to me regarding your concern about *The Autobiography of Malcolm X*. (If you don't mind, I must pause here to mention that this text is not a novel, as you put it, because it is not a work of fiction; rather, since it is an autobiography written in collaboration with the late Alex Haley, it is a work of nonfiction.)

Regardless, I am troubled to read that you believe Cayden should not study this text, which for many years my students have found to be provocative, challenging, and interesting. Teaching it is not an endorsement of anything any more than my teaching *The Great Gatsby* (which, yes, is a novel; again, I feel the need to point out the distinction between fiction and nonfiction) is an endorsement of vehicular manslaughter. Rather, it is an opportunity for my students to grow as thinkers.

If you may recall, the syllabus I handed out at the beginning of the year (which you signed) not only listed this book as part of our future coursework, but also included a paragraph about the value in teaching difficult and sometimes controversial texts. As AP Language is a college-level course that offers college credit, I have chosen to approach the teaching of it in that spirit. I trust that my students are capable scholars who are able to separate themselves from language that may trouble them on a personal level and instead focus on analyzing how the language works to a certain effect. This teaches them to become careful, critical thinkers capable of solving problems, working with others, and communicating clearly. In essence, it teaches them to be good global citizens.

I must also express some confusion over your email as I taught this text to your older son, Jayden, several years ago with no issue. In fact, if I remember clearly, he enjoyed it and thanked me for including it in my curriculum.

Sincerely,
Andrew Williams

FROM: vanessa.hollins123@hollinsfamily.com
TO: Andrew.Williams@district181.org
SUBJECT: RE: RE: Serious Concern About Book
Choice . . .

Mr. Williams,

Thank you for your response and for reminding me about
the difference between fiction and nonfiction. I confess it's
been a while since I took an English class since my parents
insisted I spend my college years studying something
"useful" LOL!

    The reason I didn't say anything when Jayden was in
your class is that I was not aware at that time about CRT
and its dangers. Trust me when I say that had I known,
I would have demanded a different assignment for
Jayden as well.

    I appreciate that you are defending the choice of this
book, but I still want a different assignment for Cayden.
Preferably, I would like you to supply me with a list of
possible texts so that I can choose the one that works best
for our family.

Vanessa Hollins

P.S. As for *The Great Gatsby*, I must tell you that it was one
of my favorites in high school. It helped me cherish the idea
of the American Dream!

FROM: Andrew.Williams@district181.org
TO: Lydia.Brennan@district181.org
SUBJECT: FWD: RE: RE: Serious Concern About Book
Choice . . .

See below. I'm fuming.

FROM: vanessa.hollins123@hollinsfamily.com
TO: Andrew.Williams@district181.org
SUBJECT: RE: RE: Serious Concern About Book
Choice . . .

Mr. Williams,
Thank you for your response and for reminding me about
the difference between fiction and nonfiction. I confess it's
been a while since I took an English class since my parents
insisted I spend my college years studying something
"useful" LOL!

The reason I didn't say anything when Jayden was in
your class is that I was not aware at that time about CRT and
its dangers. Trust me when I say that had I known, I would
have demanded a different assignment for Jayden as well.

I appreciate that you are defending the choice of this
book, but I still want a different assignment for

———————

**Lydia Brennan:** Hey just saw your forwarded email.
Texting my response. I don't even know how to begin
here. From the backhanded insult about English
majors to her ATROCIOUS and FLAWED

interpretation of The Great Gatsby, that response is a shitshow from beginning to end. I am so sorry. No parent in any of my classes has complained . . . yet. You know these people talk to each other though.

**Andrew Williams:** How the hell am I supposed to handle this? Give her what she wants? And then set this precedent that parents set my curriculum?! How is her precious Cayden going to manage in college or life if this is her approach? And to just be whiny about it, I don't want to have to come up with an entirely separate assignment/assessment because of this. I already get here at the crack of dawn every day to stay on top of grading. This is horseshit.

**LB:** Yes, it is. But you need to loop in admin ASAP. Given the Lehrer incident and Central Office's additional eyes on us right now you don't want to handle this alone. It could get nasty fast.

**AW:** I guess I should loop in Ms. Baker. I mean, she's the AP over the English department. I hate to bother her. Lately she seems sort of not herself.

**LB:** This is only my first year here, but didn't you say she hasn't been herself since she lost her wife? Regardless, you need to loop her in.

**AW:** I'm kind of wondering if I should go to Ms. Jackson.

**LB:** Why? Because she's Black?! I don't see why the guidance counselors' office should have anything to do with this. This is principal/assistant principal territory.

**AW:** I know, I know. I suppose it was stupid idea but I thought maybe she'd have some ideas on how to defuse this situation.

**LB:** My fellow white educator and friend, no. Don't put that on her. She has enough on her plate just trying to get every senior to earn the credits to graduate on time. It's not her job to hold your hand here.

**AW:** Yeah, you're probably right. But can you tell me . . . what the hell even IS Critical Race Theory?!

**LB:** It's a theory they teach in law school, I think? That racism is essentially part of all of our systems? Trust me, Cayden's mother can't explain it to you either; she's just latched onto some coded language to deal with her own racist discomfort that Baldwin High isn't as white as it was when she went here in the 90s. I said what I said.

**AW:** You're right. I know you're right. Shit, she just emailed me again. It just popped up.

**LB:** Forward it and let me see what it says.

———

FROM: vanessa.hollins123@hollinsfamily.com
TO: Andrew.Williams@district181.org
SUBJECT: Another point I would like to make

Mr. Williams,

After our last exchange I took time to review your email to me and also forwarded it to my husband so he could read it. I do not want to create a problem between us as you are Cayden's teacher and I believe that parents and teachers should be in partnership, but I admit upon reflection I do not believe it was appropriate or fair of you to try and educate me on the difference between nonfiction and fiction. The reason for my email was to get a different assignment for my son instead of *The Autobiography of Malcolm X*, which I have explained to you does not match our worldview or support the values that I am trying to strengthen in my son. The purpose was not to be taught a lesson by you.

Also, my husband suggested I add this point. In your response to me you said you wanted to help your students become "global" citizens. Are we not living in America? Shouldn't the focus be on growing American citizens? Just a thought.

I think some good books for Cayden to use for this unit might be any of the classics. Something by Ernest Hemingway or someone like him.

Please respond at your earliest convenience as I would like this resolved as soon as possible.

Vanessa Hollins

FROM: Andrew.Williams@district181.org
TO: vanessa.hollins123@hollinsfamily.com
SUBJECT: RE: Another point I would . . .

See below. Can you even believe this bullshit?! WTF! The
*audacity* of this woman to come at me like this?! After I
clarified a basic error that should be known to any fifth
grader?! She wants Ernest Hemingway. I should just throw
*The Old Man and the Sea* at her precious baby and be done
with this. I wonder if she could ever grasp that the values
she is trying to engender in her son are closed-mindedness
and bigotry. Jesus Christ I am so over this.

---

**AW:** Did you see that shit?!

**LB:** What are you talking about? Did you forward me
the email?

**AW:** Yeah, at the end of the period. Did you not get it?

**LB:** I don't see it. Are you sure you forwarded it to me?

**AW:** FUCK!!!!!!!!!!!!!!!!!!!!!!!!!!!!!!!!!!!!!!!!!!!!!!!!!!!!!!!!

---

FROM: vanessa.hollins123@hollinsfamily.com
TO: Andrew.Williams@district181.org
CC: Bryan.Hollins@enertech.com; Mark.Kendricks
@district181.org; Denise.Baker@district181.org;
Lillian.Ellsworth@district181.org; James.Espinosa
@district181.org; Melanie.Gardner@district181.org
SUBJECT: Immediate action demanded now

Mr. Williams,

As I am sure you have discovered by now, you obviously
tried to forward my last email to someone else and ended
up replying to me instead. Your disgusting response to me,
a concerned parent and taxpayer, is copied below so all
may see how you chose to talk about me.

To say that I am outraged is an understatement. On this
response to you I have CCd my husband Bryan, Principal
Kendricks, your appraising administrator Ms. Denise Baker,
my school board member Lillian Ellsworth (who happens to
be a longtime family friend and will not be pleased by this
behavior), the head of Secondary English Language Arts
Curriculum for the district Mr. James Espinosa, and the
head of all Secondary Education for the district Ms. Melanie
Gardner.

I am demanding that my son Cayden be removed from
your classroom immediately as it's obvious that you have a
personal vendetta against my family and I cannot be
assured that you will grade him fairly moving forward.

Between this and Baldwin's headline-making behavior
that occurred in the courtyard two months ago, I am really
starting to wonder if this is the right school for my son. Or for

anyone's child! I am regularly trying to convince my friends who send their children to private schools to consider Baldwin High, but your response makes me question whether I should be the one considering private school.

I will also have you know that Jessica Patterson knows me and I have already reached out to her to let her know about this situation. I am going to encourage her to create a meeting of concerned parents to review not only your book choices but the choices of all English teachers at Baldwin to make sure that they are in alignment with our community values.

Vanessa Hollins

———————

**LB:** Hey, how are you holding up?

**AW:** Drinking bourbon straight in my living room on a goddamn Thursday evening if that tells you anything.

**LB:** Understandable. I am so sorry. This is a nightmare.

**AW:** It is. And I'm an idiot.

**LB:** I want to tell you to be nicer to yourself, but it's a pointless exercise. I'd be beating myself up, too. GAH! What happens next?

**AW:** Kendricks and Baker are looped in, of course. They're putting out fires on my behalf right now and trying to keep Central Office off our backs, I'm pretty sure. Given this is happening in the wake of the courtyard incident makes it all worse. Anyway, I think the powers that be are trying to figure out if we can just appease Cayden's parents and make it all go away somehow.

LB: Appease them how, do you think?

AW: We pull Malcolm X for everyone. If we do that, then maybe we end this now and it doesn't get worse. Oh, and the kid is getting moved out of my classroom and will probably end up on your roster. He's not a bad kid, really. Gets his work in, says smart stuff. This is all the mom, I'm pretty sure. He probably just mentioned the title to her and she took off running.

LB: I'll handle it. Don't worry about that. And if we have to get rid of MX, I guess we do it. But God, I hate giving in to these assholes. It's such a rich text.

AW: It's my fault. I should have just acquiesced to her bullshit demands from the start.

LB: But you're right . . . then what? They're in charge of everything we teach? I know this is Texas, but my God, I've taught for a long time, and I've never felt so afraid to introduce certain works as I have recently. I mean, we've discussed this many times. Malcolm X makes some uncomfortable claims in that book. You know I'm not wild about some of his statements

regarding women, for example. But so much of what
he says still feels so urgent and relevant. He's an
important historical figure who is making an argument.
It's not about endorsing anything; it's about guiding
these kids to think for themselves and understand
how arguments are made.

AW: Yeah, guiding kids to think for themselves and
understand nuance is why I got into this business.
And that approach seems to be in real danger. Not just
in Texas but everywhere.

LB: Oh, I got into teaching for the money and
the fame.

AW: Funny funny. Okay, I'm going to try and get some
rest. Thanks for checking on me.

LB: For sure. This will end. It will be okay. I promise.
Hang in there, Andrew.

AW: Thanks, Lydia.

———————

Mark Kendricks: Hey, Denise. Sorry to bug you after
hours. Texting because I know it's late plus better to
talk this way.

Denise Baker: It's okay. I'm up. And I'm not surprised
you're up, too. The principal never sleeps, after all.
☺ This about the Malcolm X thing?

**MK:** Yeah. I just got off the phone with Ms. Gardner from Central Office. We're moving Cayden Hollins into Brennan's class for starters, and we're going to have to let Brennan and Williams know we can't teach Malcolm X this year. It pains me to say that, but that's how it has to be. I don't know about future years. Gardner has personally apologized to the mom and agreed to meet with her in person to let her vent and express concerns re: books, etc.

**DB:** Think that will calm her down enough to keep this off the news and neighborhood Facebook pages?

**MK:** Hopefully. Ms. Hollins is friendly with Jessica Patterson and that crowd, tho. So . . . who knows. Williams is a great teacher but man you need to be careful what you're doing on district email.

**DB:** I know. God, isn't there a food bank or something these women can volunteer for with the time they seem to have? Maybe a museum?

**MK:** Just don't email them that suggestion. In truth, a lot of our parents are really good people who mean well and advocate for our school, and I'm grateful for them. But some are just misguided. Do me a favor and loop in Williams and Brennan? So they know about the student switch and the curriculum change? I'll check in with them later, but I'm in meetings at Central Office all day tomorrow. Will probably get questions

about this along with how Ashgate is going, as well as
the usual frustrations over my resistance to toeing the
company line. Good grief.

**DB:** I'm sorry, Mark.

**MK:** It's okay. I'm hanging in there. Hope you are too.

**DB:** I'm trying.

**MK:** I know you are. And I'm grateful for you and
the fact that I can depend on you, this year more
than ever.

**DB:** Of course, Mark. You're welcome.

———————

FROM: Andrew.Williams@district181.org
TO: Lovie.Jackson@district181.org
SUBJECT: Just wanted to get your take

Ms. Jackson,
I'm sorry to bother you, but I'm reaching out in search of
some sort of guidance. Hence an email to the guidance
counselor! As you may have heard, a parent took me to task
for teaching *The Autobiography of Malcolm X* in my AP
Language class, and there was something of a kerfuffle
that followed (along with an accidental email I should never
have sent).

It appears that the text will be removed from our
curriculum, and it's really bothering me. I feel it is such an

important text with so much to say about race in America.
I've been teaching it for years and have always received
such good feedback from my students, including my white
students.

I'm pretty disheartened by this and was looking for some
words of wisdom.

Sincerely,
Andrew Williams

---

FROM: Lovie.Jackson@district181.org
TO: Andrew.Williams@district181.org
SUBJECT: RE: Just wanted to get your take

Mr. Williams,
Forgive the delay in my response. I had several meetings
this morning regarding our dual credit program.

I had heard a bit about this incident but not the
particulars. I'm certainly sorry to hear the situation has
upset you. I have actually never read the text in question,
although it is a favorite of my husband's.

In this business, we can only focus on what we can do in
the moment. We can only focus on the next good choice.
It's been my experience that this is true in life as well. We
cannot control other people or their behavior. We can only
try to do the next right thing.

I hope next week is an improvement over this one.

Sincerely,
Ms. Jackson

FROM: Denise.Baker@district181.org
TO: Andrew.Williams@district181.org
CC: Mark.Kendricks@district181.org
SUBJECT: Update on Hollins situation

Mr. Williams,
I wanted to follow up on our conversation this morning and document our discussion with this email. Thank you for your time today.

To summarize:

1. Cayden Hollins has been moved to Lydia Brennan's third period, effective immediately.

2. *The Autobiography of Malcolm X* will be replaced for all advanced junior English classes. Future use of the text will be discussed at a later date.

3. A letter of reprimand concerning your email to Ms. Hollins will be placed in your personnel file. I would like to take the time to remind you that your file is a robust one full of numerous accolades, and one letter of reprimand should not be of a serious concern to you.

Mr. Kendricks is in communication with Central Office over this incident. Cayden's parents are meeting with Ms. Gardner. Parental voices are always welcome at Baldwin and in this district, of course, so hopefully this meeting with Ms. Gardner will help to smooth things over.

Finally, a personal note. When I was a young college student, I read *The Autobiography of Malcolm X* for a sociology class I was taking. I remember finding it quite thought-provoking, and my classmates and I had many good conversations about it. I have no doubt that by including it in your coursework, you made an impact in the lives of many students. I remain hopeful that the time will come again when it can be included on your syllabus.

Sincerely,
Denise Baker

---

TO: Denise.Baker@district181.org
FROM: Andrew.Williams@district181.org
CC: Mark.Kendricks@district181.org
SUBJECT: RE: Update on Hollins situation

Ms. Baker,
I appreciate your steadying words and reassurance. Your kindness to me during this time is deeply appreciated.

Sincerely,
Andrew Williams

---

## **MR. WILLIAMS'S AP LANGUAGE AND COMPOSITION CLASS ANNOUNCEMENTS**

*ALL PERIODS: Please note an important change to the class syllabus.* The Autobiography of Malcolm X *has been replaced with an independent choice book. You should choose an autobiographical work about a person in whom you are interested. You must bring a note signed by a parent or guardian that grants permission for your reading choice. Deadlines for reading assignments and assessments TBD. Please see me with any questions or concerns.*

*Thank you,*
*Mr. Williams*

# Six

Denise Baker, the most senior of Baldwin High's eight assistant principals, sat down on the toilet first thing Monday morning and discovered that her period had started overnight even though it hadn't made an appearance in almost two months.

"Fuck this shit," she said to no one, and loudly, too, because Denise Baker lived alone without even a cat to hear her. After a few stops and starts in junior high, her cycle had always arrived politely on time. Until lately. The websites and books referred to it as *perimenopause,* but Denise just referred to it as hell. Still on the toilet, Denise cursed her ruined white cotton Fit for Her briefs and sank her head into her hands. There, she had a realization.

*A woman's late forties are the puberty of old age.*

It was a clever bon mot, one she would have shared with Kathy had Kathy not died on her three years earlier of colon cancer, a scourge only discovered after Denise had personally made the doctor's appointment and insisted Kathy try to figure out the source of her ever-worsening symptoms. But now Kathy was gone, their son was away at college, and Assistant Principal Baker was all alone on a Monday morning. She slipped off her under-pants and tossed them directly into the bathroom trash can. She would waste no time trying to salvage the unsalvageable.

———

She hadn't even pulled into the parking lot at Baldwin before her phone started pinging with the day's business, and it was still well over an hour before the first bell.

> Ms. Baker I'm sick with some sort of bug and the EducateMe portal isn't working for me for some reason. I need coverage for my first period class!!! And I guess the rest of the day too? Any chance you know how I can reset the login? SO SORRY!!!!

> Ms. Baker, I'm sorry to bother you first thing in the morning, but I just received a parent complaint because I mentioned Harvey Milk in a lesson last week. It wasn't even the focus of the lesson, just a brief mention. The mother is saying it goes against her family's religious beliefs. I know you recently had to deal with some upset parents and a text in the AP Language classes. I've forwarded you the email and wanted to give you a heads-up, but I'm too nervous to respond until you tell me what I should say. Sorry to bring this to you on a Monday. Let me know when you have a moment to discuss. Thank you.

> Denise any chance you checked the cameras on the third floor by stairwell G? Re: incident from Friday

with that ninth grader? Parents claiming he is being
bullied but girl involved claims boy threw his Takis at
her first before calling her a "fat fucking bitch." As our
friend Whitney always said . . . I believe the children
are our future! :-/ Let me know about the cameras.

Denise, I also sent you an email about this but just a
reminder that your first round of TDAF teacher
observations and conference notes are due by the end
of the week. Central Office has made it clear they will
be breathing down our necks on this deadline and
given the recent drama, we have to be really on top of
it. Just a CYA reminder. Thank you for all that you do.

Department head meeting moved to Lori's office
because Kendricks's office has some strange odor
they can't figure out???

Slinging her canvas tote bag over her shoulder as she winced
at a particularly painful menstrual cramp, Denise walked toward the building, the late November weather cool and crisp.
She responded to the last text, sent by her fellow AP Kitty
Garcia.

Strange odor like what?! Feet? Farts? Weed? Jkjk on
the last one.

Ms. Garcia's quick response (*No clue but if it's weed sure wish
I knew his dealer*) made Denise smile for the first time all morning, and she quickly applied a *HaHa* react to the text. Then she
shot off a note to Michael, a senior at UT. Her son was her

shining star and her best achievement, a brilliant kid destined for greatness.

He also seemed allergic to the idea of calling his mother.

> Hope you're having a good day, sweetie. Heading into school. Had a meeting moved because Principal Kendricks's office smells funny. The fun never stops. Give me a call soon if you can. Your mama misses you and can't wait to see you soon for Christmas. Love you.

She was reaching, she knew. Her adult son would probably not even be briefly amused that the principal's office at his former high school, which doubled as his mother's place of employment, smelled strange. But ever since Kathy had died, it seemed Denise had struggled to find ways to connect with Michael. They'd both been gripped with grief, of course, but Denise's answer to Kathy's death had been to sink deeper into isolating sadness with each passing year. Michael's solution had been to double down even harder on his commitment to overachievement: taking extra classes, racking up leadership positions on campus, committing to every volunteer and activist opportunity, even talking about running for office one day. Last summer he'd served as a congressional intern in Washington, D.C., and had come home for only one long weekend, which he'd mostly spent with his old high school buddies. Given their widely different reactions to their loss, it was no wonder they had a difficult time communicating.

As she let herself into the building and began climbing the steps to her second-floor office, the phone in her hand buzzed.

She looked down hopefully. Michael had given her last text a *thumbs-up* react. In response he'd written:

> **Maybe you need to give Principal Kendricks some extra-strength deodorant for Xmas. Will try to call tonight or tomorrow.**

Ms. Baker sent back of a GIF of a smiling dog she found amusing and hoped that "tonight or tomorrow" meant at least by the end of the week.

After unlocking her office door, Ms. Baker flipped on the fluorescent lights (one that worked, one that never did), turned on her walkie-talkie (which every AP referred to as their "radio"), set it to a low volume, and sat down with a sigh, taking a moment to curse the stuffing coming out of one of the chair's armrests. If she went through the laborious paperwork necessary to start the process of requisitioning a new chair, it might appear on the eve of her retirement. *If* she was lucky.

Determined to start the week on the right track, Ms. Baker dealt first with her morning texts and then started clawing her way through the 128 emails in her inbox from teachers, parents, and students. Several were about her TDAF observations and conferences, the bane of every assistant principal's existence. TDAF (which stood for Teacher Development and Feedback but was often referred to as Total Drivel and Foolishness or Totally Dumb as Fuck) was the time-consuming, utterly pointless, state-mandated system of rating teachers, wrapped in ribbons of red tape and consisting of three conferences and four observations over the course of a school year, each observation requiring the assistant principal to rank their teachers on a scale of 1 to 5 on everything from *Dresses in a professional manner* to *Establishes a supportive culture of warmth where learning is the focus and all students can achieve.*

Naturally, most Baldwin teachers expected to be rated a 5 on every category, even though the entire performance was meaningless, since nothing much could happen to a teacher as a result of their TDAF ratings, so long as they consistently scored a 3 overall on the rating system, which most sentient beings with half a brain could achieve. When faced with a teacher who wept over anything lower than a 5 on a particularly stupid category, Ms. Baker always wanted to shake them and say, "Look, it's not like anyone is going to get a *raise* out of this!" But in a system that didn't afford teachers much respect, several of them saw a string of 5's as their birthright, something tangible that they could point to as evidence that they were not wasting their lives teaching restless, anxious, pimply teenagers day after day. As a former teacher herself, Ms. Baker understood this, so she tried to approach every TDAF teacher conference with compassion.

Because a colleague was on maternity leave that fall, Ms. Baker was tasked with observing not only the bulk of the English department, but also several math teachers. A double major in English and education, Ms. Baker was something of a mathphobe; she'd always let Kathy be the one to factor tips at restaurants, do their taxes, and balance their checkbook, just as she'd sought Kathy's help back in college whenever an assignment involved numbers. (In those days she'd pay Kathy back in make-out sessions, which had made the entire process quite enjoyable.) The TDAF ratings system was not supposed to depend on an assessor understanding the subject matter so much as their understanding of the strategies and pedagogical choices of the teacher, but she sensed that many of the math teachers were particularly resentful of her presence in the classroom.

Mr. Fitzsimmons was perhaps the *most* resentful.

Ms. Baker grimaced at the thought of having to assess the math department's most veteran teacher, a grizzled man close to retirement who never seemed to smile, whose classroom walls were devoid of any decorations, and who—for the ten years in which she'd worked at Baldwin—had griped in every faculty meeting about the new district mandates as if he were the only one to have to endure them. She had put him on the back burner of her mind long enough, and she knew she would have to work in an observation of him in the next few days.

Ms. Baker checked the time on her computer. She had a few minutes before she had to be on morning duty. Turning up the volume on her radio, she could hear more clearly now the back-and-forths of her colleagues, the chattering of requests and calls for assistance. The radio hummed like a living thing, a squalling baby that demanded her full attention at all times.

Sighing, she knew she needed to make a move. But before she left for her duty spot, there was one more thing she felt she had to do. First, she slid out from behind her desk to lock her office door. Then she opened the bottom right-hand corner of her district-issued desk, a behemoth of a thing that must have dated back to the mid-1970s. Its drawers were cavernous and many. Ms. Baker shifted aside some manila folders and small boxes of paper clips before she found the stash of mini pinot grigio bottles she purchased regularly at a Walgreens near her house. The plastic kind whose easy twist-off cap gave off a satisfying crack each time she opened one. Glancing up at the locked door, Ms. Baker quickly opened a full bottle and tipped the sweet and fruity contents down her throat before hiding the empty back where she'd gotten it from. She exhaled, briefly savoring the taste in her mouth, shoving the shame somewhere she could ignore it for a little bit longer.

Then she popped a mint from a stash she kept in her desk, grabbed her radio, and headed out.

———————

Sitting in the cramped corner of the dean of instruction's office, Ms. Baker shifted uncomfortably in her chair, trying to get situated before the meeting of APs and department chairs began. It was more crowded in here than in Principal Kendricks's office; perhaps putting up with the noxious smell, whatever the source of it was, would have been worth it.

The pleasant warmth from the pinot had mostly faded during morning duty, which consisted of Ms. Baker roaming the hall near the auditorium and moving kids along, searching out dark corners where vaping and sexual acts were known to occur, all the while managing text after text on her phone.

> Ms. Baker so sorry but EducateMe portal STILLLLL not working for me? This stomach bug is super bad. Ms. Brennan agreed to cover for me first but I will need coverage for rest of day. Ms. Brennan is writing my lesson plans on board kids just working on vocab today so sorry.

> Ms. Baker sorry to bug but parent wants a meeting with you re: her daughter plagiarizing her last paper for me. Mom has sent a NASTY email and CCd you. This kid's essay was flagged on the MyWork portal. She basically cut and pasted from something she

found online. Should I respond to mom or let you
handle? Email so nasty!!

Denise, any chance we can switch evening duties next
week? You're on the schedule for the varsity
basketball game on Wed and I'm supposed to be here
Thurs for volleyball but I have to take my dad to an
appointment in the afternoon would be great to switch.
Let me know and thanks.

Ms. Baker briefly imagined her job before cell phones and
radios, back when schools operated by typed memos and good
old-fashioned word of mouth. Surely there must have been
fewer immediate requests, if only because people knew they did
not have the means with which to communicate every thought
and concern as an emergency. Every day was like this for Ms.
Baker, fire after fire. Often after she'd made it to Friday, she
gazed back on the week in wonder, amazed that she was still
standing. This was her twenty-sixth year in education, and every single year the bureaucratic demands and constant sense
of urgency seemed only to intensify, leaving her with little opportunity to spend time encouraging and developing teachers,
which was the main reason she'd wanted to go into administration in the first place. The only upside was that at least during
the day, it left little room to immerse herself in the grief over
losing her wife.

The biggest downside, of course, was her growing drinking
problem, something Ms. Baker continually shoved around in
the recesses of her brain, forever trying to find an unused dark
corner, a different hidey-hole where she could store what she

knew was a serious concern but one she was apparently currently incapable of dealing with.

"All right, everyone, let's get started," said Principal Kendricks, sliding into a chair and turning down his radio. An avuncular man with a tall and lanky frame, he was right around Ms. Baker's age, and Ms. Baker liked and appreciated his warm, open nature. Her sense of professional pride also appreciated that he depended on her so much, given that among all the assistant principals, she had the most experience. The two of them made a good team.

When Kathy had died, he and several of her fellow APs had attended the funeral, and a small donation had been taken up among them for the legal aid clinic where Kathy had given her time. But that had been several years ago now, before the pandemic even, and Principal Kendricks and the rest of them had all gone back to their lives, leaving Ms. Baker to linger alone in her unmanageable sadness.

It had occurred to Ms. Baker that for all the time she'd worked at Baldwin, she'd been the only out administrator at the school, but what had actually made her feel isolated and different in a significant way was the fact that now she was the only one who was a widow.

"I'd like to begin with a quick update on the Lehrer incident," said Principal Kendricks. Those in the room eyed each other meaningfully, and Ms. Baker's mind was briefly transported to that day in the courtyard, to the ashes of Mr. Lehrer flying into the face of PTO President Jessica Patterson, followed by Ms. Patterson's screams of anger and humiliation.

"As some of you know because you were required to be there, the district held a mandatory counseling session in the library last month," he informed the group. "I think it went fine. That said, I know that Ms. Patterson and some of the other parents are still"—he paused, searching for the right word—"*vocal* about their concerns. I want to reassure you that I believe if we stay focused on our good work of meeting the needs of all our kids, this will blow over soon."

There was a ripple of laughter at the phrase *blow over soon*, and Principal Kendricks winced as he realized what he'd said.

"Please, let's keep that in this space," he added, but he allowed himself a small grin.

Ms. Baker appreciated his ability to find humor in the situation, but inside she was worried about what the future held for him and, subsequently, for her. Principal Kendricks had a reputation for being smart and good at his job, but he was also something of a rebel, often incurring the wrath of his district superiors, and she often found herself running after him with a sort of metaphorical net. While she couldn't help but admire his decision to shut down Ms. Harper's toxic "counseling" session the month prior, she was one of the few who knew that his superiors at Central Office hadn't been too pleased about it, and they had let him know. Although they had never discussed the possibility out loud, she knew he was worried that his position was at risk, and she didn't think those worries were unfounded. Ms. Baker sighed, not for the first time, at the thought that she could have followed her instincts that day in the courtyard and prevented Mr. Kendricks from spreading the ashes at all, or at least stopped him from doing it in front of such an audience.

As the meeting dragged on and as she and her fellow assistant principals surreptitiously responded to the frantic, desperate messages and emails and texts on the phones they hid in their laps, Ms. Baker thought about why she'd chosen to join her colleagues in the courtyard on that day. Of course, as his right-hand woman, she'd thought Principal Kendricks would appreciate her presence. But it had been more than that. She'd interacted with Mr. Lehrer only a few times, usually when she'd been tasked with unlocking a classroom for him. (Substitutes didn't receive classroom keys.) He'd always been polite and grateful, but Ms. Baker had been struck by his apparent frailness and advanced age.

*Mr. Lehrer did not have much family*, Principal Kendricks had shared in his email inviting faculty and staff to attend the memorial. If she had to be honest, those were the words that had really prompted Ms. Baker to show up. An only child, she had lost her reserved and emotionally distant father to a heart attack when she was in her teens, and her mother—a deeply religious woman who lived with her second husband in Oklahoma—was only superficially accepting of her daughter's sexuality. They exchanged antiseptic Christmas and birthday cards, and Ms. Baker visited her mother for a long weekend about once a year. For the past several decades her family had been Michael and Kathy and all of Kathy's loud, boisterous relatives, many of whom had recently started allowing for longer passages of time in between returning phone calls and texts. In the end, they had been mostly Kathy's family, Ms. Baker realized.

When Principal Kendricks brought up the TDAF observations, she tried to sharpen her focus.

"Chairs, we need you to remind your teachers that TDAF is not a punitive thing, right?" he said. "In fact, this system was intended to be one that allows for growth and self-reflection. And APs, I know you understand the value in making sure each teacher conference is worth your time and the teacher's time." At this, Principal Kendricks smiled in that enigmatic

way he had that made it clear that he was simultaneously fulfilling a district-mandated obligation and acknowledging that it
was utter bullshit without actually saying so. His ability to pull
this off was one of Ms. Baker's favorite things about him.

But the TDAF. The goddamn TDAF. She decided she would
make it to Mr. Fitzsimmons's room by the end of the day. It had
to get done, and, after all, she might as well double down on
this miserable Monday. In an attempt to show goodwill, she
shot off a quick email to Mr. Fitzsimmons, even though he was
the type who failed to check his inbox throughout the day.

Mr. Fitzsimmons, as you know, it's TDAF time again. I am
looking forward to dropping by your classroom this
afternoon for what I'm sure will be excellent instruction! Just
a heads-up. Thank you.

Ms. Baker slipped her phone into her skirt pocket and considered the hours ahead of her. In a parallel universe—one
where Kathy had listened to her earlier, gone to the doctor
sooner, caught her cancer in time, *lived*—she would not be facing an evening in her house alone. In that parallel universe, she'd
leave Baldwin High promptly at five, maybe stopping by their
favorite Italian place for carryout. She'd have her stories and
would be eager to share them, stories about everything from
observing the cranky Mr. Fitzsimmons to the decaying animal
in the walls of Mr. Kendricks's office. Kathy, an attorney for the
city, would be dressed in her sweatpants and one of her well-
worn Rice University T-shirts, and she would pour Denise a
glass of wine, interrupting her narratives with specific questions
that revealed genuine interest in Denise's life, not just spousal

duty. She had always loved Denise's "school drama," as she'd
referred to it, going all the way back to their younger days when
Kathy was in law school and Denise taught English literature to
ninth graders. How many nights they'd spent together in that
kitchen, making dinner while drinking wine and singing along
to Sarah McLachlan and the Indigo Girls, laughing as their
son begged them to please turn down what he referred to as
"vagina music." How lovely it had all been, how warm and
comforting and cozy. How naïve she had been to believe that
such goodness and pleasure were due to her for all the years of
her life.

———————

She gave Mr. Fitzsimmons a few minutes after the bell before she headed toward his classroom on the second floor. This
would allow him time to get his students settled, manage tar-
dies, and jump into the meat of the lesson. As she opened his
classroom door (quietly, so she wouldn't disturb the instruction)
she felt her heart start to race. Why on earth was she worried
about this man's reaction? Perhaps because unlike every other
teacher she observed, Mr. Fitzsimmons would almost certainly
not mask his disdain for the process with a forced smile; in fact,
she knew that when he finally noticed her, he might even roll
his eyes.

But he didn't see her right away, because when Ms. Baker
entered, Mr. Fitzsimmons was at the chalkboard, scribbling
an equation with his back to the students. Many years prior,
the school had transitioned all the classrooms to whiteboards
and Expo markers, but, legend had it, Mr. Fitzsimmons had
refused this and had somehow gotten his way. The school had
let him keep his green chalkboard, which dated back to the mid-

twentieth century, back when the school district was still seg-regated by race and only white students went to Baldwin. The story was that Mr. Fitzsimmons was allowed to have the chalk-board, but he was responsible for keeping it clean and for buy-ing his own chalk.

"So, if you follow this formula, you'll find the answer pretty easily," he was saying as Ms. Baker slid into an empty seat at the back of the room. The staccato sound of Mr. Fitzsimmons's chalk on the board sparked a brief feeling of nostalgia in Ms. Baker for her own school years, and as she watched, she noticed how Mr. Fitzsimmons erased work with his hand, not wanting to pause long enough even to pick up the eraser. His tired red polo shirt, stretched out around the neck and tucked into a pair of worn-out khakis, was covered in little snowstorms of chalk.

*Keeps back to class, isn't turning to make sure students are en-gaged*, Ms. Baker typed on the laptop she used to take notes during an observation. Learning to write on the board while monitoring the class was a skill Ms. Baker had tried to instill in many young teachers, but one Mr. Fitzsimmons had apparently neither bothered nor cared to learn. Still, she had to admit that the rows of tenth graders in this remedial algebra class were mostly engaged, following along with Mr. Fitzsimmons in their spiral notebooks. Of course, a handful of kids were fooling around with their phones or zoning out, but that could be found in even the most active of classrooms. One hundred percent engagement was something only a person who had never taught would expect.

*Roughly 85 percent of class following lesson*, she typed as Mr. Fitzsimmons continued to explain the formula on the board. At last, he turned to assess the class; he must have caught a glimpse of Ms. Baker, yet he delivered no acknowledgment of her presence. Instead, he snapped at one of the phone users.

"Rogelio, on my desk, now," he barked. "Do it."

The offender, a short, stoned-looking young man with a thatch of unruly dark curls, rolled his eyes but immediately complied, walking up the aisle to drop his phone on Mr. Fitzsimmons's messy desk, which was covered in stacks of papers and Styrofoam coffee cups from various fast-food restaurants. The sound of Rogelio's sneakers squeaking on and scuffing against the tiled floor as he made his way back to his seat was the only noise in the room as a few other phone users wisely chose to slide their devices back into their pockets or their backpacks.

*Has command of the classroom and behavior,* Ms. Baker typed.

"Okay, so I've shown you how to tackle a couple of problems like this," Mr. Fitzsimmons said, picking up a stack of photocopies from his desk. "Now I want you to try to work on some yourself."

Licking his thumb periodically as he counted out the papers, he passed worksheets to each aisle of students, sighing deeply as he did, as if perhaps he was pausing to consider how many times in his life he had performed this action. Ms. Baker's eyes took in his old-man paunch, his unkempt shock of white hair, the smattering of white stubble on his ruddy face. She bit her lip as she wondered what rating she could give the man for *Dresses in a professional manner.* She also worried about the category *Encourages collaboration and heterogenous grouping.* Whereas younger teachers followed the newest, "best" practices and arranged the class's desks into groups, got their students up and into pairs and triads, filled their classrooms with the busy chatter of group work (and, Ms. Baker had to admit, probably a lot of off-topic conversation, too), Mr. Fitzsimmons's classroom was like a silent tomb as each child mulled over the paper in front of them. As they did so, Mr. Fitzsimmons walked up and down the aisles, pausing to check work over their shoulders. He stopped at the desk of a petite girl wearing pink cat-eye glasses that matched the pink beads in her braids.

"Maya, are you serious?" he bellowed. "Go back and look at the work on the board. You're skipping a step, my dear. You know better than that!"

Ms. Baker frowned. Calling a student out like that was not a best practice, and she made a note of it on her laptop. But Maya seemed unbothered, as if perhaps she was used to this sort of routine in Mr. Fitzsimmons's classroom. After briefly pausing to chew on her pencil's eraser, she stared at her work, glanced at the board, then sent her eyebrows skyrocketing with understanding.

"*Oh!*" she whispered to herself, quickly scrubbing out the offending problem and reworking it. Ms. Baker recognized the look on the child's face as the universal one for *I've got it!* When Maya raised her hand, Mr. Fitzsimmons meandered back to her desk.

"Yup, that's it," he bellowed. "Toldya you could do it." Then he continued on, pausing frequently to correct work and encourage students to try again, each time in that voice that made him part disciplinarian, part cheerleader.

The week before, Ms. Baker had observed a third-year math teacher who had included during one class period a digital math game using the students' phones, a YouTube video that somehow incorporated the day's lesson into an explanation of why the *Titanic* had sunk at the angle it had, and some activity that involved students moving around the room with markers and Post-it notes. In the end, when the students accomplished everything on their task list, they received a Jolly Rancher. If Ms. Baker was being honest with herself, she hadn't fully grasped the lesson, but she'd had to admit it had *seemed* like the students were learning. They'd certainly seemed to be having fun, anyway. She'd given the young and enthusiastic math teacher a 5 on almost every category, much to the young woman's delight.

There were no such bells and whistles in Mr. Fitzsimmons's classroom. He was clearly effective to a certain degree; the students were engaged and they were learning. But Ms. Baker also recognized the routine of a veteran marking time until he could finally retire. Deciding that she had enough to complete her observation, she made a few more notes on her laptop and ducked out of the room, shutting the door just as Mr. Fitzsimmons barked at another student to go back and redo their work.

———

The fires didn't stop when she went home. In fact, Ms. Baker spent many an evening in a sort of cocoon she constructed for herself out of her recliner, blankets, and a TV tray, which usually held a frozen dinner, a wine glass, a bottle of pinot grigio, and her laptop. With the television playing some mind-numbing marathon of *Law & Order* reruns on low volume, she continued answering emails, clicking through required district trainings, reviewing requests, managing, managing, managing. Naturally, the wine helped. Or maybe it didn't. It probably didn't, she knew, but she drank it anyway. That Monday evening was no different. With Mr. Fitzsimmons's TDAF observation open on the laptop in front of her, she paused frequently to take generous sips from her glass, enjoying the buzz as much as she could through her shame. She was long past the *Am I an alcoholic?* online quizzes she'd taken over and over in the past year and a half or so. There was no need for them now, but sometimes she liked to take them for the same sick reason she sometimes picked at an infected wound: She needed to know how bad it was.

Slowly but surely, since Kathy's death, she had tipped over from some problematic gray-area drinking to drinking all day during the weekends and evenings to storing bottles at work, buried deep under her office supplies. The stress of this particular school year had only made it worse. Every quiz she took now came back with a stern warning, a declaration that she was suffering from a serious case of "alcohol use disorder," which was apparently the way people were currently supposed to refer to alcoholism. She didn't like the term. It sounded too clinical, like carpal tunnel syndrome or restless leg, as if the sufferer had merely acquired the problem out of bad luck and not from bad choices. Denise knew she'd made bad choices, and every attempt at moderation, every round of mental gymnastics (*don't drink during the week, don't drink before five p.m., don't drink more than two drinks a day, don't drink more than ten drinks a week*) had only resulted in more drinking and more bingeing. In more hangovers that left her dry-mouthed and nauseous and turned her naturally pale skin a ghostly, sickly white. She was trapped in a prison of her own making; this she was smart enough to know. But she did not feel smart enough to know how to break out. The idea of quitting, of never drinking again? It was like trying to picture infinity.

So, like every other night, she drank and attended to her list of must-dos, which this evening involved tapping away at Mr. Fitzsimmons's TDAF form, clicking and summarizing and trying to finish before it got too late. It was mind-numbing work, totally soulless and serving no purpose. Ms. Baker thought, not for the first time, that she might want to spend the last part of her career back in the classroom instead of on the administrative side; at least there she could still feel like she sometimes had a purpose. But she'd become accustomed to the higher salary, and Kathy's early death had meant a loss of income, even if Kathy had been wise enough to purchase a modest life insurance policy for the both of them.

For a brief moment, she allowed herself to entertain the nightmare scenario: If Principal Kendricks was removed, even temporarily, there was a good chance that she would be burdened with additional responsibilities. The idea that in her current state she would be tasked with taking on even more sent her stomach into a spin.

Anxious to put that thought out of her mind and tired of the TDAF form, Denise decided to pour herself more wine and open another tab on her computer. She logged in to Facebook. Before Kathy died, Denise had been a frequent user of the site. In fact, she had loved it. Loved posting her wife's silly quips, photos of their dinners out, snapshots of the two of them and Michael celebrating Christmas with Kathy's family. Kathy had always gently made fun of her social media addiction, calling the site "Fakebook" and insisting that its popularity was an indicator of the apocalypse. "Why does everything have to be documented?" she'd asked, more than once. "There's something sort of nice about doing something and knowing that only you know about it." After she'd died, Denise's desire to share her life plummeted, perhaps because she felt she had so little worth sharing. Unless she was bragging about one of Michael's achievements, she was now more of a stalker on the platform.

Downing a few more swallows of wine, she searched for Mr.

Fitzsimmons. Despite his common name, she found him easily because they shared mutual work friends. She was somewhat surprised that he had an account but not at all surprised by his profile picture: a shot of him sitting in his car wearing reflective sunglasses and not smiling even a little. It seemed to be the go-to photo for many older men.

Because they weren't friends, Denise couldn't glean many details from his profile. His likes included country music artists of the long-ago past and a group for fans of the television series *Barney Miller*. She couldn't determine whether he was married or had children. She wondered briefly who he'd voted for in the last presidential election and hunted without success for clues, figuring perhaps it was best not to know the answer. There was a tagged photo of him from ten years earlier, posted by some young female relative who thanked many people by name for attending her college graduation. In the picture, next to a smiling young graduate in a black robe, a slightly thinner, younger version of Mr. Fitzsimmons peered out from the screen, but his hair—more of it back then, and not all of it white yet—was still as wild and unkempt as ever.

How odd this world was, Denise thought, where we could so easily find one another in this way. How we chose to distill ourselves down to these stupid profiles, these lists of likes and dislikes. How much we wanted to proclaim ourselves as something or someone to the world. To say that we exist and that we matter. Until Kathy had died, she'd had more than a profile pic or a job title or obligatory texts from her faraway son to prove that. Kathy had always made her feel like she mattered, in a way that was much more authentic.

And now she was gone.

Denise's head was fuzzy, her body warm. She knew she'd had enough, that she was on the verge of tipping into something that would no longer feel even halfway good. But she could not stop herself. She gave up on appearances—who was there to see her anyway?—and drank what remained of the wine straight out of the bottle. She went back to finish Mr. Fitzsimmons's TDAF. The next thing she knew, she was waking up in the middle of the night, still in the recliner and covered in a sheen of sweat. Her head was pounding and her mouth was dry; her teeth and tongue were covered in a rough, sour film. The television was still on at low volume, the *Law & Order* marathon long since finished, replaced by some early-aughts sitcom about young waitresses. At the realization that her period had seeped through her gray pajama pants, leaving a red, sticky mess, her unsettled stomach took a queasy turn. It seemed to pulse in concert with the pounding in her head. Denise pushed the TV tray away and stumbled out of the recliner, heading for the bathroom down the hall.

————

Seated at her desk the next morning, Ms. Baker took careful, frequent sips from her water bottle. A long hot shower and three Advils had helped, as had vomiting up most of the evening's microwaved enchiladas. She'd even managed two more hours of sleep. But she was functioning on autopilot this morning; she felt fragile and exposed, and while her headache had improved, a residual ache snaked through her brain. She paused to rub her temples with both hands and take a deep breath before she went back to the work of answering emails, responding to texts, all the while listening to her radio crackling from the corner of her desk.

Nights like the one before were becoming more frequent. She had to do something, but what, she wasn't sure. Maybe she could quit for one month, like a Dry January, even though it wasn't January. Maybe a reset would help her moderate more successfully next time. It was a lie and she knew it, even as she told it to herself. She had to quit.

Trying to respond to an email, she noticed her hands shaking ever so slightly, enough that she feared the tremor might be picked up by others. If she could just get through today, Ms. Baker told herself, if she could just get through today, she would go home tonight and dump out all the alcohol in her house. She would pour it straight down the sink. She would take a break. She would maybe quit for good.

She would get a handle on this.

She opened the bottom right-hand drawer of her desk and shoved the manila folders and boxes of paper clips out of the way and realized that this was as good a time as any to transfer the empties to her large tote bag to take home. She placed the three depleted mini bottles of wine on her desk, then cracked open a fresh one to try to cure her troubles.

As the first swallow of wine made it down her throat, the door to her office opened.

Standing there was Mr. Fitzsimmons.

In the following moment—a moment that could generously be estimated as lasting three to four seconds in total—it seemed several things happened almost at once. First, Ms. Baker realized she was drinking alcohol at her desk at work and, in her hangover haze, had not locked the door. Second, Mr. Fitzsimmons, whose face upon entry could only be described as "contorted in rage," had to process the fact that his supervisor was sitting in front of him drinking alcohol at her desk at work. Third, Ms. Baker yanked the bottle from her lips and, after holding it uncertainly for a beat, tossed it into the open drawer from which she'd acquired it, even though it was still mostly full.

"Mr. Fitzsimmons, could you knock?" said Ms. Baker heatedly, breaking the silence. It was a pathetic move, she knew, but she was desperate. The damage was done. There were three empty bottles sitting in front of her, and a little trickle of pinot rested on her chin. She wiped it away with the back of her hand. She didn't know what else to do or say.

Mr. Fitzsimmons still stood in the doorway, his rage transitioning into confusion. His brow furrowed, like he was trying to solve a math problem, one much more difficult than the algebraic equations he wrote on the board for his remedial tenth graders. Taking a deep breath, he squared himself and regained some of the earlier anger he'd clearly been carrying, but when he spoke, his words were clipped and measured and not as strong as Ms. Baker sensed they might have been.

"Ms. Baker, I came here this morning because of yesterday's TDAF observation," he said. "I have been a teacher at this school for almost forty years. I have lived through a lot of these absurd district things, and I have never, and I mean never, been so insulted in my life as I was by what you put on that form." His voice was the same loud bellow she recognized from observing him in the classroom, but now it was laced with something new: indignation.

The TDAF form. *Oh God*. Ms. Baker realized she must have submitted it back to Mr. Fitzsimmons for his acknowledgment, which was customary. But she had no memory of doing so.

"Ms. Baker, I recognize I'm no spring chicken, and I don't

embrace all of the latest technology and all that touchy-feely group work and whatnot," Mr. Fitzsimmons continued, his face reddening; she could tell he was trying to control himself. She also sensed his eyes every so often glancing at the empty wine bottles on her desk, as if he was trying to process that they were really there. She wanted to snatch them up and throw them in the drawer, along with the mostly full bottle that was currently draining pinot grigio everywhere, but she knew such a move would only draw more attention to the awfulness of their existence.

"I know I'm close to retirement and the administration probably can't wait to replace me with a bright young thing who costs less and who loves computers, but what I came here to say," Mr. Fitzsimmons went on, "is that to give me a 2 on my TDAF seems more than below the belt to me. It seems outright cruel. I don't put a lot of stock in state and district horseshit, but when it comes to the T-SOAR, my pass rates are some of the highest in the department. I teach kids math and they learn math. I'm good at it. I've been good at it for almost forty years." He was sputtering now, practically shaking.

Ms. Baker nodded, her mind racing, searching for what she might be able to offer Mr. Fitzsimmons to improve the situation in a way that wouldn't spell doom for her, but there was nothing. She was his supervisor, but he was more than ten years her senior and a man. And she was drinking cheap drugstore wine at work.

At last, she opened her mouth to speak.

"Mr. Fitzsimmons, if you could give me a moment to review the TDAF form, I am sure we'll be able to figure this out together, but I need time to go over it, please," she said, her voice a tired croak. She assessed how bad she sounded. She decided *pretty bad.* "I will reach out by the end of the day, I promise," she added.

Perhaps expecting a fight or some sort of defense of her actions, Ms. Fitzsimmons looked briefly surprised. At Ms. Baker's words he nodded, but his face was still stern. The man was shaken, obviously. He said nothing more, just turned to leave.

"I know you are a good teacher, Mr. Fitzsimmons," Ms. Baker muttered as he exited and shut the door behind himself, but whether or not he heard her, she couldn't know.

Then, still trying to process what had just happened, she went to the TDAF portal and opened Mr. Fitzsimmons's form, and a fresh new horror unfolded before her.

She had indeed given Mr. Fitzsimmons a 2, a totally unacceptable rating for a veteran teacher in good standing. In the large blank space for her narrative of the observation, a space that was supposed to include a lengthy and detailed summary of all she'd seen, complete with compliments for strong practice and encouraging mentions of opportunities for growth, Ms. Baker had typed the following:

*Mr. Fitzsimmmon thank you for allowing me to visit your classroom today. I enjoyed your lesson. First of all, you need to work on your dress just a little bit, like maybe make sure your shirt is watshed. I could see chalk stains on it. Please try turning around once in a while!!! Kids needs to seee your face. Good job walking around the room. Good job taking the kids phone. Good job redirecting in a positive and professional way and creating an enviroment where kids are learning and growing in a dynamic way. Please consider incorporating technology!! Thank you for your time.*

There were more spelling errors throughout the form, and one section that had been left blank entirely. It looked like the work of a madwoman or a grade schooler playing principal, not the work of an English major who, during happier times in her life, had often read upwards of forty novels a year. A 2 on a TDAF resulted in a teacher being put on a growth plan, a district-mandated hellscape of bureaucracy and paperwork that more than half the time ended in the removal of the teacher. She tried to imagine the shock Mr. Fitzsimmons had felt when he'd opened the document this morning.

Ms. Baker sank her head into her hands. No doubt Mr. Fitzsimmons was going to report her and was probably doing so as she sat here.

Not caring now that the door to her office was still unlocked or that it was almost time for morning duty or that her phone was buzzing and buzzing and buzzing in her pocket, Ms. Baker folded her arms in front of her, rested her head upon them, and wept.

---

She cried for about five minutes, and while it made her feel good in the moment, the physical act of it made her already drained body feel worse in the long run. More dehydrated, more depleted.

"Fuck, fuck, *fuck*, Denise, how could you be so *fucking* dumb!" she said to herself, her voice a whisper. She often told students in crisis to talk to themselves like they would a best friend. If she tried to follow that advice now, she could not come up with anything more than that.

In an effort to make herself feel even infinitesimally better, she tried to do some damage control. First, she went through Mr. Fitzsimmons's TDAF form and deleted everything she had written, then recalled the observation through the portal, citing "administrator error" as the reason. She knew this would generate an email to Mr. Fitzsimmons alerting him to the fact that the observation was still pending. Knowing she had only a few more minutes before having to head out for morning duty, she sent an additional email to Mr. Fitzsimmons.

> Mr. Fitzsimmons,
>
> I have recalled your TDAF observation. What you received this morning was not at all reflective of your excellent teaching abilities, abilities I know are deserving of praise. I am at fault for submitting this form, and I can only apologize profusely. I do not expect you to accept this apology. I will be completing a new TDAF observation form by the end of the week.
>
> Please let me know if you have any questions or concerns.
>
> Sincerely,
> Ms. Baker

She read it over thirty times before she sent it. She wondered if Mr. Fitzsimmons was already in Principal Kendricks's office with a printout of the original observation. Shoving the bottles of wine on her desk into her tote bag, she imagined the maligned teacher describing them in detail to her boss. Did they have the legal right to search her bag? Was there not a part of Ms. Baker that almost hoped they would?

She carried out her day's responsibilities in robotic fashion, her morning headache slowly starting to fade. But she was half-present, floating through lunch duty, administrative meetings, and a special ed conference, performing the routine of her job through a thin film that made her feel only partly there. She was empty, broken, sad, and ashamed, but most of all, she was lonelier than she had ever been in her entire life.

Each time she saw Principal Kendricks, she expected him to pull her aside, tell her they needed to speak privately in his office. She tried to sense if the other administrators were looking at her oddly, maybe even some of the teachers. But everyone seemed normal enough.

She avoided Mr. Fitzsimmons's classroom entirely. He never responded to her email. She knew they would have to meet in person for a post-TDAF conference, which she supposed they would do after she resubmitted the form. She didn't want to think about that at all.

At the end of the school day, Ms. Baker stayed in her office for a full hour after she was required to be on campus. This would allow her to walk mostly empty halls on the way to her car. Even the teachers who might have stayed to make copies, grade papers, or complete any of the other many tasks they hadn't had time for during the hectic school day would have long since left. Ms. Baker locked her office door behind her and, stopping by a private bathroom reserved for faculty and staff, shut herself inside it, checked the lock several times, and then took the unopened bottles of wine and cracked them open.

She dumped the remaining wine down the sink, along with a rush of cold water from the tap, and wondered how this liquid that she'd purchased in a Walgreens off the freeway had become her best friend and her saboteur and her lover and her biggest enemy seemingly all at once.

With all the cheap plastic bottles in her tote now empty, Ms. Baker took the steps down to the exit that led to the administrative area of the faculty parking lot. One of the few perks afforded administrators was a parking spot close to the building. When she opened the door and headed outside, she saw Mr. Fitzsimmons standing by her little silver Toyota, just next to the front of the vehicle. There was no one else around.

Her heart started pounding immediately. Mr. Fitzsimmons turned to look at her. His face was no longer twisted in anger, but Ms. Baker couldn't quite read it. Now that he had spotted her, she knew there was no turning back.

"Did you get my email, Mr. Fitzsimmons?" she asked while walking toward him, hoping she exuded confidence and sounded welcoming. Normal. Ms. Baker briefly recalled the moment she had walked in on the young social studies teacher Ms. Sanderson in one of the private faculty bathrooms: Ms. Sanderson's pants were around her ankles, her bare behind on the toilet. They had both screamed and Ms. Baker had slammed the door, shouting apologies through it. Now, whenever they had cause to interact, the two pretended it had never happened, even though it was never far from either of their minds.

Was Ms. Baker crazy to hope that what had happened with Mr. Fitzsimmons could become something like that, perhaps? That they would just never speak of this morning's interaction again?

"I got your email, yes, thank you," he said as Ms. Baker reached where he stood. He shoved his hands into his pockets. She tried again to read his face and decided it was the same expression he'd worn when he was teaching. Not patient, exactly. More watchful, like he was searching for something that needed correcting.

Since he wasn't moving or making clear the purpose of his standing there by her Toyota, Ms. Baker continued with the same tack. "As I wrote in my email, I apologize profusely for this morning," she said, using her best and most polished professional voice.

"I accept your apology," he said, not unkindly. He said it like it was easy. Like he had accepted it hours ago and even forgotten about it. Then, after pulling a beaten-up wallet that looked full to bursting from the back pocket of his well-worn pants, Mr. Fitzsimmons procured a bronze medallion of sorts, about the size of a dollar coin. "This is my twenty-year chip," he added. "From AA, I mean."

With the reason for Mr. Fitzsimmons's presence now clearer, Ms. Baker froze. She stared for several moments at the coin, swallowed up by Mr. Fitzsimmons's big, beefy hand.

"I didn't know," she said.

Mr. Fitzsimmons nodded. "Not too many people on campus do," he said. "I'm sort of private about it, I guess. But part of AA is reaching out a hand to help others in need, so I guess that's why I'm here."

Ms. Baker considered her options.

She could thank Mr. Fitzsimmons for his concern and tell him he had misunderstood the situation this morning, then politely excuse herself and get into her car.

She could nod ambiguously and reassure him that she was fine and that his next TDAF form would be glowing, as promised, and then she could leave.

She could share with Mr. Fitzsimmons that she already had a plan in place and everything was under control, even though that would be a lie, and then she could take off with a confident wave and smile.

"I lost my wife a few years back," Ms. Baker heard herself saying instead. Her voice cracked on the word *years*. She didn't know if Mr. Fitzsimmons knew she was a lesbian. She also didn't want to cry in front of him. She understood now that he was here out of kindness. An effort to help. But still, she did not want to cry in front of him. It was an act of vulnerability she could not manage yet, given the differences between them.

Mr. Fitzsimmons nodded as she spoke. He was simply listening. Something about his silence urged her to continue. As she did so, she realized Mr. Fitzsimmons was employing an old teacher trick: Always give the student plenty of time to respond. Resist the urge to speak.

"She died of cancer, and then there was the pandemic and lockdown and online school," she continued, filling the space between them. "What started as a way to unwind just . . . I don't know. It just got out of hand. The drinking at work started a few months ago. And lately, I can't stop even though it makes me feel terrible. Even though I want to. But the idea of never drinking again? For some reason that terrifies me, too." She couldn't believe she had said so much, there in the faculty parking lot. It was the first time she had ever spoken about her drinking problem out loud to another human being, and the relief that coursed through her was the first good feeling she'd had all day. "I was drunk when I completed your form last night, Mr. Fitzsimmons," she finished. "I have no real memory of filling it out."

Mr. Fitzsimmons held up a hand, waved it back and forth.

"Forget the damn form," he said. "You don't have to mention it again." He smiled just the smallest bit, the corners of his mouth briefly turning upward. "Toward the end, I kept a fifth of Cutty Sark in my desk," he continued. "Ms. Jackson could tell you about the time I proctored midterms drunk. So . . . I got stories if you care to hear them." He shrugged. "Anyway, it sounds like you've been through a lot lately, Ms. Baker."

For some reason, these words—spoken plainly and bluntly—made the lump in Ms. Baker's throat strain to the point of pain, made the hot tears pricking in her eyes threaten to spill. She took a deep breath.

"I sure could use a break, Mr. Fitzsimmons," she said. On the word *break*, her voice cracked again.

"Yeah, I'll bet," he answered, sliding his AA chip back into his wallet and the wallet back into his pocket.

They stood there for a moment. It was fairly awkward. Ms. Baker wasn't sure what to say or do next.

"Listen, that diner down the street is open," Mr. Fitzsimmons said. "If you want to get a bite to eat or some coffee . . . we could talk."

The sun was starting to sink. The only other car left in the administrative row was Principal Kendricks's. It had been an extraordinarily long and miserable day, and Ms. Baker was very tired. She shifted her big canvas tote from one shoulder to the other. The plastic wine bottles inside it knocked against one another clumsily, and she wondered if Mr. Fitzsimmons could hear them. It struck her that even if he could, it wouldn't matter.

"Yes, a bite to eat would be nice," Ms. Baker said, nodding at Mr. Fitzsimmons. "Thank you for asking."

# Seven

Ms. Jimenez was proud of her holiday gift swap, which had grown in popularity since she'd first introduced it almost ten years ago in the hopes of livening up the staff party held annually at La Casita Bonita. Every year more teachers participated, and sometimes people would start mentioning it to her as early as the week before Thanksgiving.

"Are we having the gift swap this year?" they'd ask her in the lounge or on the walk to the faculty parking lot.

"Well, as long as kids keep giving us shitty mugs and hand creams that smell like baby puke, I'd say yes," she would answer in her signature snarky tone.

This always got laughs. Ms. Jimenez liked to make her colleagues laugh.

The swap worked this way: On the evening of the last day of school before the holidays, faculty and staff would gather at La Casita before two much-needed weeks of winter break. The PTO paid for appetizers, sodas and seltzers, and chips with queso. If a person wanted booze, they had to pay for it on their own, a fact that often led those teachers who were married to lawyers or executives or people who made real money to share fantastical tales of their spouses' company holiday parties, where everything was catered from high-end restaurants and the liquor was free.

The exchange wasn't so different from your usual grab bag, except the gifts were recycled from what the teachers had received, in earnest, from students and parents that year. There were always plenty of "shitty mugs and hand creams," but what really made the swap a hit were the weirder gifts. They still talked about the year the German teacher contributed a bouquet of fake red roses that ended up being constructed of rolled-up lacy red thong underpants.

Once all the gifts were displayed on a table, Ms. Jimenez would pass out numbers, and the teachers and staff members would take turns selecting gifts. There were complex rules around the stealing of gifts, the order in which you could steal, and how many times a certain gift could be stolen. Before the swap began, Ms. Jimenez would review these rules in her clear, loud teacher voice, using hand motions for emphasis and interspersing funny one-liners that reliably got a reaction from her coworkers.

When the event was over, everyone would applaud and smile and compare gifts. Sometimes, some teacher who had started drinking daiquiris from the moment they arrived would holler, "Let's give it up for Ms. Jimenez and thank her for organizing this awesome event! Woooo, Ms. Jimenez!" And everyone would cheer for her. She liked the years when that happened.

Angie Jimenez was forty-four and had started her teaching career at Baldwin nineteen years prior, after taking a long, winding path to a bachelor's degree that included half a dozen part-time jobs, community college, and a few stops and starts at the local university. In her rare moments of vulnerability, she sometimes allowed herself to wonder if her colleagues with more impressive pedigrees thought of her as some sort of fuckup. In truth, she was simply a working-class Mexican American girl who had been the first in her family to even consider college. This had happened after her eleventh-grade U.S. history teacher at her large, underfunded Title I high school had suggested that she could probably pull it off.

"I was on the seven-year plan," she liked to tell people when the topic of collegiate life came up. "Partied a little too much." In truth, she had partied very little, and had often fallen asleep trying to study after pulling an evening shift at one of her various minimum-wage jobs. But the partying line got a better response.

On this night, after the chaotic fall semester Baldwin High had experienced, Angie hoped her swap would help lighten people's moods. As her colleagues walked inside La Casita Bonita and headed to the darkened backroom where their party was taking place—twinkly Christmas lights around the windows added a festive flair—she directed them as to where to place their wrapped presents, mimicking a cruise director or a flight attendant. "Place your gifts on this table, please," she said, pointing with both hands simultaneously. "We'll get started in half an hour or so."

She noticed that the new hire in her department, Ms. Sanderson, had arrived with the biology teacher who always looked like he wanted to cry, but he didn't seem sad this evening. Soon the two were tucked away in a booth with a few other young teachers. Ms. Sanderson and biology guy seemed particularly

cozy, and Angie theorized that they were probably sleeping together. Well, good for them. She'd had less luck in the love
department, something she often exploited for a few laughs.

"Hey, Angie," said Ms. Fletcher, arriving with several members of the English department, including Mr. Williams and
Ms. Brennan. Angie was often paired with Ms. Fletcher when
it came time to proctor the T-SOAR tests, and they had developed a mutual respect, despite being very different people. "I
have a really funny one this year," continued Ms. Fletcher,
holding up her gift and placing it on the table.

"Well, you'd better deliver, now that you've got my expectations up," Angie quipped, "or you're as bad as my first husband."

The English teachers grinned in response and headed to the
bar, and slowly the room continued to fill. Angie spied grumpy
Mr. Fitzsimmons chatting with Ms. Jackson, the head guidance counselor, both of them drinking sodas. They'd probably
leave the party relatively early. Neither of them ever participated
in the exchange, but they seemed to enjoy observing, at least.

By focusing on arranging the gifts on the table and greeting
those who were entering, Angie avoided mingling and small
talk, which was fine with her. She knew she had a big personality, and she knew she had a reputation for being loud and ir-
reverent. She had enough insight to recognize that she could
overwhelm people. But that was just who she was, she often
told herself. That was her, like it or leave it. When conversations
got too quiet or too serious, Angie didn't like how they made
her feel. They exhausted her somehow.

Finally, the swap began. She delivered directions with her
usual fanfare and received a warmer than normal reception,
which pleased her. One by one, as their numbers were called,
teachers put down their Coronas or cocktails and shoved the

last bites of tacos into their mouths before making their way to the table in the center of the room to select a present. The stately Nurse Honeycutt had drawn number one and went first, unwrapping her chosen gift methodically.

"Come on, Nurse Honeycutt!" Angie said, clapping her hands. "No need for formality here. Just tear into it!"

Finally, the school nurse put aside the paper, revealing a Funko Pop! in the form of an owl.

"What is this?" she said, holding her present up in the air, her expression curious.

"Oh," said Mr. Williams, "that's from me. From a kid in third period. I guess an owl symbolizes education?"

Nurse Honeycutt peered at the object in her hand. "I understand that, but why is his head so darn big?" she asked.

"Have you never heard of Funko Pops?" asked Ms. Fletcher.

"Happily, until this moment I had not," responded the nurse somewhat dryly, and the room erupted in laughter. They were already off to a good start, thought Angie.

The exchange continued apace as enthusiasm built (and drinks were poured). There was a bottle of pink perfume in a scent called Passion ("Why does this teacher gift feel against the law?" cracked Angie), bottles of generic hand cream from the drugstore, and an assortment of dumb mugs, including one with a cartoon chicken painted on it.

"Why a *chicken*?" asked the young Ms. Sanderson, the recipient of the gift. "What does that have to do with anything?"

"I don't know, but I'm going to steal it," said Angie, and she did.

Scented candles that emanated dubious odors, a pair of socks covered in apples, a plastic key chain that read I LOVE TEACH-ING!, and a large, smooth rock on which was painted the words

STAY STONED in bright yellow all made appearances that evening.

"That painted rock is my contribution," said Ms. Brennan, when a math teacher unwrapped it and held it up for all to see. "Joseph McManus gave it to me. He said it was a paperweight."

"That kid is high *all* the time," came a voice from the back, followed by murmurs of agreement from several teachers.

"Well, it's nice that he's creative," said Angie with a shrug.

"God bless these kids and their parents," added Mr. Williams, "but I would be happy with some cold, hard cash."

"Only then we wouldn't have the swap!" said Angie, smiling. She was having fun.

Just then, she noticed Principal Kendricks arriving. Administrators didn't always show up to this event—they knew the teachers wanted to cut loose and have a little fun—but Kendricks often did, although he usually stayed briefly, just long enough to have one drink and make the rounds. The only other member of the administration that Angie could spy was the AP Ms. Garcia. In fact, she'd walked in not long after Principal Kendricks. It was unusual to see Mr. Kendricks at a function without Ms. Baker by his side.

"Hello, all," the principal said, waving, and the crowd—relaxed by now from the food and the drinks and the festivities—responded with warmth and shouts of hello. Principal Kendricks was well liked, and for good reason. He was sensible and he cared, and whenever he could, he tried to protect his hardworking faculty and staff and treat them like human beings. Angie would never forget the year her mother had been very sick and she'd used all her district-provided days of paid leave to drive her to doctors' appointments. When she'd needed to take off one more day in May for her mom's last round of chemo, she'd shared her dilemma with Mr. Kendricks. He must have guessed (without her having to say it) that she wasn't the sort of employee who could afford to have even one day of pay docked from her check. He had told her to take her mother to the doctor and not to worry about it. She had, and her pay hadn't been cut, either.

"There's one more gift!" someone shouted, once Principal Kendricks had been appropriately welcomed. A longtime PE teacher who had the final number made his way up to the table to open the only present remaining.

"Hang on—are you sure you don't want to steal?" asked Angie. She did this for every participant, because the stealing added to the enjoyment.

"I'm good," said the PE teacher with a shrug. He picked up the small package, wrapped in red paper.

"Oh, that one's mine," said Ms. Fletcher.

"You promised us it would be a good one," Angie reminded her.

Suddenly, a panicked expression descended on Ms. Fletcher's face. Angie wondered what could be the cause of it.

"Wait!" said Ms. Fletcher, standing up from her chair. "I just thought of something and . . ."

But the PE teacher had already ripped off the red paper, revealing a small, cream-colored jar with a black lid. There was writing on the side.

Many in the teaching profession, including those at Baldwin High, were familiar with jokey teacher gifts. They had all seen mugs with the words TEARS OF MY STUDENTS printed on them, or candles labeled MY TEACHER'S LAST NERVE! The small jar in the coach's hand was in this same vein.

But this year of all years!

"ASHES OF PROBLEM STUDENTS," the coach read, and loudly, too, holding the jar up for all to see.

A few people in the room erupted in genuine laughter, momentarily forgetting the courtyard incident or the uncertainty that still hung over Baldwin High. Those who laughed loudly were quickly cowed by the nervous reactions of their colleagues— anxious chuckles or pained expressions exchanged across the room. The PE teacher, who had clearly forgotten the problematic nature of ashes at least temporarily, suddenly realized his error and shoved the jar into his pants pocket, disappearing into the crowed.

"Oh God, I wasn't thinking when I chose that one," said Ms. Fletcher, briefly covering her face in embarrassment. "Principal Kendricks, I didn't mean anything by it," she added, lowering her hands and peering at her boss.

Mr. Kendricks shook his head and laughed. In truth, it was maybe a little bit of a forced chuckle, but a chuckle nonetheless.

"Hey, if we didn't laugh, we'd cry, right?" he added, looking like he'd rather move on.

"Yeah, I think Shakespeare said that," Angie cracked, and this broke the awkwardness. Clapping her hands, she announced that the exchange was over, and she thanked those who'd participated. No one cheered her name this year, but she decided she wouldn't let that bother her.

The party would continue for at least another hour, but Angie did not plan on staying. She'd had her fill of free chips and salsa, and running the exchange had zapped her of her energy. She gathered her chicken mug and waved good-bye to several colleagues, not stopping to linger in the margarita-fueled conversations. She overheard some of her coworkers talk about getting together over the two-week break, or at least checking in via text. A few were even hugging each other. That wasn't Angie. She'd had her fun tonight, but she also preferred to keep the line between her work life and her *life* life well drawn. That felt safer somehow.

Slipping out the front door of La Casita Bonita, she crossed the parking lot and slid into her 2014 Mazda hatchback, a trusty friend who rarely let her down. As she pulled out onto the street, she slid her cell phone out of her coat pocket. Her mother answered on the third ring.

"Mami, it's me," she said, speaking loudly. Her mother was losing her hearing and refused to admit it.

When her mother responded, Angie told her that she was on her way home. She had to shout this twice. Her mother finally understood, then asked her how the swap had gone.

"It went so good," Angie answered. "Everybody really liked it." The night before, Angie's mother had helped her number and fold the slips of paper for the exchange while the two watched television. Her mom was a fan of true crime stories on cable, and over the years she'd gotten Angie into them, too. They liked to try to guess the murderer, and usually they were right. Angie didn't mention the hiccup with Ms. Fletcher's gift while on the phone with her mother. Better to pretend it had never happened.

"Have you taken your pills?" Angie shouted as she drove. In addition to being hard of hearing, her mother was also forgetful. No matter the response, Angie knew she would count the pills when she got home, just to be safe. But her mother insisted she had taken them.

"Okay, I'm getting off now, but I'll be there soon, Mami," Angie said before hanging up. She tossed her phone onto the passenger seat and settled in. The drive home would take a little over twenty minutes, giving her plenty of time to reflect on the party and what a success it had been. As she merged onto the highway, she dialed up the heat in her cozy little hatchback and turned on the radio. Ms. Angie Jimenez, U.S. history teacher and coordinator of the Baldwin High holiday gift exchange, had two weeks of winter break ahead of her, a big blank space on the calendar that would allow her to relax and unwind. Surely it was a vacation well deserved.

As a small smile ventured across her face, she wished herself a very merry Christmas.

# Eight

It was the first Friday of the second semester of the most ridiculous year of his career, and Principal Mark Kendricks desperately wanted to walk out of Baldwin High School and go home and collapse, maybe drink a beer, maybe listen to some music. Maybe just sit and stare at a wall. Instead, he was trying to manage a mountain of emails so they wouldn't completely crush his spirit the next time he walked into this office. Which, while it technically wasn't supposed to happen until Monday, might end up being the next day, depending on how bad the inbox was.

There was an email from his AP Denise Baker letting him know she was doing well and would be back by the end of January, as planned. Fortunately, that was just weeks away. He hadn't exactly been surprised when she'd shared that she was struggling with a drinking problem. While she'd succeeded in keeping it secret, he had always sensed that the grief over losing her wife had never lifted, not even a little, and she hadn't been herself in some time. Of course he was glad she'd asked for help and was taking the time she needed. But selfishly, he wanted her back as soon as possible.

As usual, there was another frustrated rant from Mr. Fitzsimmons, this time about the morning duty schedule; that could wait until later. Much later. The truth was, Mr. Fitzsimmons probably didn't expect a response. Like most members of the hardworking faculty, he just wanted to vent and be heard. Mr. Kendricks made a mental note to try to catch the veteran educator in person sometime next week before he moved on to more pressing messages.

In a few quick keystrokes he confirmed with Ms. Jackson that their meeting next week about the administration of the T-SOAR was still on. He purposely evaded addressing the part of her email that gently inquired about how Central Office had been treating him lately. Only Ms. Jackson and Denise Baker knew how tense things had been with his higher-ups recently, and he wanted to minimize anyone else's anxiety.

That said, these days his own anxiety had been off the charts. He honestly had no regrets about any of his actions this year, but he also wondered, not for the first time in his career, why doing the right thing was so often punished and toeing the company line was so often rewarded.

Trying to push his worries out of the forefront of his mind, he continued to scroll through his messages, even gathering the mental fortitude needed to respond to a frosty request about an upcoming fundraiser from Jessica Patterson. He double- and then triple-checked that his response could be considered nothing but professional and exceedingly polite before hitting *Send*.

Just then, Ms. Kitty Garcia, one of his APs, stuck her head into his office.

"Wow, Mark, you're still here?" she asked.

Recently, Principal Kendricks and Ms. Garcia had crossed over into almost constant first-name usage. It was something of a dance in the world of education—learning the first and last names of colleagues, understanding when it was appropriate to use first names and when it wasn't, appreciating that there were some veteran colleagues who commanded such respect that they would never be known by anything other than their last names, like Ms. Jackson.

"Looks like it," Mark answered.

"Sorry, that was a stupid question," said Kitty, stepping all the way inside. "I mean, obviously, you're here."

Mark smiled good-naturedly. He didn't mind when Kitty dropped by, something that had been happening with greater frequency this year.

"What's up?" he asked, pushing back from his desk, which was covered in messy stacks of papers and manila file folders and sticky notes in a variety of colors, each one representing some urgent task that had to be handled yesterday.

"That district curriculum thing I was scheduled for got pushed back to next week, but I can still make it," she said. "Given all the eyes on us, I didn't want you to worry I wouldn't."

It was a message that could have been sent via email or text, but Kitty had decided to deliver it in person. Mark appreciated her dedication, particularly since things had been so difficult lately on their campus. And, perhaps as relevant if not more so, he didn't mind the in-person announcement because in addition to being dedicated, Kitty Garcia was also cute.

No, *cute* wasn't right. Kitty wasn't a baby penguin or a newborn. She was a grown woman, and the truth was, she was sexy as hell. Funny and smart, too. About ten years younger than he was, she'd started working at Baldwin a few years prior, after transferring from one of the local middle schools. Even though they'd worked together for some time, he'd been compiling a mental dossier on her only recently, including information gathered both from their in-person interactions and from his recent, frequent visits to her social media. The act of doing so often served as a pleasant distraction in the middle of so much stress. She was divorced with one daughter, a freshman at Baldwin. Her legal first name was not Kitty but Katherine. She was a fan of sushi, mystery novels, and long, solo walks. And she was the author of several witty status updates about life and culture, but not an oversharer of personal dramas or food pictures.

"I just wanted to let you know about the date change," she continued, "in case Central Office said anything to you."

"Well, I appreciate your making the time," Mark answered, aware of the fact that his heart had picked up its pace ever so slightly.

"No problem," she said, lingering. Kitty had long, jet-black hair she kept up in a lazy twist. She wore red lipstick. Mark could easily imagine how incredible it would feel to rip her clothes off right there in his office, cup her ample breasts in his eager hands, and let his hungry mouth explore them in one frenzied moment. This vibrant visual image traveled merrily through his mind as he sat at his desk, speaking to this attractive woman who also happened to be his colleague and subordinate.

"Any plans for the weekend?" she asked, tucking a loose strand of hair behind her ear. She wasn't making any motion to leave. Mark sensed she didn't want to.

"Recovering," he answered, motioning to his messy desk. "Plus, I'll be heading back here tomorrow night for the play. And maybe tomorrow morning, by the looks of my inbox."

Kitty gave him a sad look, then leaned back against the

doorframe. "Well, I should make a move," she said, although she didn't.

Should he ask her if she wanted to walk out together? Would that be weird?

Just then, there was a ping from his cell, breaking the silence.

"Anyway, I'll let you go," said Kitty again, motioning at his phone and quietly disappearing.

Mark looked down at the incoming message. It was from his wife, Lisa.

> **If you want any half and half in your coffee tomorrow you'll need to go by the store on your way home because we're out. Also great news! The dog has diarrhea again. Happy Friday.**

Mark stared at his phone for a moment before giving his wife's text a *thumbs-up* react. He knew Lisa would understand that the thumbs-up was an acknowledgment of her message about the half-and-half, not the dog's diarrhea. It was the texting shorthand of married people.

He sighed again, answered a few more emails, and packed up some papers before turning off his office lights and shutting the door behind himself. It was after six on a Friday and he was finally heading home. His would be the last car in the faculty lot, he knew.

The entire walk there he thought about Kitty Garcia.

––––––––

To say that Mark Kendricks had ever imagined himself as a high school principal would be an inaccuracy of epic proportions. It would be like saying he'd imagined being the king of

England or an NFL quarterback with a handful of Super Bowl rings. Yet here he was. Much to his surprise.

No, he'd had no dreams of entering the field of public education. In fact, when Mark—who had recently crossed into his fifties—was growing up in the same city in which he currently served as principal, his sole ambition had been to play in a punk band. This important turning point in Mark's life had occurred during the tail end of the Reagan years; there was a vibrant punk scene in town, which he'd discovered thanks to an older cousin, and he had quickly jumped in with all the enthusiasm of a fifteen-year-old former junior high nerd who had finally found his people. Mark loved the camaraderie and the joy of the pit, the shock and the boundary pushing of punk aesthetics, and, perhaps most of all, he loved the unleashing of a fury he did not realize was buried inside him until he heard it revealed in a two-minute song made up of only three chords.

By the end of high school his bedroom was papered in flyers from the all-ages shows he'd attended at a local club called the Death Trap; his walls served as a visual catalog of bands he worshipped, from Operation Ivy to the Dayglo Abortions (the latter name so delightfully transgressive Mark could barely stand it) to a lengthy list of local acts with names like the Pain Teens and Devastation. He hung out almost exclusively with other kids in the scene, spending hours at the local record store poring over and discussing the latest 7"s. He stopped eating meat and started hating capitalism, politicians, and the police as much as he hated major record labels. He was suspicious of all those in charge, including every teacher, every school administrator, and every adult in his life, much to the dismay of his loving and congenial middle-class parents.

Punk was an ethos Mark genuinely believed in, a way of living that valued individualism, rebellion, questioning authority, and doing the Right Thing always. It provided him with direction, purpose, and a sense that he was aligned with something that truly mattered. Something that made life meaningful in a way it had never been before.

He loved every second of it.

After a couple false starts, he finally formed a band with a few other guys in the fall of his senior year. They called themselves No Tomorrow. Mark served as lead singer and guitarist, and he wrote most of the songs, too—earnest, driving anthems that spoke of alienation and rage. The night of their first gig—they were the first band in a Thursday night lineup of five local acts, not exactly a huge audience getter—right before the show, their bass player puked behind the club, from nerves. But Mark Kendricks did not get nervous. As he walked onto the stage and plugged in, he had only the feeling that he was fulfilling his destiny.

"Hey, we're No Tomorrow," he said into the microphone, a sense of purpose, even a sense of calm, washing over him. "And this song is called 'Fuck the CIA.'"

---

While he had always thought of Kitty Garcia as a reliable and hardworking AP, she had only really appeared on Mark's radar in a more significant way that fall, on a Monday morning when he was supposed to be gathering department chairs and his administrative team in his office for a scheduled meeting. Upon opening his door, he'd discovered an overpowering foul odor. As he'd walked around sniffing corners and inside desk drawers, trying to find the source of the smell (later assumed to be a dead rat inside the crumbling infrastructure), Kitty had appeared for the meeting.

"Oh wow, gross," she said upon entering. "This is bringing back memories of my nights at the Death Trap."

Mark turned toward her, startled. Her remark was enough to distract him from the stink, at least momentarily.

"You know the Death Trap?" he asked. The club had closed in the mid-aughts as part of the city's downtown redevelopment plan.

"*You* know the Death Trap?" she answered, clearly surprised.

What followed was a conversation that spilled out into the hallway as they headed to a new meeting location; it picked up again later that day when they were both monitoring the main hallway of the building during lunch. Being that she was ten years younger, Kitty's punk rock past had taken place in an almost entirely different era than his, but they shared memories of the fabled club's graffiti-covered bathrooms, frighteningly unstable stage, and infamously rude bartenders. They even realized they'd been at the same Fugazi show in 2002, a performance Mark had dragged himself to even though his oldest son had been a toddler who still didn't sleep through the night and Mark had known he would be exhausted the next day.

"So back then, were you in the pit?" she asked as they monitored the main hall. She seemed amused by the possibility. Maybe, Mark found himself hoping, even a little impressed?

"Yeah, I was in the pit," Mark insisted, enjoying himself quite a bit. "I was even in a band. We went by the name No Tomorrow."

"*Very* punk rock," said Kitty appreciatively. "I guess that all comes in handy when you're breaking up fights in the courtyard."

What began as the occasional conversation before or after meetings or when they had cause to be near each other in the building had transformed in recent weeks into Kitty stopping by his office. She always came with a work-related reason—and there were many at the ready, given the state of the district's tight hold on them this year. But then the conversation naturally meandered to other things, mostly music. One morning after Mark regaled her with a story about the time he'd been rushed to the emergency room for stitches in his chin after a particularly vicious MDC show, Kitty wondered aloud about his trajectory from punk to high school principal.

"Well, you know, life happened," said Mark. "Babies. A mortgage. Joint income taxes." He felt a twinge of guilt when he mentioned his family, for reasons he could probably articulate but didn't want to dwell on.

One evening as he was finally getting into his car after spending the hours following the final bell sorting through upset teacher emails, bullshit district directives, parent complaints (they felt weightier this year, given everything), pressing legal matters—it never ended, the work; it was totally all-consuming—his phone pinged. It was a text from Kitty.

**Look what I found! So wild. Like 20 years ago.**

Attached was a picture of a young Kitty at the Death Trap, leaning back against the bar and staring into the camera. The girl in the picture was undeniably gorgeous, dressed in combat boots, a fitted black NOFX T-shirt, and shorts paired with black fishnet stockings that snaked up curvy legs. Her expression was one of practiced insouciance. Her breasts looked incredible in that shirt. Standing by his car, keys in hand, he stared intently at the image, which made him feel slightly creepy, because even though Kitty was forty now, she was only twenty in the picture, and he was (as was often almost impossible for him to admit to himself) fifty fucking years old.

**Yowza! Blast from the past!** he typed. **I'll have to find one of mine if any still exist from that era.**

*Yowza? Blast from the past?* God, he sounded like an idiot. He slipped his phone into his pocket and started the drive home. When he arrived, he found his wife at her usual spot at the dining room table, which had become her de facto office after the pandemic made her job permanently remote. She had an actual office—the bedroom of their eldest son, who'd recently finished college and moved in with his girlfriend—but she preferred the dining room table because it was big enough for her to spread out. She worked as a grant writer for the local state university, the same one she and Mark had attended ages ago.

"Hey," she said, glancing up from her laptop screen a few beats after he'd entered the room. "How was your day?"

"The usual," said Mark. "Yours okay?"

"Mostly fine," she said. Then she yelled down the hall: "Evan, please, I am begging you for the millionth time to plug that in and take a shower." Turning her attention back to Mark, she rolled her eyes. "He is addicted to that fucking thing."

"I know," agreed Mark, heading down to his youngest son's room—their third and last boy, a surprise of a child who'd come along when Mark and Lisa had both been in their late thirties. "Evan?" He rapped on the door before opening it.

"Hey, Dad," answered Evan from his spot on the bed, his eyes not leaving his Nintendo Switch.

"Did you hear your mom?"

"Yeah."

"Did you finish your homework?"

"Yeah."

"Did you have a good day?"

"Yeah."

"Okay, go take a shower."

"Okay."

"I mean it. Now, please."

"*Okay.*"

With their oldest gone and their second son away at school, it was quieter than it had been when all three had wreaked perpetual havoc in their modest ranch house, smearing food and mud and Lego pieces everywhere they went. But Evan kept them on their toes.

Mark changed clothes and found Lisa in the kitchen, where she was staring at the humming microwave.

"Waiting for it to talk back?" he asked.

"Ha ha," she answered. "Evan already ate, but I'm heating up some of that orange chicken for myself, if you want some."

"Sure."

Once an earnest vegetarian, Lisa had given up the practice during her first pregnancy when her iron levels plummeted. Mark, out of laziness or solidarity—probably the former, if he was being honest with himself—had joined her. They'd never gone back. In many ways they were both still godless leftists who eschewed tradition; they'd gotten married on a Thursday afternoon at the courthouse after their first baby was born, and only because it had made sense for insurance purposes. But most markers of their shared iconoclastic youth had faded away, as they always must.

The microwave beeped and Lisa began spooning leftovers out into two green Fiestaware bowls. "Hey," she said, a thought occurring to her, "did you make your appointment for your colonoscopy?"

Mark winced internally. She'd been after him about this for weeks.

"Damn it, I forgot."

Lisa said nothing at first, just continued to spoon the chicken into the bowl, metal clanging on ceramic. But now the spoonfuls of orange chicken—*clang, clang, clang*—held a deeper significance.

"It was crazy at work," he started, sensing her frustration.

"It's always crazy at your work," she said, looking at him with sad eyes. No, *disappointed* eyes.

"That's definitely true," he responded, irritation creeping into both himself and his voice. "It *is* always crazy at my work." A part of him wanted to go on. To tell her that not only was it crazy, but that it sucked to live with the daily fear that he would be transferred out of his position as Baldwin principal or let go from the district altogether. What would that mean for their family? Their financial situation? It wasn't that they hadn't talked about it—they had, endlessly—but tonight, he just couldn't stand the idea of putting it out there again.

Another part of him wanted to bitch that she worked from the quiet dining room table all day and knew nothing of true stress, but all of this would make him sound like an asshole, he knew. Lisa was a good partner. She tried to understand, and she, too, worked hard every day. This he knew.

So he kept his mouth shut.

Lisa opened the silverware drawer—a little too forcefully, to be sure—and removed two forks, one for his meal and one for hers. He could tell she was formulating her response and braced for it.

"I just wish you'd take this shit seriously," she said, glowering at the orange chicken.

"Fine choice of words, given the topic," Mark answered, unable to stop himself.

"*Please* don't joke right now," she said, her voice hardening, her eyes turning toward him, boring into him. They were now in a fight, it was clear. "And *please* don't do that thing you always do where you act like some mischievous little boy and make me feel like the mean mom who has to chase you down to clean your room. I hate that dynamic and you know it."

"What, you think I *like* that dynamic?" Mark answered, incredulous. He was exhausted.

"I don't know, maybe?" she said, her voice withering. "I mean, you keep playing into it, so maybe you do. It's a simple phone call, Mark, and it's important. I think subconsciously you're avoiding it because you don't want to do it."

Mark threw up his hands. "Of course I don't want to do it!" he said, exasperated. "It's a goddamn colonoscopy!"

Lisa stared at him evenly. She always managed to remain calm in these situations, while he got worked up. It drove him insane.

"I'm going to go eat at the dining room table and try to finish up some stuff," she said. "Your chicken is on the counter." She walked past him coolly.

Sighing, Mark shoved the chicken in the fridge. He wasn't hungry now. Instead, he threw in a load of laundry, made his lunch for the next day, and continued to cajole Evan to get ready for bed. The entire time he had a sense of where Lisa was in the house. Eating her dinner, taking a shower, scrolling on her phone in the living room. But they avoided each other.

Finally, after Evan was in bed with the lights out and Mark

had eaten his orange chicken at last, he loaded the dishwasher and found a stack of Post-its in the kitchen junk drawer. He took a Sharpie and wrote COLONOSCOPY in big letters on one of them.

Lisa was in their room, sitting up in bed reading a novel, one of the thick domestic dramas she preferred. She gazed at him over the book when he walked in.

"Hey," she said. Her tone was mostly neutral, but it invited a response.

He held up the Post-it in surrender.

"Look, I made myself a reminder," he said. "I swear I'll call tomorrow."

"Since we're talking about a colonoscopy, maybe you should staple it to your ass to be sure," she said, resting the book against her chest. The tone of her voice had shifted again. She was making a joke. He could sense the ice starting to melt.

Mark climbed into the bed next to her. "If I stapled it to my ass, then I wouldn't see it."

"Here," she said, taking the note from him and pressing it firmly onto his forehead. "Now you'll see it."

Mark laughed and left the Post-it there for a moment to amuse her before unsticking it from his face.

"I'm sorry I didn't call," he said. "And I'm not just saying that like a little boy asking for forgiveness. I mean I'm genuinely sorry. And I know it's bullshit that you have to remind me to make doctor's appointments. It *is* bullshit. It shouldn't be on you."

Lisa picked up the grocery store receipt she was using as a bookmark and slipped it inside her novel, then set the novel on the nightstand. "I know you're sorry," she said, turning toward him. "It's just that I don't want you to die, you know?"

"I don't want to die, either," said Mark, taking a moment to kiss her on the top of her head. "But we're all dying."

"Gee, thanks for the pick-me-up," Lisa said, gently shoving him. The fight was truly over now. Lisa slipped down onto her back, sinking into the bed, and stared at the ceiling. Mark kissed her gently again on her forehead, then once more on her mouth. She responded, her soft lips opening slightly. Mark felt something stir in him, and he reached out and placed a hand on her left hip, squeezing meaningfully before he sent it searching inside the extra-large YMCA T-shirt she often wore to bed.

She pulled back.

"I'm sorry but I'm *so* fucking tired," she said. "And I'm really not in the mood. Let's do it tomorrow."

"Okay," said Mark, taking his hand away, the stirring inside him suddenly vaporized, his ego slightly bruised. Then he remembered something. "I have the PTO meeting tomorrow night. If I don't show, Jessica Patterson and the others will have my head for sure. So I'll be home late again."

Lisa yawned in response, the gaping inside of her pink mouth now not sexual at all but just an indicator of middle-aged exhaustion.

"Okay, so let's do it Thursday," she said, rolling over, half her face pressed into the pillow. "Can you hand me my mouthguard and let the dog out one more time?"

Mark found the dental appliance she wore each night to prevent grinding and handed it to her, watching as she slipped it in. It made her lips protrude like a prizefighter's. She told him she loved him and wished him good night, but with her mouthguard in, it came out like "I luff yah goo nah." Within minutes she'd be snoring.

As he let the dog out, he checked his phone. As always, there were half a dozen messages about school stuff, but nothing urgent. There was nothing from Kitty. He found himself pulling up the picture of a younger version of her at the Death Trap and was immediately aroused by her twentysomething bee-stung red lips, her flashing dark eyes, the fishnets and combat boots underneath tight black shorts. He gazed at the picture. His mind wandered to places that sparked pleasure and guilt in equal measure.

———

Mark had met Lisa the summer after their freshman year of college; both were taking classes at the large state university in town, a place that when Mark attended had been full of bright but not particularly ambitious young people who had applied to this school without much serious thought or consideration. During those years, applicants had only to provide a copy of a high school transcript and middling SAT scores. (As a principal, Mark had found it almost incomprehensible that this same school now seemed to require that most applicants have multiple letters of recommendation, a heavy class load full of AP courses, membership in a variety of clubs, and several examples of how the student had expressed their leadership potential.)

Mark had forged an agreement with his parents: He would take classes at the university if they supported his moving into a group home on Lexington Street, where members of No Tomorrow lived with other punks. In this house, a rambling old Victorian that had seen better days, band practice seemed to go on at all hours. The living room—its walls covered in show flyers and original artwork and political slogans (*Anarchy is order! Government is chaos!*)—was a meeting space for rotating groups of young socialists, young feminists, and young radical vegans who ran the local chapter of Food Not Bombs. Staying there made Mark feel like he was in the middle of something deeply significant, as if the house were the heart of some transformative, living thing.

On the hot July night he met his future wife, No Tomorrow had played on the same bill as a popular local band called the Tentacles, whose biggest claim to fame had been briefly touring with Black Flag before the latter had broken up. Mark felt that No Tomorrow had performed their tightest set in a long time, and the crowd had responded enthusiastically.

After the Tentacles played, he ordered a whiskey and Coke at the bar and waited for the headlining act, some band from Milwaukee that was supposed to be pretty great. As he sat drinking alone, she approached him. The first thought Mark had when he saw her coming toward him was that she was one of the best-looking girls he'd ever seen.

"Hey," she said, pausing to take a long pull of her cheap beer and sidling up next to him like she'd known him forever. "I really dug your set."

"Thanks," said Mark. "Getting to play on the same lineup as the Tentacles still feels surreal."

The girl shrugged her shoulders. "Honestly? I thought you guys were better."

Mark gave her a confused look as he dragged a hand through his sweaty mop of dark hair, which back then was full and thick and gave no indication of its future demise. She had to be messing with him.

"Yeah, right, we were better," said Mark, rolling his eyes. After all, they were talking about the Tentacles.

"I'm not bullshitting you," she answered, her voice a mix of indignation and amusement. "I mean it. I liked your set better. Especially the second-to-last song, with that weird little riff in the chorus."

So she was serious after all.

"I wrote that song," Mark was quick to inform her.

Her name was Lisa, and while they quickly discovered they went to the same university and had gone to many of the same shows and even hung out in similar circles, they'd never run into each other before, a fact that mystified both of them and that later, in their middle age, they would always mention whenever they retold their origin story. ("And to think I almost didn't go to that show," Lisa would always add.)

She was tall and had green eyes, long dark brown hair, and an interest in music that Mark found deeply appealing. She had compelling thoughts about Mission of Burma. She could defend her favorite choices off Fugazi's *Repeater* with confidence and ease. She read *Maximum Rocknroll* even though she found its emergence as the so-called bible of the scene to be disconcerting and the publication itself almost too egotistical to be authentically punk. And she put out a zine called *Fuck You, Dad.* (She told Mark she wanted to do an interview with him for her next issue.)

First tucked into a corner of the Death Trap, shouting over the music, then later in a quieter backroom where he and Lisa continued to drink and talk (they decided to skip the headlining act), Mark couldn't believe the turn his evening had taken. He kept waiting for her to mention a boyfriend, or for said boyfriend to walk up and join them, but it didn't happen. As the time moved closer to two a.m. and Lisa pressed her hand almost possessively on Mark's chest, he knew it wouldn't.

"Why don't you, like, come with me?" she asked, her voice a seductive whisper, her plump lips inviting and pink. Her left eyebrow arched, full of meaning.

Silently, Mark followed her out a backdoor and through the parking lot, the moon hanging high above them, the gravel crunching underneath their Doc Martens. They were covered in a sheen of summer sweat, and Mark's entire body was buzzing, both from the alcohol and from the sight of Lisa's ass in tight dark jeans as she led him to her 1979 Ford Fairmont, which was plastered with bumper stickers, including one that read I'D RATHER BE SMASHING IMPERIALISM!

Without a word, Lisa opened the door to the backseat and pushed him into it, then crawled in after him and undid his jeans. Before he could grasp that this was actually happening, her mouth was on him and his eyes were rolling back in his head.

It was not long after that Lisa moved into Mark's bedroom in the group house. They slept together in a twin bed underneath taped-up show flyers from the Death Trap and a tattered, photocopied photograph of the Chinese student staring down tanks in Tiananmen Square. They had sex every night, often after long, meandering debates about art, music, books, politics, and films. They participated in Food Not Bombs. They skipped class and went on road trips to see bands play. They got jobs at a local gelato place, where Mark once went down on Lisa in the supply closet during a shared break.

Lisa laughed at all of Mark's jokes, which were frequent, dumb, and often dirty. It was so easy to make her laugh. They were sardonic punks who were supposed to be too cool for sentiment, but on Mark's birthdays, Lisa would always craft homemade cards that looked like little mini zines, full of silly poems and cartoons about their relationship. In one she wrote:

*I have to say*
*You make me laugh every day*
*You're so funny to me*
*In my pants I will pee*

Mark saved it, along with the others, in a shoebox under their bed, a box that held such important artifacts as No Tomorrow's inaugural set list and a show flyer from the first time he saw Social Distortion.

They eventually graduated, Mark with a math degree, Lisa as an English major. Mark managed the gelato shop full-time, and they got their own small one-bedroom apartment after a particularly nasty cockroach infestation took over the group house. No Tomorrow kept playing gigs; they even did a short regional tour that involved sleeping in a van at rest stops and playing a long list of squalid clubs. But eventually their bass player decided to accept Jesus Christ as his personal Lord and Savior, and the drummer surprised everyone by applying to and getting accepted into law school. Replacements didn't really work out, leading to the band's slow yet eventual demise. Things started to shift perceptibly in Mark's life.

Lisa was the first to get a real grown-up job, as an editorial assistant at the university press on their old campus. She had health insurance and a retirement account, which they both made fun of even as Lisa found herself making use of them.

When Mark's mother gave him a newspaper clipping about the local teacher shortage and an alternative certification program that was accepting recent college graduates, he showed it to Lisa, but he resisted the idea at first.

"It just seems gross," he explained as they lay in bed talking about the possibility. "Like, being a part of a system that's just all about compliance and these bullshit, arbitrary markers like grades and test scores."

"Yeah," said Lisa, taking the clipping from his hands and studying it. "But I think you'd be a really good teacher. Like the kind of teacher who could actually help kids think for themselves." She also gently pointed out that their rent was going up, and his gelato shop wage wasn't exactly bringing in a lot of cash.

Lisa was right about Mark's potential as a teacher. He was a great one for the same reasons he had been a great front man. He never got nervous in front of the kids, even during his first year in the classroom. In fact, his was a dynamic presence that engaged his ninth graders and endeared them to him. They hung on his every word and trusted him, and he loved them for it. He won New Teacher of the Year for the entire district (he had to go to a ceremony at Central Office in a jacket and tie, of all things!), and in just a handful of years he was being groomed for chair of the math department. Lisa became pregnant with their first son, he got accepted to graduate school, he kept advancing, he was sucked deeper into the system, into the pension program, into an administrator's salary schedule, which was pretty useful for a household with three growing boys. His faculty and staff appreciated him for always defending them the best he could within the bureaucratic system in which they all operated, but he became the thing he'd never thought he would be: the bureaucrat.

A few years before his fiftieth birthday, he was named principal of Baldwin High, the biggest high school in the city, a position that was not just a cog in the machine, but in many ways
representative of the machine itself. He still got joy from interacting with teenagers (especially the rebellious ones), and he
still saw himself as something of a defender of the public good,
during an era when conservatives wanted nothing more than to
destroy one of the country's few remaining public institutions.

But like so many in middle age, Mark found it difficult to
not sometimes look around at the life he had built, the compro-
mises he had made, the paths he hadn't taken, and to wonder at
the strange turns that had brought him to this career, that had
brought Lisa into his life. The punk who had rebelled and
fought back and believed in a strict code of living that he swore
he'd never stray from had softened and transformed into something different, even though he trusted that a part of that boy
was still alive somewhere inside him, or so he hoped.

Mark and Lisa had grown up together, and now they were
grown. The gelato place where they'd worked so long ago had
become a Starbucks. The group house on Lexington had been
razed for high-end townhomes. And the Death Trap had
been closed and shuttered before their third child had even
been born.

———

Not long after Kitty shared that picture of herself from her
younger years, Mark made her a playlist, throwing in some of
his favorite deep cuts from the Damned and the Penetrators
that he hoped would impress her. For the last few tracks, he
added several No Tomorrow songs; the drummer turned lawyer
had digitized their early recordings a few years back. When
Mark listened to the playlist from start to finish, he had the

same reaction he always had when listening to punk now: Did he still genuinely love it, or did he only love the memory of it? It was an unanswerable question.

He sent it to Kitty.

The next morning, she came to see him before school.

"I loved that playlist so much, thank you," she said. Her cheeks were pink. She grinned, tucked her hair behind her ear. He recognized this now as her nervous habit, which meant that he made her nervous. It was flattering beyond measure.

Mark had never cheated on his wife, had never even considered it. But he could do it now, should he choose to. He had never had such an appealing possibility so easily available.

"I wish I'd seen you play in No Tomorrow," Kitty continued while standing in his office, her eyes holding his gaze, the air between them charged with possibility. Mark's entire body tingled with pleasure and excitement, like he was nineteen again.

————

The band No Tomorrow did not survive. But the irony, of course, is that there actually *was* a tomorrow for Mark. Several, in fact. And in those tomorrows Mark and Lisa had found the following (not an exhaustive list): countless broken appliances, car accidents with uninsured motorists, aging parents with early dementia, trampoline incidents followed by emergency room visits, teacher emails about failing grades in algebra, adult siblings with drug problems who asked for cash loans, nerve-racking mammogram results, colicky infants, cancer in beloved dogs, adolescent depression, a miscarriage, an urgent roof repair that coincided with an empty savings account, and a burst hot water heater that once spilled forty-six gallons of water all over their already disastrous garage.

For his fiftieth birthday, Lisa made Mark one of her old mini zines, something she had not done in ages. Although it had been years since she'd pulled out her Sharpies and rubber cement, she still had a knack for creating little photocopied gems full of witticisms and silly drawings. The zine included the top ten reasons she loved him (reason three being that he was an excellent father and reason four being that he was particularly skilled at oral sex); she also included her "Mark Kendricks's Fiftieth Birthday Soundtrack," which listed all the songs that reminded her of him, including Black Flag's "Slip It In" and "I Want You Around" by the Ramones. On the back page was one of her little poems.

*Yes, you are fifty*
*You don't think that's nifty?*
*Young we are not*
*And we've been through a lot*
*But I haven't forgot*
*That you still make me hot*
*You know it's true*
*I really love you*

On the top shelf of the hall closet he kept the old shoebox, the same one that had lived under his bed at the group house more than thirty years before. He carefully placed Lisa's creation in this sacred place, which held many of his life's treasures.

———

The Saturday after Kitty had stopped by his office to let him know about the change in the district's curriculum meeting, Mark attended a performance of *You're a Good Man, Charlie Brown* in the Baldwin auditorium. He tried to make it to as many sports events and arts performances as he could because it built goodwill in the community; it made the kids and their families feel recognized and important. Of course, he'd sat through enough crippling losses on the field and botched monologues on stage to last a lifetime, but still, he went. It was part of the job, and it was the right thing to do.

As he sat in the dark auditorium, he spotted her a few rows down from him to his right. She was the administrator on duty, charged with making sure all the students were picked up and the doors to the school were locked tight when the event was over. He knew she'd been assigned to this night, which, he had to admit, was one reason he'd decided to attend this evening's performance.

After a boisterous final round of applause for the young thespians, Mark circulated through the crowd, saying hello to the parents and students who were flooding up the aisles. Even in the midst of this year's crisis, there were many who approved of his direct nature and open leadership style. Despite the fact that his job as principal was in a precarious position, he knew that when it came to the community he served, mostly, he was liked. It was no wild crowd at the Death Trap, of course. But it was still nice.

Once everyone else had left, Mark and Kitty helped the young custodian assigned to the event clean up all the left-behind programs and other trash from the floor of the auditorium, then went through the business of shutting off lights and locking doors. Mark found himself oddly grateful for the presence of the custodian as a sort of chaperone and simultaneously annoyed at her presence for the same reason.

A few minutes past nine o'clock at night, they were free to leave the building at last. The custodian had a ride waiting. She waved to them before getting into the beat-up hatchback sitting outside the main entrance, its engine running.

It was only Mark and Kitty now.

They continued through the courtyard to the faculty lot together, their feet taking steps in unison over the pavement. It was mid-January and cold, even in Texas, but Mark could barely feel it. A gust of wind made the nearby flagpole clang. He and Kitty didn't speak to each other. Every sound and movement seemed heightened to Mark. All of it was a prelude to whatever was going to happen next, and what that would be Mark wasn't entirely sure.

They reached her Honda first. She was parked only two spots over from Mark, and of course they were the only cars left in the lot. "So," she said, turning to look at him, a soft smile on her lips, "we've survived another student production."

"We sure have," said Mark. His chest was tight. His breathing was shallow. If anything was going to happen, it would happen now. He knew it. She knew it, too. But she was waiting for him to initiate it.

He could have sex with this woman. Exciting, different, wild first-time sex. It would almost certainly be pretty great.

*And then what?* Mark asked himself. What would he be then but some middle-aged man having a predictable midlife crisis turned work affair, covering his pathetic tracks, concocting stories and hurting people he loved like some dumb ex–frat boy who'd had his bachelor party in Vegas and still quoted old episodes of *Entourage*?

Mark Kendricks had become many things he'd never expected to be, but he knew with certainty that he had never been and would never be that guy.

For a few moments he gazed at Kitty Garcia's pretty face and her red lips and understood that this marked the end of something. And then, in as friendly and professional a tone as he could manage despite the pounding of his heart, he wished Kitty a good evening and a safe drive home, and he headed to his car.

———————

Mark walked into the kitchen, where he found Lisa loading the dishwasher. Her hair was piled into a loose, wobbly bun on the top of her head. She was wearing her favorite ratty T-shirt, the one with a faded picture of Chrissie Hynde on the front and a hole in the right armpit.

"Hey," she said, pausing to wipe her wet hands on the yoga pants in which she never did yoga. "How was the play?"

"The usual," said Mark, hanging his keys on the hook where they'd been hanging their keys for decades, a reflex as familiar as brushing his teeth every morning. "You couldn't hear half the kids, and a backdrop fell over in act two. But they had fun."

"That's nice," she said, tossing in a detergent pod and getting the dishwasher started. How many times had they run that dishwasher? Mark wondered. How many more times would they run it again?

"Where's Evan?" he asked.

"At Jonathan's house. Spending the night."

"Oh."

"Want to watch something?" Lisa asked, moving toward the adjoining den and collapsing onto the couch.

"Okay," said Mark. He pulled his phone out of his pocket and plugged it into the charger on the kitchen counter without checking it for messages.

"We never watched that documentary about Mister Rogers," Lisa said, scrolling through the various streaming apps on the television screen. "What about that?"

"Sure," Mark agreed, joining her on the couch. "I've heard the sex scenes are amazing."

At this, Lisa tossed one of their throw pillows at her husband's head.

"You're such a sick asshole," she said, but she was laughing when she said it. After all these years, Lisa still laughed at Mark's jokes. Not tinkly giggles of wifely obligation, but real laughs, loud and from the gut. For more than three decades his wife had shown genuine appreciation for his sense of humor. He knew this was no small thing.

Lisa curled into a ball on her side of the couch. As she scrolled through, searching for the documentary, Mark reached over with his right foot and nudged Lisa's rear end with his big toe.

"What?" she said, turning to look at him.

This time he nudged her with his whole foot. "Speaking of sex scenes . . . ," he said.

"Are you trying to turn me on with your foot?" said Lisa, her voice coy. She was going to make him work for it.

"Come on," said Mark, grinning. "We have the whole house to ourselves."

"What about the dog?" Lisa responded, arching an eyebrow.

"We could let him watch," offered Mark.

Lisa laughed even harder than she had before. She set the remote on the coffee table. Then, in one swift movement, she pulled her Chrissie Hynde T-shirt off and threw it across the room.

Principal Mark Kendricks, former lead singer of No Tomorrow, had chosen to be here with his wife, to whom he'd been loyal for the entirety of his adult life, when even just an hour before he could very easily not have been. As he and Lisa sank into the couch and he pressed his lips against her familiar, welcoming mouth, he knew he had done the right thing. The ethical thing. Maybe even the rebellious thing.

It was the most punk rock moment of his life.

# Nine

*Mierda*, Luz Guevara said to herself when she saw the austere men in suits gathered in the hallway outside the main office, a labyrinth of conference rooms and administrators' offices. She had been headed there to fill in her time sheet—for the final time, in fact. This day in early March was meant to be her last day as a custodian at Baldwin High School. And here she was faced with her biggest fear. Was it possible that after all this time, she was in trouble? She had managed to evade any drama in this place for months for this reason, even when it had been dropped in her lap.

Luz's breathing suddenly became shallow and her stomach tied itself in knots as her mind was pulled back to the day it all began.

———

Months earlier, on that sad September afternoon after they had taken away Mr. Lehrer's body, they had made her clean the couch in the lounge. Her EZ-Clean campus supervisor had said it was because she was in charge of those rooms on the third floor, but mostly Luz thought they made her do it because the job was hard, and Luz Guevara was the hardest-working custodian at Baldwin High School.

The men from the medical examiner's office had taken his body away and the school day was already over when she was given the directive to enter the lounge and clean the couch. No one had bothered to explain to her why she was doing so. She asked what the cause was, and her sour-faced supervisor explained, openly irritated with Luz's need for a reason. Wasn't the reason for their jobs always the same? Something was dirty and now it had to be clean.

"It's some substitute," she said. "He died in there. *El viejito* that was always around."

"Mr. Lehrer?" Luz asked, and her chest started to tighten.

"*Sí, el viejito*, like I said. I don't know his name, but I think he used to teach here when he was younger, *sí*?" Her supervisor was ready to end the exchange. "*No sé que pasó, pero* . . . he died. This morning. In there on the couch." She pointed toward the door of the faculty lounge. With this limited information, she left Luz to go inside and begin her work.

Mr. Lehrer—she had tried to call him *Bob* per his request, sometimes even *Roberto* as a joke when they were practicing his Spanish—had emptied his bladder upon dying, Luz learned. While wearing thick rubber gloves and a face mask, she kneeled on the cold tile floor and attacked the stain with the industrial-strength cleaner and sponge her employer provided, scrubbing until the muscles in her right shoulder and upper back burned hot and she was forced to switch to her left hand.

After a little over a year of working as a school custodian at Baldwin High, Luz was mostly immune to the sights she encountered as part of her job. Sights like bloated pretzels swimming in pools of lukewarm milk, bread and pizza crusts stained with fuchsia lipstick and moistened with strings of saliva, and Styrofoam trays splattered with so much ketchup that they looked like murder scenes. She had cleaned her fair share of urine, too, and worse, so it wasn't even that part of the situation that made her break down that afternoon in the empty lounge.

What made Luz rest her sponge on the tiled floor, what made her rock back on her heels and peel off the gloves and weep—really weep—into her hands until the tears and snot poured freely down her face, what made her cry like she had not cried in quite some time, was the understanding that she had lost her only real friend at Baldwin High School.

———

She and Mr. Lehrer had started at Baldwin at the same time, the fall prior. He had returned to substitute and she, brand-new to the country, had been hired to work as a custodian. She'd acquired the job through her sister's boyfriend, Eduardo, whose family had connections with the people who ran EZ-Clean, the company to which the school district outsourced janitorial services. Eduardo had been born here, had the all-important status of *citizen*, and this afforded Luz certain advantages, advantages her older sister, Maritza, promised her during phone calls in which she tried to coerce Luz to join her in America.

"Eduardo can get you a job so easily, and you won't need real papers to do it," she said. "It's a cleaning job in a school, but it would just be for a little while, until I can get you a nannying job like I have. You would be amazed what you could make here in cash, no questions asked. So many rich white Americans who want their babies to learn Spanish."

Maritza had always been the dreamer, the adventurer. When they were small and their parents had taken them to El Cuco beach to swim in the cool, clear water, it had been Maritza who had swum out the farthest, dived the deepest, shouted the loudest with joy and excitement. It was Maritza who took bites of their *abuelita*'s pupusas right off the pan, ignoring their grandmother's warnings that they were still too hot. And it was Maritza who had headed north not long after their mother died in search of more opportunities, less violence. There, she had fallen in love with Eduardo. She was never going to come back to El Salvador, she declared. Not unless she was forced to.

"But there are gangs in America, too," Luz said to Maritza on the phone when her sister tried to persuade Luz to join her. "I think they hate people like us there. It is not a paradise."

"Don't believe everything you hear," argued Maritza. "And anyway," she continued, her voice losing its verve and confidence, "the United States is where *I* am, isn't it? Your family?"

There were cousins and aunts and uncles to miss in El Salvador, of course, but with their parents both gone—her father of a heart attack when they were small, her mother of an aggressive cancer only recently—Luz felt the tug of her closest family member. The idea of never seeing her sister again, ever—it filled her with dread. And so she had come, and not long after her arrival she had started the job at Baldwin.

Most of the people who worked at Baldwin High School were pleasant enough, especially the teachers, and when she hesitatingly entered their classrooms at the end of the day to begin her daily cleaning routine, they tried—in their broken, accented Spanish—to say hello, to wave her in with gratitude from their desks. (*Por favor, entre. No te preocupes.*) It was nice at least to live in a place where a surprising number of people could speak a basic level of her language. In a halting but pleasant back-and-forth with a young physics teacher probably only a few years her junior, she had taught the teacher how to write *No borres* on the board when he didn't want Luz to clean it at the end of the week.

But mostly Luz remained reserved around the school employees and even the other custodians, women much older than her who had husbands and children, several of them grown. Luz sensed that, like her, they were all working under false papers, that there existed a quiet understanding between EZ-Clean and its employees—an understanding that EZ-Clean would provide them with work if the employees provided a good enough lie. It was an understanding, Luz decided, that seemed to extend beyond EZ-Clean to the entirety of the United States. Despite the rhetoric of the country's previous president, despite the bigoted messaging and the red caps and the cries for a wall, within her first few months in America she had come to truly understand the extent to which people like her kept the wheels turning in this country, generating a constant hum just under the surface, operating from a place a person could simply choose not to see.

But Mr. Lehrer had been different. The first day she met him, a few weeks into her first year at Baldwin, she had been tasked with unlocking a classroom door for him. She was struck by his age, his stooped-over figure, his rheumy, tired eyes and liver-spotted hands. Luz was a few years shy of thirty, and she estimated this teacher had to be at least fifty years her senior. Did he need the work this much? Did American schools need teachers this desperately?

"*Gracias por abrir la puerta*," he had said to her, and Luz could tell that he was proud of himself for knowing how to thank her for what she had done. His accent was horrible, his elementary Spanish funneled through the sort of twangy cadence she had become accustomed to hearing among the older employees at Baldwin. She smiled uncertainly.

"*Sé que mi acento es terrible,*" he told her, reading her mind. At this she couldn't help but laugh gently. She answered in her tentative new tongue that her English wasn't much better.

"*¿Podemos practicar?*" he asked her, his old man hands gripping a folder full of attendance rosters as if he were afraid he'd fall over if he didn't hold it tightly enough. He went on to explain that he was a substitute teacher, here only a few days a week at most, but that if she saw him and had a few moments, they might be able to practice their Spanish and English. He seemed so eager to try that Luz felt she had to say yes.

And so they practiced. She and Mr. Lehrer would exchange words in passing whenever she had a few spare minutes during the day or in the afternoons after school when she was cleaning a classroom. (He never rushed to leave at the bell, like some teachers did. She inferred that he enjoyed simply being in the place.) Their practice sessions would be as short as a few back-and-forths, sometimes as long as ten minutes if she had the time.

The conversation was ongoing, covering topics that were mostly mundane: food, weather, the sorry state of the stairwells, where students were known to leave so much trash behind. What was the word for this, for that? How do you say this phrase, this sentence? But the moments brought Luz a lot of happiness, a sense of connection that was sorely missing during her workdays. Once, she even created a little quiz for him to test his understanding of *ser* and *estar.* He reacted with delight upon receiving it, insisting he would take the quiz without any outside assistance. (When he returned it to Luz the next day, she quickly marked it for him; he'd gotten seventeen out of twenty correct.)

Early on in their conversations, Mr. Lehrer explained to her that he had taken to practicing his Spanish on a language app on his phone. His hand trembled a bit with age as he pulled out the device to proudly show her each level through which he had advanced.

Luz pulled out her own phone to reveal that she had the same app, and soon they became "friends" on it. Mr. Lehrer used it to send her encouraging messages in Spanish when she broke through another level of English learning. His written Spanish was often riddled with errors, but he could make himself understood. Luz fought the urge to constantly correct him, mostly because she thought there was something charming about being so dedicated to learning something new, even at an advanced age, and she certainly did not want to discourage him. Of course, his enthusiasm for Spanish was not a surprise to her. Mr. Lehrer had been a teacher at Baldwin for many years, and Luz knew that the best teachers never tired of learning themselves.

Along with her conversations with Mr. Lehrer, Luz sometimes practiced her English in the postage stamp–sized bathroom in the apartment she shared with Maritza and Eduardo. Staring at her reflection in the mirrored medicine cabinet, she would watch as she spoke first in Spanish, then in her thickly accented beginner's English. When she spoke in this new language, her brow furrowed, and the skin around her dark brown eyes wrinkled. Her full lips thinned out, retracted inward or pursed angrily at every attempt at a vowel. She didn't think she looked as pretty when she spoke English. She certainly didn't think she looked as smart, and being smart was something Luz Guevara had always prided herself on. Still, she kept trying, and during her first year at Baldwin, in large part because of her interactions with Mr. Lehrer, her confidence with her new language grew with each passing month.

In addition to working hard at learning English, Luz worked hard at her job. Over time, she adjusted enough that she no longer felt like gagging each time she had to unclog a toilet or empty containers full of used sanitary napkins. It became routine, and the entirety of the situation impressed upon Luz how resilient she could really be. How much she could endure if she had to. But what would she do with all this resilience? she wondered. How far could it really take her in a country in which she was not even supposed to exist?

At home, Eduardo and Maritza made her feel welcome in their apartment; Eduardo was a kind man who truly seemed to love her sister and talked often of marrying her and having children. It was wonderful to be around Maritza again, to be the receiver of her warm embraces, her back scratches, her mugs of *atole de elote* like their mother used to make.

Still, she often felt like the tagalong baby sister. An obligation and a responsibility of sorts. And she was quickly reminded of how different she was from Maritza. How bookish and quiet she was in comparison, and how this difference had always existed between them.

One Saturday evening not long after she had met Mr. Lehrer, Maritza and Eduardo insisted Luz join them at the house of some friends. A large party was promised, full of friendly people with ties to their homeland. It would serve as a sort of welcome for Luz. There would be music and dancing and good food, too. Tamales and horchata and *panes con pollo*. Please

come, they both urged. Luz agreed, even if part of her longed
to stay in the apartment alone, enjoying the rare moment of
peaceful solitude.

Once there, Luz smiled and nodded as gamely as she could
while Maritza guided her around the party as if Luz were a child
too shy to attend her own birthday celebration. How at ease
Maritza seemed here, how she squealed in excitement at each
familiar face she encountered and embraced each friend with
enthusiasm. In a few short years, Maritza had made this place
her home, Luz marveled. After a time, her older sister became
absorbed in a conversation in the kitchen, and Luz found herself moving quietly through the noisy crowd, grateful for her
smallness, grateful for her ability to slip out of sight so easily.
She decided to hide in one of the bedrooms, and opened the language app on her phone. She found a message from Mr. Lehrer.

*Otro bueno trabajo para ti. ¡Excelente, Luz!*

Grinning, she responded.

*Thank you Mr. Lehrer. You keep going too with your Spanish.*

The bedroom door opened; it was Maritza, frowning.

"Why are you hiding in here?" She tugged on Luz's arm, pulling her in the direction of the door. "Come on back out there.
One of Eduardo's cousins is asking after you." At this Maritza
raised an eyebrow meaningfully, and Luz flushed. Maritza read
this as a signal of interest, not the rush of discomfort it actually
was. Luz had absolutely no interest in Eduardo's cousin.

Later that night, once they were finally back in the apartment and Maritza and Eduardo had gone to bed, their giggles
and chatter laced with beer and louder than normal, Luz carefully transformed the couch she slept on into her bed and
slipped between the pale pink sheets, pulling the worn-out
floral bedspread that had come from Eduardo's sister's house up

to her chin. She peered out the set of windows that ran the length of the living room and overlooked a parking lot. It was usually at night when she felt the most unmoored, almost a stranger to herself. Who was she now? She was not an American, even though she lived here. And because she no longer lived there, Luz wondered if she could even still be considered Salvadoran.

---

Toward the end of her first year at Baldwin, a chemistry teacher on the third floor whose room she cleaned regularly went on maternity leave. In her place appeared a tall, dark-haired man with a well-trimmed beard who looked to be in his late thirties or early forties. Mr. Lehrer explained to Luz that the man was what they called a "long-term sub." Unlike Mr. Lehrer, who was placed wherever he was needed when a teacher called in sick or took a personal day, this substitute had some understanding of the subject, and he would be in the same classroom every day, almost like a real teacher.

Almost instantly, Luz did not like this long-term sub. Unlike most of the teachers at Baldwin, he never said hello when she entered his classroom to clean after the bell. In fact, he did not acknowledge her at all, once brushing past her to leave the room as if she were invisible.

But what really bothered Luz was the overly familiar way he seemed to speak with the young female students, as if they were his peers. There was one in particular, a blond girl who had a streak of purple in her hair, whom he seemed to focus on especially. As Luz pushed her janitorial cart down the hall, she would often catch him outside his classroom during passing periods, joking and laughing with her. She was clearly enamored of him, Luz could tell, and a few times after the bell to begin class rang, the two would linger near the door of his classroom, talking in low tones and laughing.

At home, she shared her concerns with Eduardo and Maritza, who cautioned her to stay out of it.

"It's probably nothing," Eduardo told her as the three of them sat in the living room watching a variety show on Spanish television, Eduardo in the recliner and Luz and Maritza on the couch. "He probably just wants to be liked by his students."

Luz shook her head. "But it's always the *girls* that he talks to in that way."

Maritza reached out to her little sister and gave her a squeeze.

"I know you mean well, Luz, but it's too risky to say anything," she said. "And anyway, the school year is almost over."

Nevertheless, Luz could not suppress the sense that something was wrong and growing more wrong with each passing day.

One afternoon after the long-term sub had been there almost two months, she approached his classroom after the school day had ended to begin her regular cleaning routine. She could see that the lights to the classroom were off, but the slim window in the door did not allow her to get a good view of the entire room, including the teacher's desk, which was tucked into a corner. While she could not be sure, she assumed that at this hour the room would be empty, and she used her key to unlock the door.

There, sitting close to his desk—he in his teacher's chair, she on a small, low stool—the long-term sub and the girl with the purple streak in her hair were speaking barely above a whisper. Their knees were practically touching, and the expressions on their faces revealed a level of intimacy Luz knew in her core was entirely inappropriate.

"Oh!" shouted Luz, her surprise sincere. She stood there next to her cart, her heart beating hard.

Startled, the man and the student quickly pulled apart from each other, and Luz thought she saw a flicker of annoyance cross the man's face. Murmuring something to the man, the young woman flushed scarlet, then stood up, grabbed for her nearby backpack, and made a fast exit, keeping her eyes on the floor as she did so. Uncomfortable around the sub—who was clearly pretending to be busy with papers on his desk—Luz completed her duties in record time and left the room as soon as possible.

That entire evening at home, she could not get the scene out of her head. The next morning, before the first bell of the day, she found Mr. Lehrer in a classroom on the third floor, not far from the long-term sub's room. He was writing the lesson plan on the whiteboard with a blue Expo marker.

She recalled Maritza and Eduardo's constant warnings. *Don't bring too much attention to yourself. Don't give anyone a reason to question you. Don't get involved.* It was not just her status in the United States that was at risk, but Maritza's, too. And Maritza and Eduardo loved each other.

Still, Luz thought of the girl with the streak of purple in her hair and her flushed cheeks and that dark corner of the classroom. She recalled how close to each other she and the man had been seated. She trusted every alarm bell ringing inside her.

"Mr. Lehrer," she said, and the old man turned to look at her. He was dressed in his usual work uniform: gray slacks, a cream-colored button-down shirt, and a solid blue tie that had seen better days.

"*Hola, Luz,*" he said, smiling broadly. "*¿Cómo estás?*" When he saw how concerned Luz appeared, he stopped smiling and asked, "What's wrong?"

Luz described as best she could—moving from Spanish to English and back—what she had witnessed. Mr. Lehrer nodded, taking it in. His face read deep concern.

"I understand," said Mr. Lehrer. "This is not okay. It has to be reported."

At this, Luz burst into tears, surprising even herself.

"Luz, what is it?" Mr. Lehrer asked, alarmed.

"I cannot . . . ," said Luz, placing her hand on her chest, pressing her palm hard against her pounding heart. Her face was hot, and warm tears streamed down her cheeks. "I cannot . . . be involved."

At this Mr. Lehrer's eyes went wide. Holding up his hands as if he were attempting to stop oncoming traffic, he shook his head vigorously side to side.

"No, no, Luz, do not worry, no . . ." He struggled to find the words, and then he remembered them: "*No diré que me dijiste.*"

*I will not say you told me.*

"I will take care of this," continued Mr. Lehrer. "Right away. *No te preocupes.*"

She had never told Mr. Lehrer that she did not have papers. Perhaps he had guessed that this was the case. Regardless, he had never asked about her status. But she sensed that he knew why she felt she could not speak up herself.

Two days later, the substitute was no longer at Baldwin High School. Instead, an older woman was there. She smiled at Luz when Luz came in that day to clean.

Mr. Lehrer found Luz that same afternoon, in an empty classroom she was sweeping. He explained in the English-Spanish hybrid that was now so familiar between the two of them that he had shared his concerns with the administration, that he had said this substitute should be investigated. He had not mentioned Luz. After a bit of digging, the administration discovered that several other people on campus had shared Luz's worries but no one had known if they should speak up. While there was nothing to suggest that the long-term sub had fully crossed a line, he had been removed and flagged in the substitute system and his name shared with neighboring districts. Hopefully, he would never set foot inside a school again.

Luz smiled and thanked Mr. Lehrer. What a relief to know that the man was gone. Mr. Lehrer said he had been happy to help, but he told Luz that he hoped she would answer a question for him. In Spanish, he asked Luz how she had sensed from the beginning that something was wrong. Where had that *instinto* to look out for that young female student come from?

Luz considered giving him a simple answer: That she didn't know where it came from. That she hadn't really thought of the situation as one requiring any sort of special insight.

But she trusted Mr. Lehrer. She liked him.

And there was a not-so-small part of her that wanted to share. That wanted to let Mr. Lehrer know that the Luz he knew was not all of who she was.

She began to tell him a story.

———

In her native El Salvador, in the city of San Salvador, Luz had also worked at a school. She had taught mathematics at an all-girls Catholic institution called Nuestra Señora de Fátima. By her mid-twenties, a few years before leaving for the United States, Luz had established herself as a gifted and nurturing teacher, the type that encouraged her teenage students to excel, to challenge themselves, to grow. She was small, just over five feet, and most people outside of her school life found her unassuming and even shy. But in the classroom, she had a commanding voice and a way of delivering lessons that felt even to herself like some sort of magic. Of course, she was not so egotistical as to say that out loud. She struggled, in fact, just to admit it quietly to herself, despite the transcendent sense that settled over her when she witnessed the click of understanding blooming on a student's face.

Curious and brainy, Luz had loved school as a little girl, loved its rhythms and routines, its pure mission of learning and self-improvement. And she had loved mathematics for its certainty, its promise of a right answer lurking somewhere inside a formula or a proof. Teaching math was all she had ever wanted to do, and so she had done it, starting first at a government-run school and then moving on to Nuestra Señora. She liked teaching only girls, liked the camaraderie and solidarity that developed between them, liked the way their confidence grew over the course of the school year, a confidence Luz knew they deserved and needed.

She was firm and demanding, but she could be silly, too. Once, shortly before the end of term, she acquired a student uniform—a navy blue skirt and a white blouse with dark blue piping around the collar and sleeves—and she wore it to school on the last day before the break. The students found it hilarious, urging her to sit in a student's desk and playact like she was one of them, mimicking their confusion, their frustration, their adolescent enthusiasm and angst. Luz eagerly complied for her girls, exaggerating their movements and their sayings into magnified expressions of themselves, expressions so easily recognizable by the teenage girls that they burst into peals of unrestrained laughter, and several started to cry tears of amusement.

The director of the school, Señora Flores, a serious, brilliant woman in her sixties who held her staff to the highest of standards, once told Luz that when she taught her students, she was like an artist creating a brand-new, brilliant canvas each day. These words of affirmation would never leave her, Luz knew.

*Maestra. Profesora.* These were the titles Luz dreamed of being called for the rest of her life.

Once, during her first year of teaching at Nuestra Señora, Luz had found herself on a city bus while running errands when a student of hers named Idalia climbed aboard. A tall girl with an angular face who often seemed lost in thought, Idalia reminded Luz of herself because of her bookishness, her shyness, and her deep desire to learn. It was a Saturday afternoon, and Idalia flushed a little when she climbed onto the bus and spied her teacher. Clearly, she wasn't sure how to react.

"Come sit next to me," Luz said with a smile, setting the young woman at ease. The bus was nearly full, but Luz was sitting toward the back, and the space next to her was empty. She patted it to signal to Idalia to join her. The girl did, and as the bus bounced along, Idalia explained that she was off to visit a cousin who had just had a baby.

"How nice," Luz said. Then she commented on how hot it was. She took a tissue from her skirt pocket and blotted her cheeks and temples. Idalia pushed her dark locks away from her sweaty forehead, dotted with adolescent acne.

As Luz slipped the tissue back into her pocket, she noticed the bus suddenly lurching to the side of the road. The stomping of heavy boots accompanied the shouts of four young men as they climbed aboard; two of them were brandishing pistols. They could not have been much older than Idalia.

"*¡Esto es un asalto!*" the tallest one shouted. He held his pistol casually, with experience.

Idalia gasped in panic, but Luz had been through this before. Glancing at Idalia, she noticed that the young girl was wearing a gold chain around her neck. Motioning with her fingers and whispering, Luz calmly guided the young girl to quickly tuck the necklace underneath her top, where it stayed unseen as the four men—boys, really, Luz realized—raced up and down the aisle, snatching purses, demanding wallets, and snatching jewelry off women's bodies with grins on their faces that could only be described as cavalier.

One middle-aged man toward the front of the bus resisted, and the leader brought his pistol down hard across the man's face, sending a spray of red mist into the air. Idalia squeezed her eyes shut, and Luz was grateful that they could see only the back of the man's lolling, balding head.

As one of the assailants approached Luz and Idalia, the two young women held their hands open to show that they had nothing. The young man had a hint of a mustache, a desperate attempt to appear older. He was not much taller than Luz. He sneered and motioned at them to empty their pockets; Luz's tissue tumbled to the floor of the bus. Idalia's pocket held a few coins, which she dutifully turned over. Tucked inside her sock, the folded-up bills Luz had hidden there almost seemed to pulse. She wondered if the man would somehow read her mind and find her money, but instead his eyes lingered on Idalia, who was seated next to the aisle. Reaching out with a smirk on his face, he cupped the young girl's left breast with a rough hand and squeezed, hard. Idalia pressed her eyes shut as if by doing so she might disappear.

"Leave her alone!" Luz shouted. "If you want to bother someone, bother me." She reached over and smacked the offending

hand away. Shocked, the young man stared at her, his brain trying to catch up with what Luz had just done to him. As he at-
tempted to calculate a response, the leader of group yelled that
they were done, it was time to take off. The young man did nothing more than scowl before trooping off the bus with the others.

As soon as they were gone, Idalia collapsed into Luz's arms,
sobbing. She pressed her face—damp with sweat and tears—
against Luz's shoulder and cried.

"*Gracias, maestra. Gracias.*" Idalia repeated these words over
and over, on a loop.

Thank you, teacher. Thank you.

Luz held Idalia in her arms, comforting the girl until she
was calm again, until the last of her tears were all dried up.

---

She told this story to Mr. Lehrer while they were seated side by
side in student desks. He had understood the weight of what
she was telling him early on, and he had suggested they sit. She
had shared all of this with him in her careful, awkward English, switching over to relatively simple Spanish phrases she
knew he would understand whenever the English she knew was
not enough. He had waved a hand in the air every so often to
signal her to pause, asking her to repeat a phrase, a word. Luz
sensed it was important to him to understand every detail of the
full story.

"How scared you must have been," he told her. "But also,
how brave. You are a teacher. You know that part of being a
teacher is to look out for your students."

Luz smiled shyly, feeling truly, fully seen in this place for the
first time since she had started working there.

Then Mr. Lehrer asked her what she missed the most about
teaching. She appreciated that he did not ask her *if* she missed

teaching; being a good teacher himself, he already knew the answer. But Luz struggled to put into words what pained her most, in part because of the language barrier and in part because the sentiment seemed so difficult to convey.

"What I miss most is the feeling . . . that . . . the work is so important," she said at last. This wasn't totally right, but it was at least somewhat close.

What Luz wanted to say was that while she certainly didn't think she was above her job or better than the other custodians (her mathematical mind even appreciated the efficient design of the plastic yellow janitorial cart she pushed around—one streamlined device that could carry a trash can, a mop bucket, and a crate of cleaning supplies all at once), what she missed most was the feeling of *usefulness* that came with being a teacher. At Nuestra Señora, she'd believed that every bit of knowledge she imparted to a student floated somewhere inside that student's brain, and even if certain mathematical models and steps were lost to the passage of time, she knew that she had forever altered that young person's ability to think, to process, to deduce. Some days it hadn't even been about mathematics. She had simply been there to encourage a child. To make them feel better in a difficult moment. That child would remember her. She'd made a permanent difference. But as a janitor at Baldwin High, she was aware that every floor, toilet, or table she scrubbed clean would be dirty again, often within minutes or hours. She hated the seeming futility of it all and how ineffectual it made her feel.

Luz tried again to explain: "With teaching . . . the work is . . . good work." She shrugged, hoping her point had been made.

Mr. Lehrer nodded, agreeing with her. "*No es trabajo,*" he added. "*Es una vocación.*"

"*Exactamente,*" said Luz, smiling. He understood her after all.

Their conversations continued, as did their mutual encouragement on the language app. When Luz returned for the following school year, she was cheered to see that Mr. Lehrer was back as a substitute. The last time she ever saw him was the morning of the day he died; he was substituting for a Spanish teacher, and she saw him standing in the doorway of the classroom during passing period. Luz was pushing her cart.

"*¡Puedo enseñarles algo aquí!*" he said to her proudly as she walked by. He was smiling at the idea that he knew enough to actually teach the children in the class.

"I need to make another quiz for you to take to be sure!" she teased, grinning.

His smile, his pride in his learning. She thought back on them fondly. But what Luz knew she would never forget was that day when they had sat next to each other and she had trusted him with her past. Toward the end of the conversation, as she had gotten up to leave, Mr. Lehrer had stopped her. In his accented Spanish he had said he had been wrong to call her Luz.

"*En realidad,*" he had told her, "*eres Profesora Guevara.*"

————————

On the day that Luz was made to scrub the couch in the lounge on which only hours before had rested the body of her friend, an assistant principal by the name of Ms. Garcia entered the room and discovered her weeping. She rushed to Luz and dropped down to her knees, instinctively putting one arm around Luz and rubbing her back in a maternal sort of way.

"Are you okay?" Ms. Garcia asked. "Can I help you?"

Luz wanted to spill out an explanation in the language that felt most comfortable to her, Spanish, but she had lived in

America long enough to understand that here a person's surname was not always an indicator of their ability to speak a certain language fluently. Here, there were plenty of Americans with the last names of Garza, of Hernandez, of Rios who had lost their ancestral tongue after generations of their family had lived in the United States. She knew that Ms. Garcia was one of those people. Still, she appreciated the kind gesture.

"I am okay," she said, wiping her wet face with the backs of her hands. "I am okay."

Ms. Garcia, still next to her on the floor, looked at Luz, her expression uncertain.

"Do you need . . . *puedo llamar alguien* . . . for you?" She was trying, pulling back from the recesses of her brain the Spanish that someone had once taught her, perhaps an *abuela* or an aunt.

"No, no," said Luz, shaking her head. She took a quavery breath and tried to prove that she was fine by continuing her task at hand. She picked up her sponge and started scrubbing away again.

Ms. Garcia stood up, and Luz could feel the assistant principal staring at her, trying to determine if it really was okay to walk away. Eventually, she decided it was, and Luz was alone again.

She later heard through the gossip of her fellow custodians that Mr. Lehrer's ashes had been spread in the school's front courtyard not long after he died, and now the school was in trouble because of it. She would have liked to have been present when Mr. Lehrer's remains were dispersed into the autumn air, but no one on campus would have invited her. They could not have grasped that she could have known him or been his friend. Luz was not really seen by so many of the people she came into contact with each day. Upon her arrival in the United States,

Eduardo and Maritza had explained to her that it was shock-
ingly easy to exist in a country that did not, at least on paper,
want her there. Because the truth was that, in many ways, it
did. It needed people like Luz. It depended on them to clean
their buildings and tend to their babies and fix their homes. It
did not want to extend to them their full humanity—that was
clear. But as long as she didn't open her mouth, ask for too
much, or rock the boat, she could stay. As long as she could
agree to exist only in a *certain* way. Like, half a person.

As the school year passed, the rumors that kind Principal
Kendricks was in big trouble only increased. She worried that
more eyes on the school could mean she was at an even bigger
risk. And truth be told, without Mr. Lehrer around, going to
work wasn't the same.

Toward the end of February, Maritza secured a nannying
job for Luz. It paid more than double what she made at the
school, and it paid in cash. Easier. Safer. The parents were nice,
Maritza claimed, having met them once. And just one little
baby to care for, too. The family was friends with the family
Maritza worked for. They could take the babies to the park together. It would be impractical for Luz not to take the position,
so she did.

On her last day, Luz completed her routine on the third
floor, finishing with the faculty lounge. When she was done
cleaning the bathrooms, emptying the trash cans, wiping down
the tables, and sweeping and mopping the floor, she returned
her janitorial cart to the supply closet and headed to the main
office, where the EZ-Clean employees signed in and out on a
time sheet.

It was just outside the office that she spotted the dreaded
suits standing in the hallway. But as she continued to walk to-

ward them fearfully—she figured it was best to act normal until she knew what was going on—she saw Principal Kendricks
emerge to meet them.

At first afraid to take it all in, Luz at last forced herself to
look in their direction as they headed inside the main office,
clearly not paying her any attention. Her thudding heart began
to slow as she tentatively followed them in and walked up to the
front desk, where she pretended to search for her name on the
time sheet as she tried to assess what was happening. She saw
the principal frowning as he headed into one of the adjoining
conference rooms, followed by the others.

After a moment of immense relief that this had nothing to
do with her, Luz felt sorry for him. He seemed like a decent
man. He'd even stayed behind after the school play earlier that
year to help her clean up, which was certainly unusual for someone of his station.

But most of all, she sensed that it was good she was leaving
this place.

Yet, a part of her—the part of her that was still a teacher and
always would be—would miss working inside a school.

Carefully and with precision, she signed her time sheet for
the final time. And then Profesora Guevara left the building.

# Ten

March 8, 2023

---

FROM: Denise.Baker@district181.org
TO: All Staff
SUBJECT: Mandatory meeting after school for all
employees

Colleagues,

There will be a mandatory meeting after school in the
auditorium for all Baldwin High employees, immediately
following the final bell. After-school tutorials and club
meetings must be postponed. If you have afternoon duty,
employees from Central Office will be here to cover.

---

"Fuck, fuck, fuck," Mr. Williams whispered in the hall, his
eyes wide.

"It's Kendricks, isn't it?" Ms. Brennan responded.

"It has to be," said Williams. "They don't announce manda-tory meetings after school with just a few hours' notice to give us raises and free supplies for our classrooms."

"Do you think he's gone?" Ms. Brennan asked. "Like for good?"

Mr. Williams paused to peer into his classroom to make sure his students were not committing any crimes, then turned his attention back to Ms. Brennan.

"I don't know," he said. "I don't think they could just take him out like that. There has to be a process. A Kafkaesque pro-cess, to be sure. But still, a process."

Now it was Ms. Brennan's turn to check on her class, which was growing squirrelly.

"I believe I said we would be completing our metaphor charts, not playing on our phones and whispering with one an-other," she called out to them in a firm, crisp voice. Her stu-dents were momentarily cowed. Focusing on Mr. Williams again, she said, "I have to get back in there. But this absolutely blows. This is only my first year here, but I've liked working for Kendricks. He's smart. Not some district drone."

Mr. Williams gave her a pointed look, and in a withering voice, he said, "Why do you think they've removed him?"

---

**Jim Fitzsimmons:** Denise, I'm not going to ask questions or pry about whatever district bullshit is going on now. Although I'll take a moment to say I'm sure whatever it is, it IS bullshit! But I'm really reaching out as a friend. Whatever is happening, I am sure this is a lot of stress on you and that can be tough in early sobriety. I just want to make sure you

have support. I'm here if you need anything. You have
the right to draw boundaries and say no to protect
your sobriety. It has to come first, always. One day at
a time.

**Denise Baker:** Jim, I appreciate you. This all
happened yesterday afternoon very fast and admin is
still processing. Just got informed of much of it myself
late last night and it's a mess. I've already been in
touch with my sponsor today and I'm seeing her at a
meeting tonight no matter what. Your words about
boundaries and protecting my sobriety mean a lot to
me. Please continue to check in with me. It helps me
stay accountable.

**JF:** It's no trouble and I am happy to do it. I will text
you this evening to check in. And you call me or your
sponsor or someone if you feel like you're going to
pick up.

**DB:** I will, Jim. I promise. Thank you.

———

Kitty Garcia made her way to Principal Kendricks's office,
tucked into the back of a collection of rooms that was part of
the main office. On her way there she passed other administrators, huddled in panicked, whispered conversations.

Mark's door was closed, and she knew he wasn't on the other
side of it. Clutching some file folders to her chest, she paused
briefly and thought back to the heady days of the fall semester,
when she'd dropped by here with such regularity, drunk on a

schoolgirl crush. She let her fingers graze the doorknob for a moment. Then she continued on to a nearby single-use women's restroom, and she locked herself inside.

She'd given Mark the opportunity to blow up his life, and wisely, he hadn't taken it. After the sting of rejection had worn off (God, the humiliation of that winter night in the parking lot after the play!), she had slowly come to realize that it had been for the best. Sure, the giddy banter between them had given her a much-needed ego boost and rush. And yes, she and Mark might have been a great couple in some parallel universe that didn't actually exist. But in *this* universe, he was a married man, and until Mark Kendricks, Kitty Garcia had always thought of herself as the sort of decent person who wouldn't cross such an ethical boundary. All told, in the end she was glad she hadn't.

But after several weeks of awkwardly rebuilding a more professional relationship between them, now this. She could say with confidence that he was a good principal, one of the best school leaders she'd ever worked for. What would happen to Baldwin now? And to him?

Hidden in the bathroom, Kitty felt her chest grow tight, and she was overcome by a wave of deep sadness and loss. She gave herself a few moments to cry, running the faucet to mask the sounds.

She'd had a crush on him for a reason.

———

Ms. Fletcher ran into Ms. Jimenez in the third-floor lounge shortly after the final bell. As usual, the U.S. history teacher was wrestling with the copier.

"Heading to the meeting?" Ms. Fletcher asked, grabbing her reusable lunch kit from the refrigerator.

"Yeah, I guess," Ms. Jimenez said with a sigh, not looking up from the machine. "Although what if I just didn't go? I mean, what would they even do to me?"

Ms. Fletcher shrugged. "I suppose I want to hear what they're going to say."

As the copier continued to hum, Ms. Jimenez turned to look at Ms. Fletcher.

"I know what they're going to say," she replied. "They're going to offer up a bunch of doublespeak to defend their ridiculousness." She checked the status of her job and made sure her copies were collating properly. "Fuck it," she continued, "I'm going home. If I get in trouble, I get in trouble. Last time I looked out the front door of this place, there wasn't exactly a long line of people out there applying for my job."

Ms. Fletcher couldn't help but admire her colleague's cavalier attitude, although she didn't share it. Ms. Fletcher was on time to every mandatory meeting.

"I can fill you in tomorrow if you want," she offered.

"Sure, thanks," said Ms. Jimenez.

Ms. Fletcher started to head out, but paused by the lounge door.

"You know, I feel like this is the moment when you should crack a joke and make me feel better," she said, her voice small and hopeful. Ms. Jimenez and Ms. Fletcher were not friends, and they did not spend time together outside of school. They knew almost nothing about each other's personal lives. But Ms. Jimenez's sense of humor had lightened Ms. Fletcher's mood at work for nearly twenty years.

"Amanda," replied Ms. Jimenez, her voice filled with sadness, "I wish I could."

---

**Hannah Sanderson:** This meeting is absurd. I cannot believe we are being forced to sit in this auditorium right now and listen to this district talking head blather on about transparency and due diligence and blah blah. Jake, I'm so mad.

**Jake Rayfield:** It totally fucking sucks. When I went in to talk to Kendricks the other week about my decision to not come back next year, he was nothing but supportive and understanding. He's a cool guy and he did nothing wrong.

**HS:** God, I feel so bad for Ms. Baker up there trying to calm us all down. Trying to answer questions when she doesn't have the answers. And that district asshole not really helping her.

**JR:** So he's on "temporary reassignment" while they "complete a thorough investigation" and we just have to wait it out? I don't trust this.

**HS:** I don't think we should trust it at all. I hope he comes back. If he doesn't, who knows who they might put in as our new principal? God, I'm sad right now.

**JR:** Wanna come over to my place tonight? I can make you dinner. And think of ways to cheer you up.

**HS:** Yes please. Although it feels weird to flirt during this depressing meeting.

**JR: Yeah. But I think it's finally coming to an end at least.**

**HS: Not soon enough.**

About two hours after the torturous all-staff meeting, Ms. Jackson finally managed to leave her office and head for home. On the way out to the faculty parking lot, she crossed paths with Nurse Honeycutt. The two women had very different roles at Baldwin, and they did not have frequent opportunities to interact, but they respected each other as hardworking professionals. They had both seen so much during their decades of service.

"Let's walk out together," said Nurse Honeycutt.

"Please," said Ms. Jackson.

On their way down the long main hall, Nurse Honeycutt asked Ms. Jackson how many principals she thought they had seen during their shared tenure.

"Of course, you were here for a few years before I got here," added the nurse.

"Yes," said Ms. Jackson. "I started under Mr. John Graham. He was the first principal of Baldwin to hire Black employees, as I understand it."

"After Graham we had Donovan, then Kaplan," recited Nurse Honeycutt.

"Oh Lord, don't mention Kaplan," said Ms. Jackson, shaking her head. At this, Nurse Honeycutt laughed.

"Well, we survived at least," said Honeycutt. The two women exited the building into the parking lot, still trying to finish the list.

"After Kaplan they brought in Martha Page," said Ms. Jackson. "Baldwin's first female principal. She was smart, but she didn't stay long. They moved her up the pipeline to Central Of-fice, of course."

"Then there was Vickie Torres and that guy Sawyer," replied Nurse Honeycutt. "I can't recall his first name now, all of a sudden."

"It was Frank," said Ms. Jackson. "After him Juan Martinez and, finally, Mr. Kendricks." She sighed. "Poor Mr. Kendricks."

The two women were now standing together near their re-spective cars. March was usually quite pleasant in Houston, but if a person stood still long enough, they could sometimes sense just a touch of the humid summer months that would soon en-gulf them.

"I really thought I'd retire under Mark," said Nurse Hon-eycutt. "I like him."

"I do, too," said Ms. Jackson. "And I'm worried for him."

"We can only hope for the best," replied Nurse Honeycutt. "And expect the worst."

"Sometimes I wonder if that's how we've survived so long in this business," answered Ms. Jackson, her voice almost mourn-ful. Nurse Honeycutt responded with a rueful laugh. Then, af-ter wishing each other a good evening, both veterans got into their vehicles and drove home, leaving Baldwin High School—now nearly empty—sitting quietly in a growing darkness.

# *Eleven*

Since 1985, Nurse Honeycutt had steered Baldwin High through more than thirty broken appendages, multiple paranoid reactions to ingested hallucinogens, countless bouts of stomach flu, the birth of a baby in a student bathroom, poor Mr. Lehrer dying in the faculty lounge, *and* a global pandemic, and yet the first thing students, alumni, and even teachers thought of when the sixty-eight-year-old school legend had cause to cross their minds was how easily her name could be adjusted to Nurse Honeybutt. She was referred to in this manner frequently and casually, but not without kindness, to be clear.

Nurse Honeycutt was beloved.

For decades, the tall, slender woman inhabited the clinic on the first floor, near the school's main intersection, and kept order with a cool and collected demeanor. She let her hair turn gray naturally, and for many years now she had worn it in a bun pulled back tight from her face. She was kind but firm, quiet but commanding. She had won the state's School Nurse of the Year award multiple times. She often wore scrubs covered in small honeybees, and every year she gratefully accepted presents from students and faculty members in the form of small jars of honey, small ceramic bees, bee-shaped earrings, and mugs with bees that playfully insisted the reader buzz off because the drinker was drinking coffee.

She was known to slip students with upset stomachs peppermints and cups of cold, fizzy ginger ale (she stocked both items in the clinic with money out of her own pocket), and she could be depended on to whip up the perfect ice pack for a muscle strain in thirty seconds flat, but Nurse Honeycutt was no fool. Decades of school nursing had calibrated her bullshit detector into a finely tuned instrument, and she knew exactly when a student was truly in need of her services and when they were just faking it, the latter being the case about 40 percent of the time. The biggest offenders were the freshmen, who had not yet learned that Nurse Honeycutt had the ability to stare into your soul with her green eyes, rest a cool hand on your forehead, and wait three beats before saying, "Please head back to class, but feel free to take a peppermint on the way out."

In short, Nurse Honeycutt believed in following policy, keeping impeccable records, and maintaining order at all times. Even during the past stressful month and a half without their leader Principal Kendricks on campus, Nurse Honeycutt had gone above and beyond to make sure that she was compliant in all areas and communicative with interim principal, Ms. Baker. She had continued to try to serve as a stabilizing force in the middle of a storm.

But there was one area of care where Nurse Honeycutt bent the rules, and she did so for the girls.

A handful of times a year, a young woman would venture

into the Baldwin High clinic, and without the girl needing to say much, Nurse Honeycutt would understand the predicament even when the student had not really been able to admit it to herself yet. The pained expression, the pale face. Tears often already lining red-rimmed eyes. A few times in Nurse Honeycutt's career the girl simply folded over and puked, breakfast vomit splattering all over her pink tiled floor.

Even though she knew she was not supposed to do so, inside a cabinet Nurse Honeycutt kept a black duffel bag filled with pregnancy tests she purchased at the local drugstore. Better the girls know the full truth, and the sooner the better, reasoned Nurse Honeycutt. While stocking these tests was a gray area when it came to the rules, Nurse Honeycutt figured she was simply helping speed along an already difficult process. After all, there was nothing holding these girls back from going and buying a pregnancy test on their own.

Locking the clinic door so as not to be interrupted, Nurse Honeycutt would unfold the test's paper directions like a map to some as-yet-unknown destination, walking the girl through each step. Then she'd send her off to the clinic bathroom, test in anxious hand.

Sometimes it was blissfully, beautifully negative, and there were screams of delight from inside the bathroom. Nurse Honeycutt would remind the young woman of the importance of testing again in a few days if her period had not arrived, and she would stress the need for birth control and suggest where the student might acquire it. Pregnancy tests were something Nurse Honeycutt might be able to explain to the school board, but condoms, unfortunately, were something else entirely. Nurse Honeycutt was still mostly a rule follower, after all.

When the test was positive, those two blue lines looking at them as if they were proud of themselves, Nurse Honeycutt would give the young woman a moment to sob, to stare, to collect herself as best as possible. She would jot down the names of different websites, then, and phone numbers, too. And she would always urge the girls to go home and speak to their parents, even when she knew some of them would have to talk to some other adult in their lives. There were various outcomes for these girls. Some would continue coming to school until their bellies swelled, and some Nurse Honeycutt would spot months later, their adolescent stomachs as flat as boards, their youthful minds occupied with grades and boys and teenage triviality.

But things changed. Elections happened. And one morning in mid-April, about six weeks after Principal Kendricks had been removed, a twelfth grader named Isabella came in and said her period was two weeks late. She eventually found herself sitting in a metal folding chair, holding a positive test in her hand, and from the look on her face, Nurse Honeycutt knew the situation was particularly bleak.

"My father is going to kill me," said Isabella, who had not cried yet, even though Nurse Honeycutt knew the crying was inevitable. Isabella was a tall girl with big lips and big hips, pretty and careful about her appearance. Her creamy white skin was free of blemishes, her mouth stained with berry-pink lipstick, her eyelids painted a shimmery copper.

"You don't think your parents would be open to listening to you?" said Nurse Honeycutt, mostly just to buy time. Despite all the signs that she should not risk it—this year of all years, with everything that had happened—despite all of that, the wheels in her mind were already spinning.

"No," said Isabella. "My parents won't listen. I mean, my mom *might*. But my dad, definitely not. And my dad . . ." At this, Isabella squeezed her eyes shut.

"What about the boy?" asked Nurse Honeycutt. She purposely did not use the word *father*.

"He's an idiot," said Isabella, brown eyes opening, her face a sudden scowl. "I realize that *now*, of course. Like, a month too late." She paused and considered Nurse Honeycutt before delivering the final, humiliating detail: "I'm not his only girlfriend."

Nurse Honeycutt nodded sympathetically but tried to keep her facial expression judgment-free. She reached over and patted Isabella on the back a few times as a signal of caring, then withdrew. Nurse Honeycutt wasn't much of a hugger, in part because she didn't consider it professional and in part because she respected the fact that some children did not want to be touched.

"Do you want to carry this pregnancy?" Nurse Honeycutt asked, her voice quiet, careful not to lead. It was a question she didn't used to ask, back in the days when she could write down websites and phone numbers and wish the girls luck. At that time, the girl's answer had not been any of her business. But given the circumstances in which they were currently living, the answer now seemed more pressing. More dire.

The young woman gazed at Nurse Honeycutt. Isabella was eighteen years old. Her backpack was covered in patches that the nurse had come to learn represented different pop bands from South Korea that were popular among many of the students. When the young woman opened her mouth to take a deep, shaky breath, Nurse Honeycutt caught a glimpse of a retainer.

Now came the inevitable tears.

"No," said Isabella, shaking her head to punctuate it. "No, Nurse Honeycutt, I don't want this baby. I know that I don't."

———

In the summer of 1970, when Nurse Honeycutt was a fifteen-year-old girl named Nancy Carter, America was shifting. In flux. Chaotic. The American government was slaughtering college students on campus. Women, young people, and minorities were flooding into the streets to demand their rights. People were boycotting grapes. The war in Vietnam still raged.

But that summer Nancy's world was as still as her community pool after hours. Unchanged. Steeped in tradition. Despite changes in neighboring districts, Nancy's school had already announced that it would still not allow girls to wear pants to class that coming fall. Nancy's mother continued to sign her name *Mrs. Thomas Carter.* And even though the debut of *Ms.* magazine was only two years away, Nancy fully expected that she would grow up to be a nurse, teacher, or secretary; those were the only three available options. She hoped for nurse, as she didn't get queasy at the sight of blood and she liked helping people.

Nancy was the youngest of three children, a change-of-life surprise who was the only child left at home during the summer she was fifteen. Her parents were kind but somewhat distant. Her mother still dressed for dinner, and her father, an attorney, still led grace at the start of every meal. But there was security in Nancy's world. She wanted for nothing. The summer of 1970, she spent the lazy June days cutting out pictures of Bobby Sherman and the Jackson 5 from *Tiger Beat* and making her own facials out of oatmeal and egg whites.

Shortly after Independence Day, a new family moved in to

the house next door. Nancy's mother asked Nancy to help her make two apple pies, one for them and one for the new neighbors. As Nancy cubed the butter, broke up lumps in the flour with a fork, and sprinkled sugar on the finished pie so that it fell like a miniature blizzard, she caught glimpses of her mother, quietly humming to herself as she worked alongside her daughter at the kitchen counter, a red-and-white checked apron tied tightly around her trim waist. Mrs. Thomas Carter had spent all her adult life humming and busying herself around this three-bedroom home, keeping it pristine and peaceful, almost trapped in time. She maintained a schedule, written in careful black cursive in a small leather notebook she kept on her nightstand, of when to rotate the mattresses, when to wash the windows, when to restock the medicine cabinet, when to defrost the freezer. Nancy's mother didn't watch news programs or read the paper because she said it bothered her. Every Election Day, Nancy's father wrote out the list of candidates that Nancy's mother should vote for, and Nancy's mother tucked the paper into her purse and headed off to the local elementary school to pull the levers.

Later in her life, Nancy Carter would view all this with a sort of dumbfounded amazement. But the summer that Nancy was fifteen, it had just seemed normal.

The delivery of the apple pie revealed that the next-door neighbors had a boy just a year older than Nancy. His name was John, but he went by Jack. Jack Harris. And he was cute, Nancy decided. Not as cute as Bobby Sherman, but handsome in his own way. He had a slim runner's build and big hazel eyes and a crooked front tooth that was more charming than off-putting. When he came over a few days after moving in and asked Nancy if she wanted to ride bikes down to the local pool, Nancy was surprised to hear her mother say it was all right with her as long as Nancy was back by dinner. But Nancy's mother had been so busy flipping mattresses, defrosting the freezer, canning vegetables, and baking pies that she had seemed to miss the fact that her youngest child was growing hips, developing breasts, dreaming of boys, and lacking in critical information about everything that came along with all of it.

Nancy wore her peppermint-striped suit to the pool, so on their first outing Jack jokingly referred to her as Candy, like a candy cane. (But after that, he always called her Nancy. Much to Nancy's delight, Jack quickly proved himself to be the sort of boy who knew how to do just the *right* amount of joking.) He did flips off the high diving board to impress her. She proved to him that she could hold her breath underwater for a minute. They debated whether the band Bread was corny. (Jack said yes but Nancy said no. In truth she thought their song "Make It with You" was the most romantic thing in the world.) Jack bought her piping-hot French fries from the snack bar, and after she ate them, he reached over and gently took one of her hands in his and licked the salt from each of her fingertips. At this she felt a warm, quivering, melty sensation all over her body that could only be described as exquisite.

Jack was old enough (and had permission!) to drive his father's heritage-green Oldsmobile 98, a hulking mass of a car that made Nancy feel so grown up when he picked her up for dates, once they'd both decided they'd like to do more than just spend time at the pool. Jack was the sort of boy parents liked. He could stand inside the Carters' well-appointed living room and shake hands with Mr. Carter and compliment Mrs. Carter, and the two adults were pleased and even delighted to see their daughter leave the house with him. He was literally the boy next door!

*I have a boyfriend. I have a boyfriend. I have a boyfriend.* The words zipped through Nancy's mind on a loop that summer, and sometimes she found herself whispering them to herself in the bathroom mirror, even pinching herself once on the arm, hard, to make sure it was all real. Having dug out a black-and-white composition book that she'd intended to use as a proper diary but rarely did, Nancy would curl up in a warm, secret ball under her bedspread and write things like *Mrs. Jack Harris* and *Jack and Nancy Harris* and *When Jack kisses me he makes me feel like I'm going to explode. I want to touch him all over his body (yes even there) and I want to let him touch me all over my body (yes even THERE!!!!!!) Just writing those words makes me dizzy. I know it's a sin but how can it be a sin when being with Jack is so perfect and good?*

The back of the heritage-green Oldsmobile 98 was roomy and comfortable and smelled faintly and pleasantly of Jack's father's Tareytons. Jack Harris was a genuinely nice boy. It must be said that when it came right down to it, he really was. And it should also be said that Nancy Carter did not do anything she did not want to do. In fact, she was a willing participant and, in addition to that, she liked it. All that summer and into the fall, Nancy wondered if there was something wrong with her because she liked it so much. The story she had always been told was that boys were the ones who really wanted it. Did this make her unusual or dirty? Or was it just that girls and boys were not really that different in this regard? For a time, Nancy decided it must be that. Fervent nights in dark backseats must be a universal pleasure.

Until, unfortunately, the moment came when Nancy was forced to remember that in one important way boys and girls were very different indeed.

————————

Isabella left Nurse Honeycutt's clinic dejected, with a vacant sort of expression on her face. Before she did, Nurse Honeycutt had asked the girl, point-blank, if she wanted to hurt herself. Legally, it was the right thing to do. Morally, it also was, and Nurse Honeycutt believed in doing the moral thing. Isabella had whispered that she did not want to hurt herself and she would not, but Nurse Honeycutt had written down the number for a teen crisis line on a scrap of paper just in case. It had felt like putting a Band-Aid on an oozing third-degree burn. Isabella had taken the paper wordlessly and shoved it into her jeans pocket. She had glanced at the pregnancy test still sitting on the table in front of her and had then gotten up to leave. Nurse Honeycutt had wanted to say something else. To offer some sort of encouragement, perhaps, but what words would those be?

So Nurse Honeycutt had said nothing. She'd just watched Isabella slip out of the clinic and into the crowded hallway full of shouts and the squeaks of sneakers. Then she'd glanced at the large calendar she kept on her desk. She counted days and weeks. Made calculations. She thought about that emergency all-staff meeting in the auditorium weeks ago, and about how rudderless the school had felt recently without their well-liked principal. She thought back to the events in the courtyard, to Mr. Lehrer's ashes all over Jessica Patterson's face.

Nurse Honeycutt had worked with Mr. Lehrer back when he had been a beloved English teacher, not just a substitute, and she had always found him amiable. Kind. Focused on the kids. How frustrated he would be if he knew that Central Office had

turned his death into a reason to make things more difficult for
his colleagues and, by extension, more difficult for the students.

But if she was being honest with herself—and she almost
always was—Nurse Honeycutt knew that if anyone could read
her mind in this moment, they would accuse her not only of
risking more of Central Office's wrath, but of something much
more serious.

She examined the calendar again and tapped the eraser head
of her pencil rat-a-tat on her desk. She remembered Isabella's
crushed expression and her tears. She thought and thought.

---

At the home for unwed mothers, Nancy spent most of her time
absolutely bored out of her skull, which is a terrible thing to be
when a person is already horribly sad and lonely, which Nancy
also was.

The matron was named Mrs. Broussard, and all the girls referred to her privately and regularly as Mrs. Blowhard. Mrs.
Broussard was *not* beloved. In fact, she was despised, because
she seemed to believe that her entire life's purpose was to remind Nancy and the other girls that they were dirty, that they
were failures, and that they were absolutely unfit to be mothers
even though they were carrying babies inside them.

"The best thing to do," said Mrs. Broussard when she was
lecturing her trapped audience, "is to remind yourself that this
is your punishment for not waiting for marriage, but that you
can redeem yourself by giving this baby a safe and healthy home
to grow up in. A home with parents who can actually do the
hard, thankless work of parenting. You should be grateful that
God has granted you the opportunity to be redeemed in this
way." Mrs. Broussard was a short, squat woman with dark red
hair that she kept in an out-of-style beehive, and she had an

annoying habit of clasping and unclasping her hands as she spoke. Nancy used to try to focus on her hands instead of her words as a way to distract herself from Mrs. Broussard's hatefulness.

Nancy received cards from her parents. They never said much. They were blank-on-the-inside cards with flowers on the front, or a painting of a colorful bird. Inside, in the same careful script she used to list her chores, Nancy's mother would write some variation of *Your father and I are praying for you every day.* The message would always be signed *Mom and Dad.* But never *Love.* Nancy reminded herself that her mother and father were not a *Love, Mom and Dad* type even before all of this. She pinned the cards up on the small bulletin board by her bed in the dorm room she shared with five other girls, all of them young, all of them sad, all of them secreted away to this place where no one visited because it was too painful. Where the only way to leave was to leave your baby behind.

When Nancy had first suspected she might be pregnant, she had fleetingly hoped that Jack would marry her, even as she knew the notion was absurd. There had always been a few girls in her high school who left during senior year to get married. One girl had even graduated as a married woman before she had started to show. But she and Jack were still so young. And anyway, their parents would never stand for such a scandal.

The night she told Jack, the Olds 98 went from being a romantic, dreamlike space in which nothing bad could ever happen to the scene of a claustrophobic nightmare starring two terrified kids.

"I'm so sorry, Nancy," Jack said, holding her hand, the same hand he'd once tenderly taken at the pool, had once gently touched his pink tongue to, carefully licking the salt off each fingertip. He was sorry because it was happening to her, to Nancy. Again, to be clear, Jack Harris was a nice boy. He was kind and respectful and he cared about Nancy, but in the end, the problem was Nancy's problem. It was always the girl who was going to have to pay.

Pay she did, and quickly, too. The speed with which her parents made the arrangements was shocking, her father not looking at her once, her mother tight-lipped and forever organizing, carefully writing out a list of all the items Nancy would take with her and packing the suitcase with impressive precision. There was a quick hug from her mother on the day she was dropped off. From her father there was nothing.

At the home, the days rolled by, one into the other. Hours were spent watching *Room 222* and *The Young Rebels* on a small black-and-white in the dayroom. A halfhearted attempt was made at keeping up with studies through a correspondence course. The girls tried not to cry, because when you did, inevitably someone would tell you to shut up. Not because they weren't sympathetic, of course. But tears were terribly contagious.

Nancy tried not to think about Jack or the strange flips and kicks inside her body and the source of them. Instead, she watched television and went for aimless walks in the poorly maintained garden. She played Go Fish and Crazy Eights with a brunette named Barbara, who was replaced by a blonde named Mary after Barbara's belly swelled to its capacity and then one day she was gone. When Nancy was gone, Mary would play cards with someone else.

Nancy gave birth alone in the county hospital with a gruff doctor who checked on her periodically, as if she were a laboring cow. Her parents did not come, of course. No one explained anything. The pain was horrific, a hot, burning split up the middle of her teenage body, the screams from her mouth not ones she could have ever predicted she would be able to make. When her baby was born—pink, squalling, and wriggling—it was taken away in a rush. A sympathetic older nurse with a moon face and thin lips was the one to tell Nancy that she'd had a boy.

"Try to forget this, sweetheart," she said, her kind voice soft and whispery. She pushed Nancy's sweaty, dark hair off her face and offered her a cup of ice-cold orange juice. "Try to forget it and get on with your life."

When Nancy returned home, the Harris family had moved away. No one would tell her where Jack had gone, and she had no way of finding him. He knew her address, of course, but even though Nancy lingered over the mailbox when her mother wasn't looking and sorted hopefully through the day's letters and cards, there was never anything. Jack Harris simply disappeared.

Some evenings after heading to bed, always careful to shut the bedroom door tight behind her, Nancy would tug her composition book from its hiding spot in her closet and flip to the pages where she'd written Jack's name over and over, along with all her secret confessions about him. She ran her fingertips over her girlish scrawl, as if by touching it she could absorb and make real again in her mind those months with Jack. Whether it would be easier or harder to let Jack slip from her thinking was a question she couldn't answer, so he just stayed there, always on the outskirts of her brain.

So did the baby, of course. Nancy's glimpse of his chubby pink body kicking and wailing was on a forever loop in her consciousness.

All of her old friends had been ordered to stay away, to see her as tainted and infectious. Not that she would have gone to school with them again anyway. Instead, Nancy's parents sent her to an all-girls Catholic high school in a neighboring town, where she made the sort of school friends you can talk about assignments and homework with, not the kind you have over for sleepovers. She suspected that some knew the truth about her, but blessedly, not one girl ever brought it up. (Nancy also suspected that perhaps she was not the only girl at the school in her predicament.) At least once a week, Nancy remembered the words of that nurse, the only person who had been nice to her at the birth of her son.

*Try to forget this, sweetheart. Try to forget it and get on with your life.*

A former B student with a middling interest in academics, Nancy decided to devote all of her energy to her studies as a way to busy her mind and tend to her broken heart. Papers were turned in before their due dates. Class projects fulfilled every requirement and then some. Assigned readings blossomed with careful annotations. It turned out Nancy Carter was quite bright. She made the honor roll. She was named salutatorian. She was accepted into her first-choice university's nursing program at a college some distance from home. (She had always thought nursing would be her path, but the kind, moon-faced woman sealed the deal.) Once she graduated, she stayed where she was, visiting her hometown twice a year and never for more than a week at a time. Nancy Carter followed all the remaining rules laid out in front of her and surpassed every expectation placed on her in her professional life. After working at several middle schools, she became the nurse at the biggest high school in the city, and she performed this role exceptionally. She was a deeply respected and admired woman.

And on the day her mother died of a quick-moving cancer that ended her life far before anyone had assumed it would, Nancy came home to help. In her mid-thirties at the time, a few years into her career at Baldwin High, accomplished, independent, mostly happy at last, she sat by her mother's bedside. Some of the last words her mother said to her daughter were these: "Nancy, dear, in spite of everything, I'm proud of what you've made of yourself."

---

Nurse Honeycutt had ordered the pills from overseas. She had done so the summer before, not long after the headlines hit. That awful moment when things had gone so horribly awry. When the great undoing so many had simultaneously predicted and denied could ever happen, happened.

On that terrible June day, Nurse Honeycutt exchanged a few despairing texts and calls with some like-minded friends. Women from her book club. A cousin she'd reconnected with in middle age. Some of her fellow school nurses. Nurse Honeycutt had never been particularly political. She had never marched or protested, and she had eschewed labels like *feminist* even as a college student in the '70s. But she followed the news carefully, she read the paper each morning, she made donations to causes that mattered to her, and she had opinions about many things.

And on Election Day, when she voted, she knew exactly who she was voting for and why.

On the Thursday in mid-April when Isabella came to see her, Nurse Honeycutt went home to the small, tidy two-bedroom apartment she had once shared with her late husband, Howard, and where she now lived with her dog, a lovable mutt named Trixie. After a meal of grilled chicken and vegetables and a sin-

gle glass of red wine, Nurse Honeycutt powered up her computer and printer and sat down to type.

She started the note this way:

> It has come to my attention that you are pregnant and in
> need of assistance. I want to help you. These pills will help
> terminate your pregnancy. In other words, they will cause an
> abortion. If you want to continue with your pregnancy, do not
> take them. These pills are safe and approved by the FDA,
> but given our state's abortion laws, we must be careful.

Nurse Honeycutt typed up detailed instructions for taking
the pills in clear, numbered fashion like a trained and proper
nurse would do. At the end of the note, she added the following:

> **A slight fever is normal**, as is intense cramping and
> bleeding, but should your fever rise or the bleeding or pain
> become extreme, it is important that you go to your closest
> emergency room. These pills cannot be detected in your
> blood or urine, so the hospital will not be able to tell that
> you took them; you can tell them you believe you are
> experiencing a miscarriage and leave it at that.
>
> This is an option if you no longer want to carry out this
> pregnancy.

> I am praying for you.

Through one of the school's databases, Nurse Honeycutt had
access to every student's locker number and combination, and
she had made sure to secure this information on her computer

at home. The next day, long before the sun came up, Nurse Honeycutt crossed the front courtyard, entered the building, and headed straight for Isabella's locker, which was located on the third floor.

As she made her way down the empty hallway, hoping that she was the only soul in the building, she walked past the faculty lounge, its door shut tight. Always busy in the clinic, she had not had cause to be inside the lounge since the day she'd drawn a white sheet over the body of Mr. Lehrer. The image of his grizzled face, etched with worry lines and the strain of living, skated through her mind. Her heart pounding over what she was about to do, her mind suddenly immersed in all she had seen and done in this place, Nurse Honeycutt was flooded with some grief—but also relief—that she was closer to the end of her career than its start.

The inside of Isabella's locker was a messy explosion of teenage girlhood, charming in its earnestness. Magazine cutouts of boy bands taped haphazardly to its inner door, a rainbow of chewed and hardened gum blobs affixed in careful formation along the back wall, and a note to self on a pink Post-it that read, in capital letters, DON'T TALK TO THAT FUCKHEAD NO MATTER WHAT.

At the top of a precarious stack of spiral notebooks that threatened to collapse at any moment, Nurse Honeycutt placed the brown paper bag with the pills inside it. Her anonymous typed note was carefully stapled to the package. After surveying her work for a moment, Nurse Honeycutt took a deep breath and carefully shut the locker, spinning the combination lock more times than necessary.

It was the first time she had done this absolutely crazy, utterly dangerous thing. But as terrifying as it was, she did not feel she was violating any of her ethics. In fact, she felt she was living them.

Before the end of the school year, she would do it once more.

Walking with purpose as she always did, she headed around a corner and almost ran into Ms. Fletcher, who often came in early to catch up on her grading. Nurse Honeycutt startled and uttered a small shriek.

"Oh my God, I am so sorry!" said Ms. Fletcher, who was surprised to see the normally unflappable nurse so rattled. She was also curious about why she was on the third floor, but Ms. Fletcher didn't pry. Nurse Honeycutt was far too respected to be questioned.

"Don't apologize, please, Ms. Fletcher," answered Nurse Honeycutt, straightening herself up and laughing off the interaction. "I think I'm just ready for the weekend."

"Aren't we all," said Ms. Fletcher, nodding and smiling. The two parted ways, and as Ms. Fletcher headed to her classroom, she wondered how on earth their school could survive without the hardworking, dedicated, beloved Nurse Honeybutt.

———

In addition to a professional life that had brought her much satisfaction, Nancy eventually knew much personal joy, too. She had many rich, deep friendships, and after a few false starts with men who never seemed to be what they were at first glance, she had met Howard Honeycutt in her late thirties. Upon their first introduction, at a holiday house party held by mutual friends, he had extended his hand toward her and said, "Hello, I'm Howard Honeycutt. I realize my name sounds like a character from a children's show on PBS, but I swear to you, it's mine."

Within six months they were engaged. A few months later,

married. It seemed silly to wait at their age—Howard was already forty—especially because they both wanted children. A month into their courtship, Nancy had revealed the saddest part of her past to Howard while the two sat eating Chinese takeout in her living room. Howard had pushed aside his sweet-and-sour chicken and pressed up next to Nancy on the couch, leaning his head on her shoulder almost as if he were the one who needed to be comforted, after hearing such a sad tale. He'd taken her hand, squeezed it tight.

"Nancy, honey, I am so sorry," he'd said, his voice cracking only just. He never pushed with questions, and he was always willing to talk about it or not. Which was exactly what Nancy needed.

But mostly they did not talk about it. Instead, they simply had a wonderful marriage. They traveled frequently, hosted foreign exchange students, volunteered at the local animal shelter, and attended interesting lectures at a nearby university. They enjoyed a rich and vibrant sex life. They had the same sense of humor. Howard got Nancy into hiking, and Nancy got Howard into thick British mysteries with clever twists. For twenty-five years it was a real love affair.

Kids were not in the cards, as Howard liked to put it when nice but nosy strangers asked if they had children. In those early years they'd tried, of course, and seen all the doctors. Done all the tests. The findings suggested that Howard was fertile, and obviously Nancy knew she was. Or had been once, at least. But the years had passed, and perhaps her window was closing.

Just as the doctors and the books and the expectations started to push them toward the vast and frightening landscape of infertility treatments, just as they as a couple could have gone on some possibly never-ending odyssey with too many depressing, soul-crushing outcomes, Nancy felt a sudden sense of peace come over her. An answer. One evening over dinner not long after their most recent appointment with a specialist, Nancy told Howard that while she would pursue treatment if Howard really wanted to, she thought maybe a married life—just the two of them—would be enough. More than enough.

"Howard," she'd said, after slowly and carefully explaining her thinking and extending her arm across the table, palm up, "I love you so much. Being with you. It's such a gift."

Howard had looked at Nancy, and after a beat or two, he'd reached his hand across the table and squeezed his answer.

With the advent of social media, Nancy would sometimes see viral posts of adults holding up posters with identifying information, asking if anyone in the great, wide online world could help them find their birth parents. Nancy's eyes would linger on the faces of the men who fit the right age range, but some gut instinct—she felt strange calling it *maternal* instinct—told her no, not that one. Howard would sometimes rationalize that a baby whose life had worked out, whose adoptive parents had been loving and kind, would be less inclined to look for his birth mother. This brought Nancy a certain sort of comfort. After all, she had never made any real effort to look for the baby, and wasn't it true that she had mostly had a very happy life?

A handful of times, Nancy had also looked up the names *John Harris* and *Jack Harris*, trying her hometown and nearby locations. But the results were overwhelming. It was such a common name, and the social media pictures showed dozens of men, many who were far too young to be him. Others were far too old. She'd reached out with her fingertips on some of the possibilities, expanded some of the profile photographs, stared into the eyes of balding, bloated men in their fifties or sixties, searching for what, she wasn't sure. To think of handsome, young Jack Harris as a middle-aged man was depressing, even though she herself was also middle-aged. So eventually she stopped looking. After all these years, she still kept the composition book in a closet, although she never looked at it anymore.

Not long after their twenty-fifth wedding anniversary, Howard died of a stroke, a sudden, quick, and painless death that brought Nancy to her knees in grief. He had been such a good man. Such a good partner. He had been the biggest blessing of her life. That school year she'd thrown herself into her work, staying after hours to reorganize the clinic files, volunteering for every special school and district committee. It had helped, and after a time, she'd been able to carry on. She ached for him, of course, but she was grateful for him and for her long and happy marriage. She was thankful for decades in a fulfilling career, and for the ongoing sense of purpose Baldwin gave her.

But even though so much of her life had turned out so well, her long-ago past was still there, hovering. It came up in the strangest of moments. The most unexpected of times. Not long after she'd placed the pills in Isabella's locker, she went for her annual mammogram, and there it was again, in black and white on the simple intake form.

Age at first pregnancy:
Number of pregnancies:
Number of full-term deliveries:

She'd written the answers down with a cheap ballpoint pen borrowed from the front desk.

15
1
1

Her eyes stared in wonder at the number 15 written in blue ink. She was sixty-eight now, and some part of her had to strain to accept that it could even be true. But it was true, of course, and it had happened to her, Nancy Carter.

———

A little over a week after Nurse Honeycutt left the pills in Isabella's locker, she found herself at her desk after the final bell, organizing paperwork before heading home.

There was a knock on the clinic door. Students never knocked. They barged in or crept in, but they never knocked.

"Come in," she said, looking up from her desk.

Standing in the open doorway was Jessica Patterson, dressed in a plum shirtwaist dress that showed off her trim figure. Nurse Honeycutt's first thought was how much her daughter resembled her. The same creamy, blemish-free skin. The full lips. Even the coppery eye shadow.

"Yes, Ms. Patterson," said Nurse Honeycutt, "how can I help you?" The unflappable nurse's heart thrummed in her chest. But she invited Ms. Patterson in. The woman stepped inside the clinic and shut the door behind herself.

"Nurse Honeycutt, I need to talk to you," she said, her voice clear and confident as always, her body language full of her usual assuredness.

"Yes?" said Nurse Honeycutt. Her heart only pounded harder.

But then the mother opened her mouth to speak, and no words came out. Instead, she paused and placed a manicured hand on her chest, just under her collarbone. Everyone on campus knew Jessica Patterson. She was not the sort of woman to suffer a loss for words. Something about how she was behaving now made Nurse Honeycutt breathe a little more easily.

"Would you like to sit down?" the nurse asked, motioning to the same folding chair Isabella had sat in not very long ago.

Jessica took her seat, knees pressed closely together, feet crossed at the ankles. She shifted her chic brown leather handbag from her shoulder to her lap and held it close to herself, as if it served as some sort of protective shield.

"Nurse Honeycutt, I want to . . ." She paused again, took a deep breath. "This past weekend, Isabella and I had a little talk." Her voice was strained, her word choice deliberate. "I sensed something was going on with her." She stopped here, gazed around the clinic, as if taking in her surroundings for the first time. Perhaps she was processing the idea that her own daughter had sat here not long ago, grappling with the worst sort of news. A wave of pain seemed to take over Jessica, and she closed her eyes briefly.

"At any rate, I finally got her to talk to me, to tell me what happened," she continued, her voice dropping to almost a whisper. Her hands clutched her handbag more tightly. Then the words came out in a shuddering rush: "She told me she'd only told you. That she'd gone to you as soon as she thought it could be true. But I wish she would have come to me first." Her voice cracked on the word *me*, and her eyes glassed over. "I can't understand why she wouldn't."

In one crisp movement, Nurse Honeycutt drew two fresh tissues from the box on her desk and passed them to Jessica. The mother pressed them carefully to the corners of her eyes in a failed effort to hold back her crying, then gave up and allowed the tears to fall freely down her cheeks. There was part of Nurse Honeycutt that could not believe she was seeing this campus powerhouse look so broken.

"I always thought . . . she could tell me anything," she said, her voice breaking again as she spoke. "I thought we had that sort of relationship."

Nurse Honeycutt nodded sympathetically. "I've worked with teenagers for a long time, Ms. Patterson," she said. "Sometimes they are just too scared or too nervous to speak with their parents, even when they should. I'm sure what you're feeling right now is painful. I understand that."

Jessica took a shaky breath and then gathered herself and dried her face with the tissues. "I know what she told you about my husband, and the truth is, she's not wrong," she said. At this she looked down toward the floor, and Nurse Honeycutt sensed the woman was embarrassed. She wanted to tell Jessica there was nothing to feel ashamed of, even though she herself couldn't imagine being married to a man like that, but she did not know if this was the time or the place for that.

"He would not have reacted well at all," Jessica continued, her gaze finally lifting toward Nurse Honeycutt. "If he had found out . . ." At this Jessica shook her head firmly, apparently trying to push an idea out of her mind. "Of course, I would have found a way to help her, had she come to me. I would have flown her to Europe if I'd had to, and we would have managed to keep it from him. But she didn't, so I can only say that I am grateful that she came to you instead. And I am grateful you were able to assist her, even at enormous risk to yourself."

Nurse Honeycutt wasn't sure how much to acknowledge or

admit to out loud in this conversation. So she simply said, "It's a gift to be a school nurse here at Baldwin High, Ms. Patterson. And it's a privilege to be able to serve my students."

Jessica nodded, then folded the used tissues neatly into a square before throwing them away in a nearby trash can.

"Isabella is doing well, I gather?" Nurse Honeycutt asked. From the attendance records she'd checked, she knew the twelfth grader had been absent on Monday, but she'd been in school the rest of the week.

"She is," said Jessica. "She's feeling good. She's looking forward to graduation."

"And I look forward to seeing her there," said Nurse Honeycutt.

"It will be a good day," replied Jessica, standing up and shifting her purse back to her right shoulder. It was obvious to Nurse Honeycutt that the woman was trying to compose herself completely before leaving. She made it to the clinic door, then turned back and said, "Thank you, Nurse Honeycutt. Thank you so much."

Nurse Honeycutt nodded and offered a small smile.

After Jessica left, the nurse allowed herself a deep exhalation, then let her mind flutter to the graduation ceremony she and Jessica had just discussed. It was only six weeks away. She always had to work the event, which took place at the school district's field house. She would arrive early and set up in the tunnel through which the graduates would march; her station was always right on the perimeter of the action, and she stocked it with a cooler full of Gatorade and bottled water, her medical kit, her supply of sanitary napkins and tampons, and her smelling salts for the occasional fainter.

Nurse Honeycutt was always prepared.

When at last the members of the Baldwin High orchestra began to play their instruments in a careful, workmanlike manner, and the opening strains of "Pomp and Circumstance" floated toward them from a distant corner of the field house, the graduates would march onto the floor.

At that year's ceremony Nurse Honeycutt would keep her eyes open for Isabella. It would make her heart lift to see her, her coppery eye makeup carefully applied, her blond hair laboriously styled into big, bouncing curls. Her mortarboard would threaten to slide off for a moment, and Isabella would tug it back on, laughing as she did. And then, just as quickly as she appeared, she would be swallowed up by the sea of students that was flooding the field house to cheers and applause.

Nurse Honeycutt had attended many high school graduations, and she would know the order of things as well as she knew how to make an ice pack in thirty seconds flat or sense a fever with the cool touch of her hand. Soon there would be speeches, and clapping, and shouts of pride from the families in the audience. And soon Isabella Patterson would climb the steps to cross the stage, her red robe flapping around her, her young, colt-like legs uncertain in her brand-new high heels, her fresh young face as wide and open as her future.

# Twelve

Washing her hands at a sink in one of the faculty bathrooms, Ms. Lovie Jackson caught a glimpse of herself in the mirror. How many times had she washed her hands at this very sink? she wondered. Certainly, the bathroom looked identical to how it had when she'd started at Baldwin, more than forty years ago. One more look in the mirror at her deepening crow's-feet had her wishing she did, too.

Ms. Jackson's knees and her heart had been in such top shape when she'd first started at Baldwin in the fall of 1977 that she could jog swiftly up the stairs to her third-floor classroom without trouble. Decades later, she'd had knee-replacement surgery on her right leg and took medication for high blood pressure, but her status as head counselor was legendary. The school was large, and she couldn't always keep up with the names of all the younger teachers who hadn't been at Baldwin long. But they all knew her name, usually within their first week, and she could sense the deference with which she was approached. The days of racing up to her very first classroom as a naïve young math teacher simultaneously felt like yesterday and part of another lifetime.

She left the bathroom and headed for the library, where she was due for a meeting. The final bell of the day had rung not long ago, and even though the halls were growing empty, she swore she could feel the buzz of an impending summer. Graduation was looming, the end of the academic year rapidly approaching. Although she'd gone through this season dozens of times at Baldwin, the speed and fury with which it always arrived still surprised her. She likened the end of the school year to the sensation of running down a steep hill.

This year, it held an even more destabilizing sensation, one that she didn't quite know what to do with whenever it gripped her, as it was doing now. She took a breath and tried to ignore it as she entered the empty library. She was the first one there, and she began to pull chairs into a circle in preparation for the important meeting that was about to take place. (She smiled when she thought of the meeting's purpose and of the good secret she held.)

That she would have worked anywhere else but in a school had never been a consideration for her. To Ms. Jackson, education had always felt like the family business. In addition to an older sister who had taught geography for years, both her mother and her father had been teachers; in fact, they had met while teaching mathematics at what had once been the largest high school for Black students in the city, the same school Ms. Jackson herself had attended. Loath to let go of segregation even in the face of federal directives, Houston schools had started to integrate in a meaningful way only several years before Ms. Jackson began her teaching assignment at Baldwin. And back then, the school had still been mostly white, a fact she'd been well aware of when she had applied for the job. But Baldwin's reputation as a learning institution was strong, and Ms. Jackson had been an overachiever and an excellent student all her life. She had wanted to work at one of the best schools in town, so when she was offered the position at Baldwin, she had accepted it immediately.

After switching out one chair that had a large, anatomically incorrect phallus carved into its seat and sliding an unmarked one into position in the circle, she checked her watch. It would be mere minutes until the courtyard crew (as she had come to think of them) made their way in. She smiled again at the news that was in store for them, and briefly shook her head at the thought of the wild year they had just endured. That it had all started because of Mr. Bob Lehrer still amused and confounded her. He had been the source of a story from early in her career that she still thought back on from time to time.

During her first year at Baldwin, Mr. Lehrer had found her in the faculty lounge during an off period, planning out a lesson. Back then she'd been a few years from meeting and marrying George and had been known as Ms. Washington. A type A person through and through, she had used every moment of her off periods to claw her way through an ever-increasing list of tasks and concerns, forever focused on trying to be the best first-year teacher she could possibly be. Not only was she naturally this sort of person; she felt the additional weight that came with knowing there were certainly members of the all-white administration who believed she should not have been hired in the first place.

"I believe it's Ms. Washington, yes?" Mr. Lehrer had asked as he approached. At that time he had been in his late thirties, with a well-earned reputation as one of the most beloved teachers on campus. Not particularly handsome, but not awful-looking either, he was of average height, with a head of dark brown hair that gave the impression that it was not long for this world, and clear blue eyes.

"Yes, I'm Ms. Washington," she answered, putting down her pencil and looking up at him. He was interrupting her work, but at least she didn't have to correct him when he called her by the last name of one of the handful of other Black faculty members on campus. Predictably, that had happened to her more than once.

He didn't sit. Rather, he sort of leaned on the table in an effort, perhaps, to appear thoughtful and casual.

"Not sure if you know, but I'm an English teacher here," he said, "and I was wondering . . ." He paused, apparently trying to formulate a question. "Well, I was wondering if you could recommend any novels by Black authors? Works you might find compelling and important? I thought I might consider them for use in my classroom."

An uncomfortable silence sat between them as she considered what to say next. It had been less than a year since the adaptation of *Roots* had aired on television, and white people were apparently suddenly very interested in books by Black authors.

Ms. Washington had recently finished the latest book in the Dragonriders of Pern series, and she was thinking about again cracking open her beloved, well-worn copy of *The Lord of the Rings*, if ever she could find a bit of free time amid her voluminous teacher prep. There was also a book she had heard good things about entitled *Patternmaster* by a new writer named Octavia Butler. The last had been written by a Black person, but

Ms. Washington knew that high school English teachers often shied away from teaching fantasy and science fiction, which was what she read almost exclusively.

"Well, maybe *Roots*?" she suggested, shrugging uncertainly.

Mr. Lehrer nodded sagely, as if she had named the most compelling book in the history of the entire written form. "Excellent choice, yes. Thank you very much, Ms. Washington." And then he left the lounge.

During the early days of her relationship with George, she'd had cause to share the story of this interaction with him, and the entire thing had become something of decades-long inside joke between them, with George forever finding funny moments to ask if she had "any of those Black books" on hand.

She'd thought back on that moment with Mr. Lehrer when Mr. Williams had emailed her that fall about the incident involving *The Autobiography of Malcolm X*, even though the situation involving the angry mother was totally outside her purview on campus. Well-meaning white liberals like Mr. Lehrer and Mr. Williams were always so eager to seek validation that they were some of the Good Ones. Over the years at Baldwin, many things had changed. But some had not.

That said, she loved the work, and she enjoyed most of her fellow colleagues, even the earnest, left-leaning white people. They were all overwhelmed and underpaid. There was a sense of solidarity among them that was built around the noble goal of helping young people learn and thrive in the face of constant bureaucratic absurdity and nefarious external forces. Ms. Jackson wondered if group cohesion might be easier to achieve in a field like public education, which few respected anyway. Public school employees always felt like underdogs.

A knock on the open library door startled her into focus, and Ms. Jackson looked up to find Mr. Williams, of all people, standing in the doorway, along with several other teachers who had been part of the courtyard incident all those months ago.

"May we come in, Ms. Jackson?" Mr. Williams asked. "Or are we early?"

"No, no, please sit," she said, stepping back and motioning to the circle of chairs.

"If I may, what exactly is this meeting about?" Ms. Brennan asked, taking her seat next to Mr. Williams. "The email was just to a few of us, and it said to report to the library right after the last bell."

Ms. Jackson smiled. "I promise it's good news," she said. "I can say at least that much. But you'll have to be patient."

Just then, Ms. Jimenez walked in, her teacher tote bag full of papers.

"Thank God it's not another meeting with that lady from Central Office," she muttered as she took her seat. "What's that old saying? When I go, I hope it's during professional development because the transition to death would feel so seamless?"

The group laughed, including Ms. Jackson. People continued to trickle in, and soon the circle was nearly full. Nurse Honeycutt was there, as was Assistant Principal Garcia. There were the English teachers, as well as the two young instructors, still clearly very much enamored of each other. Mr. Fitzsimmons took his place next to Ms. Jimenez. They gazed around expectantly at one another, waiting for something to happen. Ms. Jackson continued to glance toward the door of the library.

Then, as if by magic, Principal Kendricks appeared. He walked in, in his calm and easy way, Assistant Principal Baker by his side.

"May we join you?" he asked. He was smiling widely, and so was Ms. Baker.

"Principal Kendricks?" asked Ms. Sanderson, sitting up straighter, her eyes wide with happy surprise. "You're here!"

"Yes, I am," he responded, and he took his seat in the circle, Ms. Baker pulling up a chair next to him. "And if you were to check your work email in a few minutes, you'd find an all-campus message letting you know about the district's decision to reinstate me as principal of Baldwin." He looked around the room as he spoke, taking in the familiar faces he had not seen in two months. "I confess that Ms. Baker and Ms. Jackson already knew about this, but we thought it might be nice to share this news with all of you in person first, since you were with me on the fateful day in the courtyard."

There were murmurs of approval and wide grins, and Ms. Jimenez said, "I can't believe I've finally worked here long enough to see Central Office make a smart decision."

"First time for me, too," agreed Mr. Fitzsimmons, and they all laughed.

"Thank goodness," said Ms. Brennan, her voice filled with relief. "We needed this before heading into summer. There's enough uncertainty in this life as it is."

"Yes, the school needs you back," said Ms. Garcia, her voice even, a soft smile on her face. "This is good news." And Principal Kendricks nodded at her appreciatively.

"What a relief," added Ms. Fletcher. "But what about Jessica Patterson?"

"It seems our PTO president's concerns have been sufficiently addressed," Mr. Kendricks continued. At this, Ms. Jackson noticed a small grin spreading over Nurse Honeycutt's face, and she briefly wondered about its source. Principal Kendricks continued: "Ms. Patterson has also been asked to join the district's parent advisory council, and I suspect such accolades have her focused on bigger fish. I also think the situation at Lanthrop might have factored into Central Office's decision. They can only manage so many crisis situations at once, I guess."

The group shared amused glances. Just last week it had emerged in the headlines that the rooftop garden club at their rival, Lanthrop High, had been tending to a robust crop of marijuana plants. Their sponsor, a well-meaning but admittedly naïve older woman, had taken pictures to proudly share on the school's social media, leading to the club's downfall. It was later discovered that the students had been selling the marijuana to buy more gardening supplies, as well as Taylor Swift tickets.

"Well, I'm really glad it worked out," said Mr. Rayfield, who then shared with the group that he'd recently taken a position as a lab technician and was thinking about graduate school. "Even though I won't be returning next year," he added, "I want to say that I'm glad for the school that you'll be here."

Principal Kendricks thanked him, and then told the remainder of the group that he didn't want to keep them, that he knew the end of the school year was jam-packed with concerns and must-do tasks. Gathering their things, the Baldwin faculty and staff members made their exits, chattering excitedly with one another about the happy news.

"I think we managed to put them in good moods, right?" Principal Kendricks asked Ms. Jackson. Ms. Baker had taken her leave with everyone else, but Mr. Kendricks had hung back to speak with his head guidance counselor.

"I think we surely did," Ms. Jackson answered.

Mr. Kendricks gazed at her curiously. "I admit I was surprised," he said, "that when Mr. Rayfield shared his news about leaving Baldwin, you didn't want to share yours?"

That destabilizing sensation that had held her in its grip just before the start of the meeting returned.

"Do you mean, why didn't I share that I'm retiring?" she asked. There was the word. *Retiring*. It felt strange even to say it out loud.

"Yes," said Mr. Kendricks. "I know you told me you didn't want a big production, and I can respect that. But are you sure you don't even want to tell people?"

Ms. Jackson shook her head no; her body language was firm. "I've thought about this," she said. In truth, she'd avoided thinking about it too much, because doing so made her feel so discombobulated. "I'll be here over the summer to train my replacement, but then I'd just like to make a quiet exit. When they find out in the fall that I haven't returned, they can reach out to me then, if they'd like."

Principal Kendricks nodded, although his somewhat sad expression revealed that he didn't fully understand. The two walked out of the library together, but Ms. Jackson said she needed to head in the opposite direction as Mr. Kendricks. She intended to drop by her office to gather some things.

"Well, I'll let you go then," he said. "Thank you for arranging this meeting today."

"Of course," she answered. "And I'm so glad you're the principal under whom I'm leaving. I'll sleep better at night knowing that's the case."

"Well, thank you," answered Principal Kendricks. "Although it is hard for me to imagine what this school will look like without you." At this he extended his hand. Ms. Jackson took it, and the two shared a warm, firm handshake. Then Ms. Jackson headed off.

———————

Alone in her office off the courtyard, Lovie Jackson assessed (not for the first time) the papers and supplies and desktop tchotchkes she would soon have to pack or do away with. It was good that student files were digital now, of course. That made life a little easier. When she had started in this profession, she had spent countless hours in dusty, musty records rooms, sorting through boxes. As a young teacher she had used a mimeograph, once destroying a favorite blouse with spilled ink.

She was proud of her ability to keep up with the changing technology over the years, but she also knew that she was beginning to be outpaced by it. She had to ask for help from younger colleagues far too often, and she didn't like how that made her feel. It was one of the reasons she had begrudgingly accepted that it was time to retire. She thought back on the teachers and staff members who had not managed to keep up, who had become burdens in many ways on their coworkers. Who had softened and decided to phone it in, running out a play clock. She knew that people talked about such colleagues behind their backs, whispering about how much better off the school would be when they left.

She had never wanted to be viewed in that way.

It was time to go. She knew that it was. She had grandchildren to visit, and George spoke longingly of traveling to countries they'd talked about but never seen. Still, as retirement loomed and she began to wonder what would come next, she couldn't help but envy her husband, who had worked for forty years as an accountant and who had retired without any doubts or even much concern. The work had been solid and predictable and had supported their family. He had been good at it, but he had not loved it. Had not felt *called* to it. It had been so easy for him to let it go. To transition seamlessly into a life post-career, which he filled with watching news programs on television, trying out new recipes, and—in a move that still surprised her—a step aerobics class for seniors at the downtown YMCA.

Her time at Baldwin—from that first year as a young math teacher fielding Mr. Lehrer's clumsy inquiry about books to this chaotic year filled with strife—had been so much more than a job or even a career for her. It had been something bigger than that. Her identity, perhaps.

She gazed around at her office, and as had become habit in recent months, she was pulled back into the past and into reflection.

———

By the early 1990s, after teaching for a decade and a half, Lovie Jackson had developed a reputation at Baldwin as a firm but fair math teacher who prepared her calculus students very well. She and George had welcomed two daughters, who would go on to attend and graduate from Baldwin themselves. Lovie enjoyed her work and knew she was good at it, and while there were times when it could feel slightly repetitive to run the same lesson multiple times in a day, she figured she would teach for ten or fifteen more years, retire, and collect her pension after a career well spent. Sometimes Lovie thought about the fact that her time at Baldwin could have ended that way, and that would have been fine. More than fine, really.

But in the fall of 1993, a young woman named Anh Dinh had appeared on her roster. The slight young woman went by the Americanized name Annie, wore her hair in a perpetual ponytail, and chose to sit in the first row. Lovie noticed how she had a curious habit of lining up her Ticonderoga No. 2's at a forty-five-degree angle, sharpened points to the front right corner of the room. She asked excellent questions and worked through problems with an ease and fluency that was a joy to witness. Once, when Lovie paused after explaining a problem on the overhead projector and asked if there were any questions, Annie smiled and said, "Ms. Jackson, it's just beautiful to watch you solve that equation. I mean, the way the numbers work like that. It's just beautiful to me."

This reaction was followed by a round of snickering from Annie's classmates, something Lovie shut up with a single, pointed look.

"I agree, Annie," she replied, offering the young woman an affirming nod. "Math can be beautiful."

Teachers, when pressed by their students, would say they didn't have favorites. But, of course, this was a lie. Within the first few weeks of that fall semester, Annie Dinh quickly became one of Lovie's favorite students of all time.

During conversations she would sometimes have with Annie in the final moments of class as students packed up their things, Lovie learned the young woman's parents were part of a wave of Vietnamese immigrants who had arrived in Houston in the 1970s. She also discovered that they worked in a Vietnamese restaurant and that their English was not very strong. Annie shouldered additional responsibilities at home because her parents worked late hours; she was often responsible for making sure her two younger brothers did their homework, ate dinner, and got ready for bed.

When Lovie asked her about her future plans, Annie admitted that she had thought about taking classes at the local community college while working part-time, maybe at the same restaurant where her parents were employed. Understanding Annie's full potential and knowing how rare it was, Lovie decided, that fall, to help the young woman with applications for a four-year college and financial aid. She dived into the project with all of the drive and focus afforded to her by her naturally type A personality. But she was also driven by something else. She knew Annie deserved more.

It was the early '90s and there was no accessible Internet. Nothing in the long, complicated college applications process was easy to figure out or understand, and things had changed since Lovie had applied to college, many moons prior. Still, although she had two children at home, papers to grade, and aging parents to fret over, she found the time to help Annie. She researched schools with good math programs and grappled with how to fill out a FAFSA. She marked up Annie's college essay and monitored looming deadlines. She wrote her a glowing letter of recommendation.

It wasn't that the counselors at Baldwin hadn't wanted to help Annie themselves. But because Baldwin was a large public school, they had limited time to devote to each individual student, and they were often overwhelmed by the parents of more resourced children who hovered anxiously over their sons' and daughters' applications like nervous bugs. And even though Annie's parents surely cared about her, there were barriers in their way when it came to advocating for her.

That year, George gently joked that Lovie was going to bring Annie home for Christmas dinner, she talked about her favorite student so much, and Lovie laughed. But she thought that even George didn't understand how much it meant to her to help Annie Dinh.

One afternoon after the final bell when she and Annie were

going over Annie's college essay one more time, her student paused and, with a furrowed brow, said, "I don't mean to sound rude or ungrateful, Ms. Jackson. But why are you helping me so much? I know you've got a lot to do."

Lovie nodded. It was a good question. She did have a lot to do. But she answered Annie directly and honestly.

"I think you have a gift for math, Annie, and I believe that if I don't step in and help you now, it might not be fully realized."

Accepting this response, Annie got back to work. Lovie wondered briefly if her answer made her seem egotistical or like she had a savior complex. But the truth was, Lovie believed her answer was correct. How many more chances would a young woman like Annie get before being consumed by the arbitrary, fickle world? How many more opportunities would she have before she was forced to settle down with something good enough? Annie was at an inflection point in her life, and Lovie knew it.

But Annie's question gave Lovie pause. It sparked an idea in her mind that she couldn't quite let go of. The truth was that she was almost forty years old. She hadn't been a student herself for a long time. She had one child who was still in elementary school. But that evening after the girls were in bed, she told George she was thinking about going back for her counseling degree. She could make it her mission to support Baldwin students like Annie. And Baldwin students who looked like herself. She could encourage the counseling department to find ways to prioritize and assist them.

Annie Dinh was now older than Lovie had been when they'd first met. She no longer went by Annie but by Anh. Actually, she went by Dr. Dinh, having earned her doctorate in computer science. She still sent Lovie Christmas cards and updated her every so often on her busy, successful life.

That her star pupil's abilities in mathematics now surpassed her own was one of the singular joys of Lovie's life.

———————

A text from George caused her phone to buzz. He was working on a new recipe for dinner. Something Greek, he said, and he wanted to know when she would be heading home.

*Leaving very soon*, she responded, and she made a promise to herself to mean it.

Scanning her inbox one last time, she saw emails that could be dealt with the next day. There was one from Jim Fitzsimmons, probably some gruff diatribe over something that she could not control. She honestly didn't mind that he sent her these sorts of messages. She liked him. He had once occupied the classroom across from hers, and she'd witnessed his descent into problematic drinking and his recovery. She'd observed his ability to work with kids who were resistant to math and needed extra help. She knew from experience that he was a good teacher. And while she was realistic enough to know that they would not keep in touch after she left (after all, could she really imagine getting a coffee with Jim Fitzsimmons?), she was glad that she had shared space with him in this building for decades, each making cameos in the other's stories of work life. They had guided the same students for nearly forty years, an astonishing number when she really stopped to think about it. And now those days were coming to a close.

She shut her laptop and stood to pull down the blinds covering the window that opened out onto the courtyard, where Mr. Lehrer's ashes now rested. Like Jim Fitzsimmons, Mr. Lehrer had understood what mattered in this job and what didn't. And then he had retired. To what? To end up as an aged substitute whose death had become a campus fracas? The thought pained her.

She had spent so much of her life as Ms. Jackson, Baldwin High School institution. Mr. Lehrer had been an institution, too. What happened to institutions when they were no longer needed? What happened to legends when they retired? With each passing day, these questions haunted her more and more frequently.

There was only a matter of weeks left now, Ms. Jackson thought. A collection of days on a calendar. Summertime was calling, but what came after that, Ms. Jackson did not know. She prayed that whatever it was, it would be sweet.

Then she switched off the lights to her office and headed out.

# *Thirteen*

The vibrator was cotton-candy pink, and it belonged to his eleventh-grade English teacher.

THE SATISFYHER! was stamped in gold-foil letters at the base in a jaunty, proud-of-itself, all-caps font. Emilio stared. Was he shocked by what he was seeing? Or was he disturbed by the fact that his precise, quiet English teacher, the only person Emilio knew who understood when to use the word *whom*, would purchase a product labeled with such a corny and obvious pun?

In a situation such as this, he wondered, should he really be expected to have to choose a singular feeling?

He should not.

It sat there, THE SATISFYHER!, nestled in the middle of Ms. Brennan's neatly organized nightstand drawer, next to what he was really supposed to be looking for: a spare set of keys attached to a tired-looking, plastic blue key chain in the shape of the number 1. The key chain read NUMBER ONE AUNT! in a sad little typeface that paled in comparison to the sassy letters on

THE SATISFYHER! If the key chain was the tepid voice of a tired toddler giving up the fight, THE SATISFYHER! was head cheerleader at a pep rally.

THE SATISFYHER!

"Emilio, did you find the keys?"

It was Ms. Brennan's voice over the phone pressed to his ear, a voice measured and formal, very much the voice Ms. Brennan used in the classroom when she was lecturing on the meaning of Gatsby's green light or how to formulate a clear thesis statement. At the sound of it, Emilio was suddenly transported back to the present, to the task he was supposed to be completing. After all, in this scenario he was functioning not as Ms. Brennan's student but in another role: house sitter, cat sitter, and next-door neighbor.

"Yes, ma'am, I have the keys, Ms. Brennan," answered Emilio, taking the NUMBER ONE AUNT! keys into his hand, fully aware that as he did so, his right pinkie finger grazed the head of the vibrator, its silicone tip as soft as velvet.

"Terrific," said Ms. Brennan, still cool and all business. "I'm so sorry for the confusion, but those should work for the gate, and the lawn guy should be able to get back there now. I can't believe I forgot he would be showing up while I was gone."

"It's fine," Emilio answered, already heading outside to meet up with the lawn crew, Ms. Brennan's orange cat, Sylvia, trotting along at his heels. It was probably his imagination, but it almost seemed like his pinkie finger was pulsing in the spot that had made contact with THE SATISFYHER!

"And, Emilio," continued Ms. Brennan, "you can just leave the gate keys on the kitchen counter, in case you need them again. There's no need to put them back in the nightstand drawer."

There was subtext in this request, Emilio knew. Emilio knew this because Ms. Brennan had been the person to teach him what *subtext* meant.

"Okay," he said. "No problem."

Emilio made it to the front door and opened it. It was only Memorial Day weekend, the very start of summer, but already the humidity gripped him instantly. It was Texas, after all. With his left foot, he gently guided Sylvia the cat back toward the safety of the house as he shut the door behind himself. The mechanical drone of the yard crew's idling equipment grew louder as he approached the guy waiting for access to the backyard so he could complete his work.

"Emilio?" Ms. Brennan's voice bled through the buzz; she was now shouting to be heard. "Make sure you call or text with any other questions, okay?"

"Yes, ma'am," he answered, tossing the keys in the direction of the lawn guy, who caught them with a nod. He unlocked the gate and quickly lobbed the keys back at Emilio.

In the middle of this exchange, Ms. Brennan ended the call, and Emilio slid his phone back into his jeans pocket before glancing toward the yellow-and-white Craftsman bungalow where his English teacher lived. Technically, his former English teacher. Ms. Brennan had taught him junior English up until two days ago, but that was over with the arrival of summer. Emilio was now a rising senior, his seventeenth birthday just a few days behind him.

Walking back toward the house to put the NUMBER ONE AUNT! key chain on the kitchen counter as requested, Emilio could not stop thinking about THE SATISFYHER! Honestly, how could he stop? How would he ever think of anything except his English teacher's vibrator for the rest of his natural-born life?

For the sake of accuracy, it should be stated that this odd state of affairs had really started one year ago this month, when Ms. Brennan bought the house next door to his, just before starting her job at Baldwin High School. Before Ms. Brennan purchased it, the house had been owned by the Taylors, an older retired couple who had decided to move into an assisted-living facility; they had been Emilio's neighbors all his life, giving out full-sized candy bars on Halloween and never minding the persistent barking of Grover, Emilio's family's mutt.

Emilio's parents and Emilio and his little sister, Maisy, had been sorry to see them go, but they were full of curiosity about who would move in next door. They didn't have to wait long. Two weeks after the Taylors moved out, a moving van rolled up. Emilio's nosy (she would say curious) mother insisted that the entire family troop over together so they could welcome their new neighbors.

A petite brunette answered the door dressed in khaki shorts and a faded forest-green T-shirt that read MOUNT HOLYOKE in white letters. Her hair was pulled back into a neat ponytail, and her face was covered with a sheen of sweat. Behind her was a mess of open cardboard boxes. Like most adults, she could have been twenty-five or forty-five; Emilio wasn't sure. She simply looked like a grown-up to him.

"We're the Gonzalez family next door!" Emilio's mother said cheerfully, as well as loudly, too, Emilio thought, cringing.

"I'm Lydia Brennan," the brunette answered, wiping her hands on the seat of her shorts before reaching out to politely shake hands with all of them, even eight-year-old Maisy, who'd been eagerly chewing on her fingernails when Ms. Brennan opened the door.

Emilio stood there mutely as his mother and, to a lesser extent, his father made boring adult small talk with their new neighbor. Ms. Brennan seemed quiet but pleasant, polite enough to eagerly accept the fancy cookies his mother had purchased and repackaged to give the appearance of homemade, but distracted enough to give the impression that she wanted to get back to the task of unpacking.

"Is it just you who's moved in, or . . . ?" Emilio's mother asked, letting the unfinished sentence linger as her eyes scanned the room behind Ms. Brennan.

"Just me," Ms. Brennan answered, but she didn't offer any more information.

"No kids?" Emilio's mother persisted, her question followed by Emilio's father's gentle chiding.

"Just the ones at Baldwin High," Ms. Brennan explained. "I'll be teaching junior English there this fall."

"Maybe you'll have Emilio!" his mother said, pushing her oldest toward the front door as if Emilio were a specimen to be inspected. "English is his favorite subject!" At this Emilio smiled gamely, but inside he was cringing again.

"How funny that you might live next door to your teacher," Ms. Brennan said. "I promise I won't treat you any differently." She gave him a friendly yet conspiratorial look and added, "I won't even tell anyone we're neighbors."

Emilio just smiled stupidly, unsure how to respond. Just then an orange tabby wandered to the front door and Ms. Brennan scooped it up, introducing it as Sylvia. After some additional awkward banter about the cat, Emilio's father suggested that Ms. Brennan probably wanted to get back to unpacking, and the four of them walked back to their house, Emilio's mother prattling on about how old Ms. Brennan might be, whether she was single or divorced, and how she could afford that house on a teacher's salary.

That had been a year ago, and Emilio *had* gotten Ms. Brennan for English, and Ms. Brennan *had* kept her word about not making a big thing about their being neighbors, even pretending that she didn't know his name on the first day of school. She'd just smiled at him kindly, treating him like anyone else.

The truth was, Emilio didn't mind others knowing he lived next door to Ms. Brennan, and he'd been known to mention the fact to a few of his friends, all bookish nerds like him who loved Tolkien and chess and had never kissed a soul. She quickly established herself as a well-liked teacher at Baldwin because she was engaging and fair and could explain things in a way that made you feel like you had always known them, that they should come naturally to you and they would, if only you trusted her methods. Organized and steadfast in her approach, she taught Emilio and his classmates how to structure essays using highlighters, which she demonstrated by marking thesis statements (lemon yellow), text evidence (lime green), and commentary (sky blue). Her written feedback always appeared in careful black cursive in the margins, critical but encouraging, and always using the pronoun *we*, as if the student and Ms. Brennan were a team striving toward a shared goal. (*We could have more robust commentary connecting this text evidence to the thesis. We could elaborate here. We could avoid this redundant language in the conclusion.*)

She never raised her voice and didn't need to; she commanded the classroom even though she was small in stature. She dressed professionally, in creams and grays, with a single gold chain around her neck at all times. Her hair was always

pulled back off her face in a tight ponytail or twist. But her enthusiasm for literature and language was evident in every
planned lecture, every pause that lingered over a certain phrase
or clause that clearly brought her a feeling of satisfaction. Or
perhaps validation. She was anything but robotic. In fact,
Emilio would never forget the afternoon her voice cracked as
she read aloud the last few lines of *The Great Gatsby*, and her
eyes seemed to fill with tears that never quite fell.

"Forgive me," she'd said, holding the book to her chest and
briefly closing her eyes, taking a moment to exhale. "But is that
not utterly exquisite?"

Emilio's mother had been right. English *was* his favorite
class, and Ms. Brennan made that true again during his junior
year. It occurred to him in certain fleeting moments, like when
she tucked a loose lock of dark hair behind her ear or tilted her
head as she considered something a classmate said (it was always a classmate; Emilio was too shy to speak), that she was
what some would consider an attractive woman. But even though
he saw her in more human moments—rolling out her city gar-
bage can dressed in that MOUNT HOLYOKE T-shirt, carefully
stringing white Christmas lights along her azalea bushes during the holidays, watering the spider plant that hung on her
porch—she still seemed otherworldly somehow. Like an ab-
stract painting you admire from afar but don't fully understand.
It wasn't at all like when the young French teacher Ms. Toussaint crouched down next to his desk to check his conjugations,
her breathy, whispery voice sending shivers down his spine, the
warmth of her body enveloped in the scent of vanilla, her deli-
cious, ample bosom tempting Emilio to glance just once.

No, she wasn't Ms. Toussaint.

Even when Ms. Brennan had approached him in the front

yard the week before as he was doing the weeding, per his father's orders, and asked if Emilio could check on her house while
she was away that coming weekend (her usual house sitter was
unavailable), she had carried herself with all the properness of a
teacher assigning an essay.

"It's just a getaway to celebrate the start of summer, and I'll
be back by Tuesday afternoon at the latest," she'd explained. "It
really only involves going over once a day to get the mail and to
feed Sylvia." Even though the job was easy, she'd jotted down
instructions for him in the same careful black-inked script that
Emilio recognized from his marked essays.

"Of course, Ms. Brennan, I'd be happy to help," he'd said,
honored to be asked. Emilio had wondered for a moment if she
would have asked him if he were just any old student and not
someone who had earned an A on his final analysis paper, his
chosen text Faulkner's "A Rose for Emily." (*We have a lovely
command of the language here, Emilio, and a well-crafted, insightful argument. I enjoyed reading this!*)

So now here he was, back in the house, placing the NUMBER
ONE AUNT! keys on the kitchen counter, already knowing what
his next steps would be. Without contemplating whether it was
perverted or creepy—in fact, he could not contemplate because
he felt compelled—Emilio walked down the short hallway to
Ms. Brennan's bedroom; like the rest of the house, it was clean
and impeccably organized, decorated in muted tones, all precise
lines and right angles. As in the living room, there were several
bookcases lined with countless books, their well-creased spines
evidence of a library well loved.

Did part of him hope it wasn't there? That what he'd seen
hadn't been a vibrator at all but perhaps a handheld thermome-

ter like the kind his mother used to use on him and Maisy when they were small?

Or was there a part of him that could not wait to see it again?

His heart racing in a way that was not at all unpleasant, he opened the drawer and found THE SATISFYHER! peering up at him, stretched out in all its rose-gold luster like a woman sunbathing on the beach, longing to be admired.

He memorized its placement there in the lower-right corner of the drawer, next to the space where the keys had been and below a collection of electric chargers and several black pens. For a moment he wondered if he should take a picture of it, so he could be absolutely sure he'd place it back correctly. But then he would have a photograph of his English teacher's vibrator on his phone, and that seemed wrong, somehow, even if he were to delete it later. That would be more of a violation than he felt comfortable with.

Unable to resist, his hand reached out and picked up THE SATISFYHER! by the handle. It was heavier than he'd expected; it contained a sure-of-itself solidness. There was a round button on one side that Emilio assumed was the on switch; it sat underneath something that looked like a volume control, although even never-kissed-a-girl Emilio knew it was a different type of controller altogether.

He realized he was holding his breath and his cheeks were flushed.

As curious as he was, he didn't dare turn it on for fear he wouldn't be able to turn it off. Outside, the drone of the lawn crew's equipment seeped through the windows, covered in gauzy white curtains. Sylvia the cat sauntered in and leapt onto the bed, immediately arranging herself into a small orange fluffball on Ms. Brennan's taupe bedspread; Emilio gave silent thanks that she could not rat him out.

Standing there in the middle of Ms. Brennan's bedroom, his heart still thumping, he held the velvety silicone head of THE SATISFYHER! close to his face, not so close as to touch it, but close enough that he breathed in deep, searching for what he did not know, but he thought he might be able to sense it when he smelled it at last.

———

"Jesus Christ," said Lydia Brennan, tossing her phone onto the hotel bed and lifting her hands—no rings, fingernails clipped short and neat—to her face. "My student found my vibrator."

Next to her in bed, Sean allowed his book (a dog-eared copy of *Time Regained* by Proust) to fall back against his naked chest. He leisurely readjusted the pillows behind him.

"Please explain," he answered, a smile building on his lips. Lydia dropped her hands and gazed at him. She could see a gleam in his hazel eyes; he was eager for a good story, and Lydia had it. It was the sort of story that Sean would tell his friends—probably with some colorful flourishes for increased engagement—who would go on to tell *their* friends, and so on, a new urban legend passed on at happy hours and small gatherings, a sort of old-fashioned virality. The high school boy who discovered his teacher's vibrator. It was irresistible, really.

"And after everything that's happened at my school this year," she said. "After we just got off the district's radar and our principal was reinstated!"

"The courtyard incident?" asked Sean. That story had become his story, too.

"Yes," answered Lydia glumly.

"Well, explain this vibrator tale and allow me to determine if it really is the undoing you think it is," he coaxed.

"Let me get coffee first, at least," said Lydia, sliding out of the bed fully nude. Sean took the time to admire her curves and nicely shaped ass as she fiddled with the hotel coffeemaker. She was rounder and softer than you'd think when you only saw her in clothes, dressed like some librarian from the 1950s.

Back in bed, she sipped her drink as she explained the events of the morning, pausing to answer Sean's questions and requests for clarification, including why she would keep the keys to the back gate in her nightstand. ("Because I keep the keys to the file cabinet and the safe on the same key chain, and those things are in my bedroom!") Lydia could sense Sean mentally taking notes, perhaps already embellishing certain details in his mind. He would command the room with this story at some point in the near future, she knew, eager to be the center of attention. The realization irritated her.

"Try to view this like an English teacher, like someone who loves a good narrative," he said, perhaps sensing her prediction. "It's a terrific little chestnut, if you think about it. And I don't think it's going to cause a scandal."

Lydia sighed, then took a large, last swallow of her coffee before setting the paper cup on her nightstand. "I'm absolutely positive he's never even kissed anyone. Maybe he didn't know what it was."

Sean arched an eyebrow. "Lydia," he said, "the Internet exists, you know."

Lydia groaned in embarrassment and slid under the covers, still processing the morning: the buzzing of her phone, startling her out of her half-sleep; Emilio's explanation that the lawn crew needed access to her backyard; the awful moment when she—not yet fully awake—directed him toward her nightstand drawer; and the near-simultaneous horrific jolt of realization that she experienced as she remembered what he would see when he opened it.

Sean took the opportunity to set aside the Proust. He scooted under the sheets to join her.

"So, tell me more about this vibrator," he said, dropping his voice to a whisper, a grin spreading over his handsome face. Traces of the morning sun streamed in through the white sheets, warming up their toasty little tent. Lydia turned slowly to face him, already beginning to unwind. Sean pressed his mouth to her neck, under her right ear, which he knew she liked.

"Well," said Lydia, her voice soft and coy, "if you must know, it does the trick in under two minutes flat."

The scent and feel of her flooded his senses, and Sean pressed closer, reached for her breasts. "Is this some sort of demand," he said, "for a competition?"

At this Lydia laughed and spread her legs wide open, already ready for him.

Later, while Sean was in the shower, Lydia took stock of the situation and tried to convince herself it all wasn't as awful as she feared. Surely this could not be as bad as the ashes incident. It wasn't as if she kept her vibrator in a desk at *school* and Emilio had found it there, for God's sake. After all, he was no longer even her student, and she wasn't teaching seniors next year. She would never have to face him in the classroom again. He didn't have a slew of little brothers with whom to share this story— surely he would not tell young Maisy about this—so she did not have to worry about future Gonzalez boys eyeing her on the first day of school with a knowing smirk.

He did have his band of nerdy friends, of course, but there was something about Emilio that led Lydia to believe that he might be the type to hold fast to some outdated gentleman's code of honor. On his last essay for her, an analysis of "A Rose for Emily," he'd exhibited such empathy for spinster Emily—a murderous necrophiliac, for God's sake!—that she'd been touched.

True, he was her neighbor, but their paths didn't cross all that often, and soon he would be off to college, hopefully a school at least a few hours away. Although he was quiet in class, his writing revealed that he was a bright boy—that was certain. Lydia reminded herself to make his requested letter of recommendation of the highest quality. Anything to ensure his admission to the out-of-state college of his dreams.

And honestly, even if somehow the story came out, what was wrong with a thirty-seven-year-old woman owning a vibrator? With all the male-centered pornography easily available, perhaps it was good that a teenage boy learn that there was nothing wrong with a woman keeping her sexual satisfaction a central focus in her life. Certainly Lydia always had.

At this thought her mind turned to Sean, who was still in the shower. She stretched out in the hotel bed, not minding one bit if they stayed in it all day. She and Sean had planned this beach getaway to Galveston Island for as soon as school was out—he taught senior English at an all-boys Catholic high school in town—so the summer stretched out ahead of them both, open and inviting.

He was the sixteenth man she'd slept with since her divorce five years ago, and certainly one of the best in bed by far. Moments ago, he had given THE SATISFYHER! a real run for its money. She smiled to herself at the thought of it.

True, he was also an aspiring novelist—with an emphasis on "aspiring"—and he could be a little full of himself at times. But Lydia enjoyed his wry sense of humor and his intellect. He'd never been married and had no children; in the dating world of a woman in her late thirties, he was something of a unicorn.

Itching for more coffee, she forced herself out of bed to make another cup. The drumming of the shower bled through the closed bathroom door. Sean was singing in Italian, something from an opera. He had a loud and terrible voice. As she struggled to open the plastic packet of coffee, the buzz of a phone caught her attention. It was Sean's, face up on the nearby dresser. Lydia could not help but let her eyes scan the incoming text, which came from a woman saved in Sean's phone only as Hot Amy.

*Had so much fun on Tuesday. Like So Much Fun. Let me know when you're back in town.*

Lydia was grateful she had the privacy to prepare her reaction. Otherwise, it would have turned into a scene from a bad film: Her, naked, holding the phone toward Sean, screen facing forward, her voice building into a shout as she demanded an explanation. Him, walking toward her, trying to put his arms around her, the "Baby, baby, baby, please" that might follow.

No, Lydia wanted none of that. Instead, she slipped on her cream-colored linen sundress and dug into her purse for her hairbrush and an elastic tie, slipping her dark hair into a neat and well-practiced twist. By the time Sean came out of the bathroom, hotel towel tied loosely around his trim waist, his dark blond hair still wet and dripping, Lydia was seated at the foot of the bed, legs crossed, arms crossed. Her heart was pounding, but no one would guess it by looking at her.

Sean stared at her, confused.

"So," Lydia said, her voice cool and polished, the sort of buttery, practiced tone you might hear through the headphones of an audio tour at an art museum. "Is there someone in your phone saved as *Ugly* Amy?"

She relished the confusion on his face, the growing awareness that something was wrong, very wrong, and he was responsible for it. Then, the realization of what it was. Lydia uncrossed her arms, leaned back slightly on the bed. Took a deep breath and wished it hadn't sounded so shaky. Her throat ached.

But Sean did not "Baby, baby, baby, please" her. Instead, he recalculated. Composed himself. Walked over to the phone and calmly read Hot Amy's message as Lydia waited, her mouth dry, her cheeks flushed.

"Lydia," he said, turning to face her, the phone still in his hand, his voice soft, as if he were talking to a lost child or a frightened puppy, "hey, sweetheart . . . we never said we were exclusive, did we? I mean . . . we're both adults here, right? I thought you knew I was seeing other people."

And then he came and *sat down next to her* on the bed, turned toward her, tilted his head in a way that indicated only pity. Pity for her! This was all wrong and not at all how Lydia had planned it. With one calm reaction, Sean had the upper hand. He was the rational, mature, straightforward man. She was the histrionic, idiotic, needy woman. They had been sleeping together for three months. She had been stupid to assume that a unicorn would have the desire or need to be exclusive.

"You have to leave," Lydia said, rising and taking her purse and one of the plastic hotel key cards off the dresser. "The hotel is on my credit card, and I won't bother you for your half. But I need you gone by the time I come back." She slid her feet into her slip-on flats.

"We came in your car," said Sean, still seated on the bed, apparently not motivated enough to even stand up. His voice was calm and steady. Perhaps he was already reworking this moment into a scene for one of his cocktail party stories.

"Figure it out," said Lydia. And she left the hotel room.

––––––––

Whatever scent Emilio thought he might find, it wasn't there. Just a trace of something chemical and plastic. He didn't know if he was disappointed or not, but he carefully placed THE SAT-ISFYHER! back in the drawer and stared at it for a moment, trying to align it with the mental picture he had in his mind. There was no way Ms. Brennan would know that he had touched it. He shut the drawer gently and stood up straight, looking around Ms. Brennan's bedroom with fresh eyes. On the bed, Sylvia the cat stretched and rearranged herself.

Ms. Brennan was not the sort of teacher to share much personal information, but in class once she had told the students that her cat was named after Sylvia Plath, a poet. Although she had never taught them any of Plath's work, nerdy, curious Emilio had looked some of it up on his own and been immediately drawn in by some of her punch-in-the-gut lines and her haunting, confessional tone. He never shared any of this new knowledge with Ms. Brennan, but he found it sad that she would name her cat after this depressed woman whose true love had abandoned her and whose own tortured soul had driven her to suicide.

Perhaps it was telling, too.

Poor Ms. Brennan, thought Emilio. It was clear to him now as he walked through the small two-bedroom bungalow, absorbing more proof that his English teacher was a tragic case. The home was neat, maybe too neat. Evidence of a compulsive person with too much time on her hands. The few pictures on the walls and refrigerator were of what Emilio had to assume were her nieces (NUMBER ONE AUNT!), identical twin girls younger than Maisy with hair the color of butterscotch and matching missing front teeth. In the photos, Ms. Brennan smiled, but Emilio did not think the smile reached her eyes.

She had moved here all alone from Austin and had never mentioned a husband, a partner. His mind went to THE SATISFYHER! sitting in the drawer, ready for use. Had she not referred to his paper on "A Rose for Emily" as *insightful*? Insightful because, perhaps, she could relate to old and lonely Emily Grierson, shut up from the world, a spinster?

How had he missed all this? Ms. Brennan had taught them to analyze characters with such precision, but he had never correctly analyzed Ms. Brennan herself.

A new thought occurred to Emilio: Despite the attractive face, the poised and sophisticated outfits, the composed and polished air, could it be possible that Ms. Brennan—smart, together Ms. Brennan—was a *virgin*, just like him?

Emilio was suddenly convinced that this had to be true. The evidence was there in spades. She had never known a lover. Perhaps she had never even been kissed.

Why else would a woman need THE SATISFYHER!?

But unlike Emilio, who had every reason to hope that college would be where his love life would finally blossom (surely in *college* girls would be attracted to the shy and intellectual type), poor Ms. Brennan might not be so fortunate. The prime of her life might very well be behind her, Emilio thought. She might be destined to live out the rest of her days in this yellow-and-white bungalow comforted only by a machine.

The thought crushed sensitive, well-meaning Emilio. It didn't seem fair or right. Ms. Brennan was smart and not unattractive. She was interesting, intelligent, and sometimes even funny in her wry, understated sort of way. She deserved something more than a vibrator in her bedroom drawer.

Emilio felt consumed with sadness for his teacher. He glanced once more around the little cottage before leaving, making sure the front door was locked tightly behind him.

———

Lydia spent the remainder of her trip in only three places: sleeping in the luxurious hotel bed, stretched out on a towel and reading on the beach (*Brief Interviews with Hideous Men* by Wallace), or drinking bourbon, neat, in the lobby bar. On her last evening at said bar, she engaged in flirtatious conversation with a decent-looking man with salt-and-pepper hair named Kenneth; he said he wasn't married although he probably was, and after three and a half drinks she invited him back to her room, where they engaged in sex that was about as satisfactory as a Netflix binge of a show she'd already seen twice.

After she asked him to leave, she punished herself by browsing Tom's social media, where he was frequently pictured with his new wife and new baby. At the park. In the mountains. On the baby's first birthday. The child was truly adorable, with apple cheeks and red hair she'd obviously inherited from Tom's second wife. In every picture, Tom looked so happy.

She couldn't even be mad at Tom. He hadn't been a terrible husband, and she hadn't been a terrible wife. They had simply discovered too late that they were wrong for each other in all the tedious, typical ways so many people sometimes are. He'd been decent and generous in the divorce, giving her more financial stability than a public school teacher typically had. And now they were "friendly" with each other, connected on social media, co-owners of past mutual friends. It was all so modern and sophisticated, Lydia thought, not long before she crawled into the hotel bathroom to puke up the evening's drinks.

———

Groggy and slightly hungover the next morning, Lydia paid extra for a late checkout, texting Emilio to let him know she would be later than planned. As she hit Send, she winced at the memory of the vibrator incident. Hopefully the young man had mostly forgotten about it. Of course, thinking of the vibrator also brought the image of Sean to the forefront of her mind, although in truth he had been thrumming in the background since the moment she'd kicked him out of the hotel room. She wondered how many people had already enjoyed his story at her expense. She hoped he'd had the decency to change the names.

By the time she pulled into the driveway of her home, the sun was setting. She was anxious to do laundry, unpack, put things where they belonged. Lydia enjoyed imposing order on inanimate objects during times when there was little order inside her head and heart.

She shifted the car into park and decided to check her phone before heading inside. A flash of panic seized her when she saw an email from Principal Kendricks with the subject line "Please read this."

This struck her as strange. They usually didn't get much email traffic in the summer. Lydia opened the message, cursing the time it took to load; after a little while, she realized it was blank. There was nothing. No words. No attachment. Upon closer examination, she wondered if the email had been sent to more than one person, perhaps using BCC? But she couldn't tell for sure.

Oh God. Had her hidden vibrator sparked yet another crisis, as she'd feared? Had Emilio said something to his parents, and they'd complained? (Mrs. Gonzalez was something of a nosy neighbor, to be sure.) Was Principal Kendricks sending out some sort of email admonishing her? Would she become the laughingstock of Baldwin High?

Half frantic, she sent off a quick text to her colleague Andrew Williams, asking him if he'd received the strange communication and knew what it was about. Then she slipped the phone into her purse and, trying to quell the anxiety Principal Kendricks's strange email had sparked, gathered her things from the car and headed inside. After a quick cuddle with Sylvia, she immediately set to emptying her luggage, doing her laundry, and making a shopping list for tomorrow's grocery store run. While she was at it, she reorganized her medicine cabinet, rearranged her underwear drawer, and rifled through her refrigerator, making sure everything expired was tossed.

With no tasks left with which to distract herself, she turned on the television to some mindless true crime show. When her phone pinged, she startled. Upon picking it up, she saw a text from Andrew Williams.

> Sorry for the delay. Was out with family. Monica and
> the kids demanded Italian tonight! Yeah, Kendricks
> tried to send an email and I guess he made a mistake.
> Anyway, he sent out a corrected version just now. You

should read it, despite a few errors I've managed
to spot. ;-)

As quickly as she could, Lydia opened her work email and
read Mr. Kendricks's latest message. As she took it in, she exhaled a sigh of relief. Her paranoia had been for naught. In fact,
Principal Kendricks's email put a smile on her face.

Setting her phone down, she thought she heard some shuf-
fling or noise on the porch, followed by a light knock. With
Sylvia at her heels, Lydia made it to the front door and opened
it just wide enough to peer out. Although it was dark, she
caught a glimpse of young Emilio making his way across the
strip of grass that separated their houses.

At her doorstep was a small bouquet of yellow sunflowers,
clearly bought from a grocery store, and tied with the sort of
cheap red ribbon a person would use to wrap a child's Christmas gift. Next to the flowers was a square white envelope with
*Ms. Brennan* written on it in the chicken scratch of a teenage
boy who had been born too late to have learned proper cursive.

Taking both items inside, she set the flowers on the kitchen
counter before sinking onto the couch in the den, envelope in
hand. Inside was a piece of loose-leaf paper folded in fourths.
She opened it.

*Ms. Brennan,*

*While I was house-sitting for you these past few days, it
occurred to me that I do not think I ever took the time to
properly tell you how much I enjoyed your class this year.
I know I never spoke much in class (because I am shy), but
your lectures and your lessons always held my attention and*

*expanded my love of literature and the English language. You taught me to look past the obvious, surface-level interpretations and seek deeper understandings. What you taught me will stay with me for a lifetime.*

*If I may be so bold as to say that I sense perhaps the world has not been as kind to you as it should have been. That perhaps you are lonely. As I write this, I worry that I've offended you. Perhaps you might say my thinking is incorrect, not supported by text evidence. If so, I can only apologize.*

*No matter what, I just wanted to remind you that you are a special person.*

*Sincerely, your student,*
*Emilio Gonzalez*

The ache in Lydia's throat was so painful, the only solution was to cry immediately, which she did. Starting from her elementary school years, certain words had always had the power to make her weep.

Not fifty feet away from all this, in his bedroom, Emilio lay flat on his belly reading a paperback novel (*The Return of the Native* by Hardy), but his mind was mostly elsewhere, floating through his bedroom window and hovering over Ms. Brennan's bungalow, wondering if she had discovered the flowers and the card yet. Wondering what she might do when she did.

He was rereading a paragraph for the third time, almost about to give up trying to focus, when the phone on his nightstand buzzed. Reaching for it immediately, he smiled as he read the waiting text. It was formatted formally, as if it were a letter.

Emilio,

I am very touched by your card and flowers. Perhaps
more than I can say. Thank you for being such a good
student and neighbor.
Have a restful summer.


Your teacher,
Ms. Brennan


Emilio smiled with the pleasure that came with making
another human being happy, and after a moment or two, he
reached again for his book.

In her den, Lydia read and reread Emilio's note. She placed
it face up on the coffee table and stared at it. Just then, her
phone rang, the name of the caller exploding on the screen like
fireworks demanding to be admired.

Upon realizing who was calling, Lydia despised her initial
reaction, which was delight. She couldn't help but think about
Sean's dry wit. His abilities in bed. His impassioned defense of
the criminally underrated Anne Brontë. As her phone continued to ring, she tried to ignore her memories of the crushing
sensation she'd felt upon seeing the text from Hot Amy.

Next to her ringing phone sat Emilio's note.


*No matter what, I just wanted to remind you that you are a
special person.*


In one swift motion Lydia rejected the call, and without
pausing, she blocked the caller and unfollowed him on every

social media platform. Then she turned her phone off and went to the kitchen, thinking she might pour herself a glass of wine.

There, she realized Sylvia had discovered the sunflowers on the counter and was peacefully chewing on one, small fragments of velvety yellow dotting her sweet orange face.

"No, no, Sylvia," Lydia said gently, tugging the flowers away and finding a vase to put them in. When she was done with that, she scooped the cat into her arms and nuzzled its neck. The cat purred appreciatively.

As she stood there in her kitchen, Lydia reflected on the day she'd had and on the wild school year that had preceded it. She'd made good friends at Baldwin, and together they had endured so much. She'd taught kind and curious students like Emilio, and next year she would surely teach many more. But right now it was summer. For Lydia Brennan, the flowers standing proud in their vase were a reminder of this season that unfurled before her, a time full of countless chances for her to discover who she was and who she might still want to be.

May 30, 2023

---

FROM: Mark.Kendricks@district181.org
TO: Lovie.Jackson@district181.org; Denise.Baker
@district181.org; Katherine.Garcia@district181.org;
Nancy.Honeycutt@district181.org; Amanda.Fletcher
@district181.org; Hannah.Sanderson@district181.org; Jake
.Rayfield@district181.org; Lydia.Brennan@district181.org;
Andrew.Williams@district181.org; James.Fitzsimmons
@district181.org; Angela.Jimenez@district181.org
SUBJECT: Please read THIS email

Colleagues,
My apologies for any confusion that my previous blank
email may have caused anyone. I think my emailing skills
are a bit sluggish after some time away, however, I think I
have it this time.

Below please find an email I received today from Matthew Lehrer, the son of Mr. Bob Lehrer, our substitute and former colleague who made this year so memorable in so many ways. I thought perhaps those of you who were in the courtyard on that fateful day would want to read it. I personally found it to be very kind and a nice way to kick off the summer.

I hope all of you are having a wonderful summer and finding the time to relax, recharge, and so on.

Take care,
Mark Kendricks

---

FROM: matthew.r.lehrer@yourmail.com
TO: Mark.Kendricks@district181.org
SUBJECT: A note of thanks

Dear Mr. Kendricks,
My name is Matthew Lehrer. Bob Lehrer was my dad. I'm sorry to only just be getting around to sending you this note, but time has gotten away from me. It's been difficult to wrap up everything since I live out of state, but I've got it almost all taken care of now. This was one of the last things on my to-do list.

I wanted to thank you and everyone at Baldwin High School for celebrating my dad and spreading his ashes. When I heard from his lawyer that this was what he wanted, I almost decided to ignore it. But my dad was a good guy, and I know how much it meant to him. Thank you for fulfilling his wishes.

My mom raised me in Arizona to be near her family, and I still live here. But I spent the summers with my dad when I was a kid. He was always trying to make me into a big reader, but I inherited my mom's math and science mind, and I turned into an engineer. During the summers, I remember how he'd talk about the upcoming school year at Baldwin, sometimes even drive me by the school to point out which classroom windows were his. He'd reread the books on his syllabus that he'd taught a million times already. When I asked him why, he said he didn't want to ever get rusty. Sometimes he would come up with lesson plan ideas and ask me for my opinion. It was so obvious to me even as a kid how much it all mattered to him.

He wanted to retire while he was still sharp, I think. Plus he had other plans he wanted to pursue. Traveling and writing and so on. I think he mostly enjoyed retirement, to be honest. But I don't know that he was ever so fulfilled as he was when he was at Baldwin High.

When he told me he was going back to substitute, I was worried for him. He seemed too old to be doing that kind of work. But I want you to know he really loved it. He was really happy doing that.

As I was cleaning out his condo, I found so much stuff he'd saved of mine. All my school photos. This space shuttle Lego kit I put together the summer I was ten. But I also found that he'd saved stuff from his students. Essays that I guess he found especially insightful. Letters and cards from kids he'd taught. I'm sorry to say I had to throw all that out. You can't keep everything. But as I sifted through it, I wondered (not for the first time) what it would have been like to have been my dad's student as well as his son. I think I would have liked it.

Anyway, please forgive my delay in sending you this note of thanks.

Sincerely,
Matthew Lehrer

# *Epilogue*

*August 1962*

Bob Lehrer stepped through the front doors of Baldwin High School on a Friday morning in late August with an eager and anxious heart. Just twenty-two and fresh out of school, he was not due to report to his first teaching job until the following Monday, when a week of teacher in-service days would begin, followed by his first year in the classroom as a high school English teacher. But as a brand-new employee, he'd been asked to stop by the school a little earlier to pick up his room key and fill out a few personnel forms.

"I'll be there all day on Friday," the school secretary had explained when she'd called his apartment, her warm, welcoming voice not unlike his grandmother's. "So just drop on in when you can."

He'd been to the building only once before, earlier that spring, for his interview with Principal McDonough and a few other administrators. Central Office had set up meetings for all the student teachers in the district in the hopes a match would be made between prospective teaching candidates and schools that had openings. Bob had attended them all in gray slacks, a short-sleeved white dress shirt, and a dark blue tie. After each interview he'd washed the shirt in his kitchen sink and carefully ironed it, so it would be prepared for the next one. It was the only good shirt he owned.

Bob had enjoyed meeting with Mr. McDonough, who had struck him as both sensible and kind, and who had asked thoughtful questions. Bob had tried to offer answers that painted him as both insightful and hardworking. But he knew Baldwin High was a large school with a strong reputation in the community. Surely they would not take a chance on a greenhorn like him, whose only experience had been a semester of student teaching in a small semirural high school on the outskirts of the city, student population two hundred. But not long after his interview, he received a call with exciting news.

"Somebody over at Baldwin saw something in you," said the woman at Central Office over the phone. "They want you to start in the fall. You'll be teaching tenth graders."

Bob hung up the phone, stared out the window of his small, first-floor apartment, and smiled at the oak trees that lined his street. It was a plum assignment, he knew. He called his parents and a fellow student teacher who had become a friend to share his good news before he sank into the sofa and came to the realization that this was all happening. He was going to be a teacher. It was still something of a strange turn of events when he stopped to consider it.

Bob Lehrer had headed off to college without much of a plan in mind other than to major in English. He'd been a decent student in high school, a strong writer of term papers and essay exams, a lover of novels and short stories. He enjoyed Russian literature during a time when enjoying Russian literature was considered mildly transgressive, yet that hadn't stopped him from plowing through thick hardcovers with such speed and enthusiasm that he often found himself dreaming of the characters. Occasionally, he felt compelled to try his hand at writing his own fiction, huddled over the Royal typewriter he'd received from his grandmother as a high school graduation present. He spit out little bits of prose here and there and read them out loud to himself while his roommate was at class. What he wrote was fine, but what he really craved was reading the work of others and making sense of writers far superior to him. There was a magic to it, and a warmth. He came to know certain books so intimately that on some level it still occasionally surprised him that the characters inside those pages were not real.

That there were more books in the world than he would ever have time to read was equal parts comforting and troubling.

Bob went on dates but never had a steady girlfriend. He attended class but could not determine a career. Graduation loomed, and his well-meaning father continued to suggest that Bob join him in running the family's small chain of hardware stores. The idea of spending the rest of his adult life thinking about hammers and bolts and fifty different types of nails made Bob Lehrer grit his teeth with anxiety. Yet he feared this might become his future.

Affable but a little shy, Bob found that his popularity increased as he became known as something of a go-to man when it came time to writing papers or making sense of dense texts, even in courses in which he wasn't enrolled. Once, when a member of the university's football team asked him to explain a passage from a history textbook and Bob complied—the ability to do so coming to him rather easily, to be honest—the football player had gazed at Bob with an expression that was almost one of wonder.

"You know, Bob, you always make this junk more clear to me," he said appreciatively. "You make it more clear than some of the professors in this place."

"Well, the better choice is I make it *clearer*," he told the football player. "But thank you."

The exchange made an impression on Bob Lehrer.

And then, on a bitterly cold January day in 1961 when Bob was a junior in college and feeling as uncertain as ever about his future, a young and impressive new president asked his fellow citizens to consider not what their country could do for them, but what they could do for their country. Watching the speech with his floormates on a small black-and-white set in the common room of his dorm, Bob found the line particularly moving, a strong example of chiasmus. A moving and emotional appeal. His mind traveled back to the compliment the football player had paid him, as well as the ease with which he approached the analysis of the written word. The next day he inquired about a program his college offered that would allow him to graduate with his teaching certificate and an English degree.

And so that brought him to now, to entering Baldwin High School on this August afternoon. To heading down the polished floor and into the main office, where the school secretary who had telephoned him earlier—a Mrs. French—greeted him warmly.

"Principal McDonough is in a meeting at Central Office," she explained, "but he sends his regards and says he can't wait for you to start on Monday." She supplied Mr. Lehrer with a key and a stack of personnel forms, which he worked through efficiently in a small conference room at the back of the main office.

Upon giving his papers back to Mrs. French, he asked if he might be able to take a quick peek at his classroom up on the third floor.

"Of course," she said. "Feel free to look around."

Baldwin High had been built a few years earlier as the city expanded. The launch of *Sputnik* had lit a fire in towns and communities across America that had prompted them to pour money into their public schools in an effort to keep up with their sworn enemies on the other side of the world. The students at Baldwin had benefitted. The building was clean and modern and fresh. Inside the library, Bob found rows upon rows of brand-new hardcover books. The tall windows gleamed. Every corner of the building seemed to suggest that this was a serious place where young people came to learn about serious things.

On the way to his classroom, he passed a room with a small sign affixed to it: ENGLISH DEPARTMENT BOOK ROOM. Inside, in careful, well-organized stacks, he found all his old friends. *The Last of the Mohicans* and *Jane Eyre* and *Romeo and Juliet* and *Great Expectations*. They were all here. He picked up a copy of *Pride and Prejudice* and flipped through it carefully, imagining what it might be like to dig through the text with his students. He wondered what books would even be assigned to the tenth graders. And how could he possibly be ready for them in just a few days? Bob put the book back and tried to settle the wave of anxiety that rolled through him.

Just a few doors down he found his classroom, functional and orderly. In an effort to keep the room cool during the warmer months, there were rows of awning windows that could be cranked open to let in fresh air. Tucked into a corner were two metal file cabinets, and along the back wall were several built-in bookshelves and another small cabinet for storage. At the front sat a heavy, imposing wooden desk and a straight-backed teacher chair. The student desks were arranged in careful rows, facing front, toward the chalkboard. It took Bob a beat to remember that the teacher desk was meant for him.

He walked to the front of the room and turned to face the empty rows.

"Good morning," he said. Then he tried once more, projecting his voice a bit louder this time: "Good morning!" He tried to imagine the faces that would soon be in these seats, looking up at him. Expecting him to teach them something. He couldn't believe that people in positions of authority were actually letting him do this, and he half-expected someone to walk in and say there had been a mistake and there was no need for him to return on Monday.

Finished with his brief tour, his mind littered with necessary preparations and questions and concerns he knew would simply have to be answered in due time, Bob stopped by the main office on his way out to say good-bye to Mrs. French. The mechanical punches of her Smith Corona were put on hold for a moment.

"Well, we'll see you Monday, Mr. Lehrer," she said with a wink. "Ready or not."

Mr. Lehrer. The title startled him as much as it excited him. *Mr. Lehrer.*

"I don't know if I could ever be ready," he confessed to Mrs. French shyly. "There's so much I still need to understand."

The school secretary laughed gently but not unkindly. Taking a loose pile of papers and knocking them into a neat stack against her desk, she smiled at him.

"No one is ever really ready for the first day," she said. "So the best you can do is show up and hang on."

He nodded and thanked her for the advice, then left the main office.

As he made his way down the wide hall, the freshly waxed floor glimmered as if it were showing off. A growing sense of pride filled him as he walked past polished wooden cases with glistening glass fronts that held tall athletic trophies and burnished silver cups and elaborate plaques engraved with the achievements of Baldwin students. Of course, he was new here, and he wasn't sure if he was exactly entitled to this feeling just yet. He hoped he was.

But it wasn't just pride, he realized. It was something else. A feeling of purpose and of belonging. A sense of committing to a cause much bigger than he.

He allowed himself a brief smile as he made his way to the end of the hallway.

After pushing open the main doors and heading out into the front courtyard, lush in its summertime greenness, he stopped and turned to look at Baldwin High. At its red brick solidness. At its presence, both utilitarian and dignified. On Monday it would be filled with other teachers joining him in meetings, in lesson preparations, in classroom rearrangings. And then, in what he was sure would be sooner than he could ever imagine, the students would arrive, pimply faced, anxious, eager, or perhaps not so eager. Could he ever really be ready for them?

*No one is ever really ready for the first day*, Mrs. French had told him. The words brought him some comfort, but not nearly enough.

For a beat or two longer he stood there in the courtyard in that thick August heat, surrounded by the nervous buzz of cicadas. He gazed at Baldwin High School, almost willing it to hear him as he silently hoped that he would not fail or at least not fail miserably, as he quietly prayed that he would be the sort of teacher who did right by his students and always gave his best. Then, the sense of purpose he had felt in the hallway coursed through him again. He took it as a sign that perhaps he had been heard, and he was reassured.

Here, in this place, he would become Mr. Lehrer.

Here he would do good work.

# *Acknowledgments*

Many thanks first and foremost to every adult who works in a school, from teachers to cafeteria workers to librarians to paraprofessionals and everyone in between. Those who work in a public system are especially worthy of praise. Despite the bureaucratic and often oppressive structures in which we must operate (created by people who could not do our jobs for even a day), you show up and it matters. Thank you for all that you do.

So much gratitude to my amazing agent, Kerry Sparks, for seeing something in my very early pages and telling me to keep going. You and everyone at Levine Greenberg Rostan have been such champions of my books and career, and it means so much.

A million thanks to Lexy Cassola for exceptional guidance and understanding as we worked together to shape a loose collection of stories into an actual novel. Working on this book with you has been a dream, one that my writer's soul needed more than I can properly express.

Le

Thank you to Tamarie Cooper and Jeff Waller for reading early portions of this book and providing critical, insightful feedback. This story is better because of you both. And many thanks to Marta Flores de Gómez, Ana Comayagua, and Natalia Martinez for their help with Luz's story.

I have so much gratitude for my writer friends, especially Marit Weisenberg, Jeff Zentner, Cristina Henríquez, Katie Cotugno, and Jessica Taylor, for always being there to talk shop, commiserate, and motivate me. Many thanks to Blue Willow Bookshop in Houston for being so supportive of my career from day one.

To my second family at Bellaire High School, I remain so grateful for the opportunity to work with such a committed and creative group of people. In so many ways, this book is for you.

And finally, thank you to my sweet son, Elliott, and to my husband, Kevin, who has always, always believed.